A Nov

WITH YOU

FALL SERIES

J.S. HODGSON

Coming soon by J.S. Hodgson

Fall Series
FOREVER WITH YOU

Desire Series
BURNING DESIRE
BEAUTIFUL DESIRE

Dangerous Series
DANGEROUS LIES
DANGEROUS LOVE

A Novella
BACK TO YOU

Listen to the playlist that inspired and assisted in writing every single chapter on Spotify.

To those who read the first book.
Thank you.
It means everything.

CHAPTER 1

AVA

I can't stop shaking. My leg is bouncing up and down, causing my keys to jingle loudly in the empty waiting room. There were two women before me who have already been called with their partners by their side. The secretary gave me a sympathetic smile when she gave me the paperwork I needed to fill out before seeing the doctor. Fort Worth is a small city when it comes to my family. Everyone knows my uncle and my step-aunt, who is the best OB-GYN at the private doctor's office in town. I wasn't planning on telling anyone, especially my dad, but I couldn't just go to the hospital. One person who knows my uncle, cousin, or dad will say to them they saw me in the pregnancy ward. So, of course, here I am to see my aunt.

I've been in denial. I know I have.

I've been in denial since I was in Seattle.

I missed my period during the first two weeks of being away from Gabriel. I can't even look back and remember when my last period was. I have never wished so hard for cramps, bloating, and tampons in my life.

"Ava Thompson?" A nurse calls, and I can't stand. I'm looking at the blonde woman with the pixie cut smiling politely at me, but my body won't move. My brain is screaming at me to get up and walk over to her, but that means I'll find out the truth. There will be no more denial. The baby *will* be real.

The baby *is* real.

"*Ava?*" She asks and gives me an encouraging smile as if she needs to prove she can be trusted.

I nod and stand up very slowly. I can feel the secretary's eyes on me, but my eyes are locked on the nurse who begins to walk down the hall. I pass each room, some with doors closed, some open and those are empty. She pushes through a door and leaves me to follow her.

"Dr. Thompson, your patient Ava Thompson." The nurse announces as my aunt is typing away on her computer.

She looks up and smiles at me. "Thank you, Natalie; please give us the room."

Natalie nods her head and leaves the room without a word.

"Hi, sweetheart," she says with her Texas twang. "Now, I promised I would keep this to myself, but you do plan on telling your daddy at some point, *right*?"

She begins to turn on machines and pats the leather chair with the stirrups. I sit down and start to chip at my nails nervously.

"I do...I may not even be pregnant. Who knows?" I say unconvincingly. She gives me a sad smile, and I know she doesn't believe me either. Missing one period means one thing...usually.

"We're going to do a vaginal ultrasound because it may be too early to see anything with a regular one." She stands and pulls a hospital gown from the drawer. "Change into this; there's a private bathroom behind that door. I'll be waitin'."

My body moves in slow motion as I change in the bathroom. I stare at myself in the mirror and wonder how the hell I got here. Gabriel consumed me so quickly that I hardly had time to wrap my head around anything. We did years worth in a matter of months. I let my guard down willingly and basked in the world he brought me into.

I love him, I honestly do, it never went away even after all this time, but a girl can only take so much.

I take a deep breath and set my palms against my flat stomach. "If I am pregnant," I whisper. "I will put *you* first. I will protect you."

I exit the bathroom and sit on the chair, lifting my legs. I'm shaking, and my aunt notices, placing her hand on my knee.

"Sweetheart, no matter what happens, I will be there for ya." She gives me a genuine smile and begins to instruct me how it will feel, but I can't focus on her voice. I'm looking at the screen, waiting to see what I know will be there. Everything moves in slow motion as I feel the pressure of the wand. I can hear my heart racing as I wait, and then...

"There it is." My aunt says with concern.

The dread I was waiting for didn't come. Instead, my heart expands when I see the small figure on the screen. That's my child, and I will do anything to protect him or her.

Nothing matters anymore. Not Elizabeth, not Gabriel, not the heartache. Just this child who is now relying on me to keep it alive.

"Oh my god," I mumble and look to my aunt, who's waiting to see my reaction. "That's *my* baby."

She nods. "Yes, sweetheart. You're about six weeks. Very early." She places her hand on mine. "Are you okay?"

I nod and wipe away my tears as I watch the screen. "I should be afraid, but I'm not."

She gives me a sympathetic smile. "Darlin', you're not a child like last time. You're an adult, a *strong* woman who can do this with or without a man." She stands and kisses my forehead. "Congrats, sweetheart. Let's get you cleaned up, and we will go over everything you should be taking from now on. There's a lot of information out there. I'll have the prints ready for you in my office."

I take one last look at the screen and wish *he* was here.

"So, you're really not going to tell him?" My cousin Drew asks.

I shake my head as I brush Luna's mane. "I don't know. He *cheated* on me, Drew; it's not like I wanted to leave. He left me no choice."

Even though I have never really lived in Texas full time, my uncle and dad bought me a horse to keep here for whenever I visit. As a kid, I saw Drew with his horse *Sunny*, and it looked so free. Watching a human be one with an animal, there's a sense of trust and unity that I have never seen before. They need to trust one another so they both can do their jobs.

When I was eight, it was my first time riding a horse, and of course, I chose Sunny. We couldn't go as fast as Drew was able to go, but it was terrific.

For Christmas that year, they let me pick out my own horse. I wanted her to be the opposite of Sunny, hence, *Luna*.

He leans against the railing. "He has a right to know even if the prick can't keep it in his pants. He should be here taking care of you, not letting you work the farm. Don't make me tell your, daddy, girl. I've caught you once already working the field when you should be resting."

I roll my eyes.

So much like my dad and my uncle.

They believe in hard work and letting their wives "rest" and "relax." They're too much of gentlemen to let a pregnant woman work.

"I'm hardly pregnant, Drew. I'll be fine." I make my way to leave the barn, but he grabs my arm.

"Are you sure you're okay? You won't talk about him. You don't even let me say his name when you're around. I want to make sure you can handle this."

He looks worried, and I know half the reason is that I won't tell my dad yet. Drew doesn't understand. I faced him when I was seventeen without Gabriel, and here I am again ten years later, once again pregnant and without Gabriel. I don't want him to be disappointed in me. My aunt was happy, but it's because I'm not her actual child. I'm afraid my dad will tell me this is a mistake, I need to do this with Gabriel, but I can't.

I can't just think of myself anymore. This baby has to come first, even if that means I keep this a secret. I can't promise that Gabriel will love this child. I know what it feels like to be hated by your parent, and I never want this baby to feel that way. I want it to be loved and only know love. I haven't forgotten that someone out there is looking for me... or Gabriel, which means I have to keep my distance. I need to keep this a secret so no one can use this to hurt me.

It's been hard, having my phone stuffed in a drawer somewhere, ignoring his calls and texts. Even though I don't want to miss him, and I shouldn't miss him, I do. Even though I chose to leave this time, it didn't mean I wanted to. I should have given him a chance to explain, but I saw it with my own eyes. Elizabeth naked in his apartment while he was in the shower washing off their sins. I don't even want to imagine what they did to one another.

I smile. "It's going to take time to get over him, but I'm okay. Texas is just what I needed."

During our first summer here, I fell in love with the simple life my uncle has—sweet tea, horses, farming, and all the other great things Texas has to offer. I wanted to move here, but my mom never allowed it. My dad never wanted to leave his construction business behind or rip me away from everything I knew back in Portland.

Being back here is giving me a sense of tranquillity. Maybe, being here will help me get over him.

I want to laugh at myself. As if I haven't been crying over him for almost two weeks. Lately, it's been getting easier, but that makes the emptiness hurt even more. Soon, he'll be nothing but a distant memory that I have to look back to when I miss being adventurous, when I miss travelling... when I miss him.

I make my way into the house, and my dad and uncle are sitting at the table while my aunt serves them her homemade fried chicken. My stomach growls very loudly, causing my dad to look at me in surprise.

"Hungry, bug?" My uncle asks and pulls the chair out for me.

"Even if I wasn't, you think I can pass up Margi's homemade fried chicken and sweet tea?" I ask with a smile.

"See, this is why I need a daughter." My aunt says she places a plate in front of me and puts a prenatal vitamin in my hand when she hands me the sweet tea. She gives me a slight wink as I take the pill, drowning it with the delicious sweet tea. "You boys are too caveman for me."

My dad rolls his eyes. "Trust me, there's nothing harder than raising a teenage girl."

I swat at his arm, causing him to laugh. My uncle points at me with his fork while glaring at his wife. "See, my brother knows what life is like with a girl. Besides, my hands are full enough with you, darlin'." He blows her a kiss, and she swats it away.

I can't help but grin as I watch their playful banter. This is what I wanted, and I wanted it with Gabriel. I pick at my chicken as Drew comes through the door. He takes off his cowboy hat, hanging it on the hook beside the door. My aunt has rules here, and the men respect them.

No hats indoors.

"Well, looks like ya'll started the party without me," Valerie says as she makes her way toward us. She kisses the top of my dad's head and sits beside him.

I love Valerie for my dad. She's the best of both worlds, just like him. She brings out a side in him I've never seen. He's playful and... in love when he's around her. I never saw him this way toward my mother.

She wouldn't have deserved it anyways.

I can feel Drew's eyes on me as I rip through the chicken. A second ago, I lost my appetite, but now it's back with a vengeance. I can't get enough of the delicious fried chicken. I reach for a biscuit but stop to look at Drew.

What is his problem?

He gives me a worried look as he scans the table to make sure no one is paying attention.

'*Slow down.*' He mouths, and I look at everyone else's plate to see them slowly eating and enjoying their food. I haven't even bothered to serve myself the side dishes before ripping into my chicken like an animal. I place the biscuit on my plate and wipe my mouth.

This baby will change everything about me, and the most challenging part is I have to make sure no one else catches on.

Not yet.

CHAPTER 2

GABRIEL

I've been going through the motions. I've been trying to stay focused, knowing that a company is relying on me. Although, how much can one man take?

I haven't seen her in a month. Not one word, not one peep or sound that tells me she's still alive. After I left her apartment two weeks ago, I went back a few days later. This time I had persuaded the super to let me into her apartment. I lied and said I was her boyfriend, that I hadn't heard from her. I was worried.

When he opened the door, it was empty.

I stepped out to make sure this was her apartment. It had to be. This is the number Isabella gave me. She was the only one who stepped foot in her apartment.

I got angry, punched a hole through his door, and then gave him cash for the damages.

She left without a fucking trace.

I have no idea if she even left the city or just the apartment. Every time I phone her, it goes straight to voicemail. At least before it used to ring, giving me a sliver of hope that she will answer.

Now, I'm just numb.

I tell myself that I don't need her. That I can survive without her because I survived ten years without her. This is the same. The only difference is she left me this time.

But I know I'm a fool.

I've drunk enough for all of Seattle, but it's the only thing that keeps me going. Elizabeth has tried to convince me to move on and has even proposed we get back together. I told her I couldn't be with anyone who wasn't Ava. She doesn't give up, however. She's the only one who continues to even speak about Ava. She isn't afraid of me or my reaction.

My sister, on the other hand, I know, wants to ask me. She wants to know what happened to her friend, but I can't tell her. I'm ashamed of myself. I know she will side with Ava no matter how much I explain.

I thought we had a chance; I really did. I hear my front door open, and I know it's Elizabeth without looking. Isabella stopped coming by weeks ago. I only see her when I visit my mum or at work. She doesn't know what to say anymore to help me.

I don't blame her.

I want everyone to run away from me.

"What are you doing here?" I ask while exhaling loudly. I want her to know I'm annoyed with her presence. This is not who I want walking through my front door.

I want Ava.

She throws her coat on the barstool and gives me a slight pout. "Well, someone isn't in a good mood. Haven't had a drink yet?" She asks.

I lift my glass that's filled almost to the brim. "*No*, I have. You're just not who I want to see."

I'm harsh, I know, but this is who Ava despised. I can't seem to surpass my coldness even if I wanted to.

She rolls her eyes. "Are you going to be a drunk forever, Gabriel?" She isn't happy now. *Good*, I would love to fight. "She's been gone for a month now. That *bitch* didn't deserve you anyway."

I scowl but decide I need more alcohol before I proceed. I stopped sipping on my whiskey the day Ava walked out. "I cheated on her, Elizabeth, with *you*. She had every right to leave me. It's *I* who doesn't deserve *her*."

I begin to pour myself another glass.

She scoffs. "You seem to be forgetting who *you* are. You're a rich, successful, powerful man who can get anything he desires from material items to any woman."

That's why I never loved Elizabeth the way I loved Ava. Ava didn't want me to spend a cent when we were together. She didn't want gifts or money. Ava wanted me and only me, anyway she could have me. She loved me unconditionally and didn't care if I had money to my name. Elizabeth needs riches. It's what defines her. She needs to have luxurious cars, fancy homes and jewelry but doesn't want to work for it. All she sees is my riches.

"That's why I love her. She didn't care about any of that."

She rolls her eyes. "You have got to be kidding. Don't be foolish, Gabriel; of course, she cared about that. She was faking it. She couldn't get Scott, so she settled for you."

"*Stop*," I say through my teeth as her words fill me with rage. She has no idea what she's talking about. Elizabeth is threatened by the slightest thing; she didn't know Ava the way I did. I won't let her tarnish her name as if we aren't the ones who caused her to leave. Ava should be speaking ill of myself and Elizabeth. We are the ones who deserve it.

I can't even stand to look at myself in the mirror, knowing I hurt Ava; knowing I hurt Ava with Elizabeth is the cherry on top of this self-destruction and self-hatred cake.

"You have no idea what you're saying, and I won't let you bad mouth her. I love *her*, Elizabeth; when will you understand?" I'm angry now, and the alcohol isn't helping. I chug back the whisky and serve myself another glass as if it's water. "She loves me."

Elizabeth crosses her arms over her chest. "*Loved*."

I stop, the glass hovering over my lips as I take in her words. "*What*?" I ask, confused and set my glass back down.

"You're saying *love*, which is present tense. But who are you kidding, Gabriel? She isn't me. She isn't the type of girl to looks past this. You two weren't even officially together when I sucked your dick, and she ran off crying. Do you honestly believe she still loves you?"

"Stop."

She laughs. "You do believe she still loves you." She says with amusement.

"Enough," I say through my teeth.

She shakes her head with a grin. "You're a bigger fool than I thought."

I grab my glass and turn my back to her, throwing it and smashing it against the wall. "*Enough!*" I yell while panting. I turn to face her, but she hasn't flinched.

"You're pathetic. What happened to you, Gabriel? You never used to let some girl affect you."

That's what she doesn't understand.

"Ava isn't just *some* girl. *She. Is. Everything.* She is the only person I will ever want." I try to calm my breathing, but her snarky grin isn't helping my temper.

She collects her coat while shaking her head with disapproval. "Getting rid of her was the best thing I have ever done." She mumbles softly.

But I heard her.

I make my way around the breakfast bar and grab her arm. I need her to look me in the eye when she repeats it.

"What did you just say?" I ask as my body begins to shake with boiling rage.

If she's behind this...

She sticks her chin up, but I see the fear in her eyes. She wants to take it back, but it's too late.

"I got rid of her." Her voice is smaller now.

I clench my jaw. "Explain."

I can't form any words bigger than that. I'm telling myself that she's a woman.

I don't hit women.

She pulls her arm out of my grasp and adjusts herself. "I sent her away."

Bloody woman.

"I know that!" I yell. "I'm fucking confused here because she left over me cheating on her. How the fuck are *you* the one who made *her leave*?"

She smirks. "She came back here and caught me naked. She took one look at me and left."

At that moment, it feels like I'm falling down a black hole. I walk away from her to the first thing I can find. I pick up the barstool and throw it across the living room, not caring what it hits. I hear a crash, but I don't bother to look. I don't watch what I break. I grab the other chair and throw it again.

"*Gabriel!*" She screams, bringing me back to reality.

Which isn't good for Elizabeth.

I look at her to see fear written all over her face. "You lied to her! You made her believe I was fucking you when I was fucking heartbroken!" I make my way to her, and she begins to back up, tripping over her feet and falling onto the ground, but I don't care. I want her to hurt.

"You will leave here and never come back," I snarl and bend down so we are eye to eye. "I never want to see you again. Everything between us is over. I don't care if you starve for the next fucking century! *GET OUT!*"

I can feel my face redden as I yell, my veins popping, my fists clenching. Ava was right. I should have ended this friendship a long time ago.

Tears well up in her eyes. "You're really choosing her?" Her voice breaks between her words.

I laugh angrily. "That's the funny thing. *You* were *never* an option. *Get. Out.*"

She swallows hard and stands, sobbing as she walks out, but guilt doesn't come. Instead, I begin to cry as well. The pain in my chest growing bigger, knowing what Ava must have felt at that moment. She came back, she came back for me. Elizabeth had ruined everything.

How could I have not known?

Two weeks ago, when I had returned from Ava's, I entered my living room to find Elizabeth naked. She begged me to fuck her; I almost had to throw her out of my apartment without her clothes. She wouldn't take no for an answer, but I remained polite, not having the slightest clue that Ava was there before I had come downstairs. Elizabeth saw her chance to end us for good and took it with no hesitation.

Madwoman.

I take my whiskey bottle and slide down to the floor with my back against the breakfast bar. I look at the two broken bar stools and the now broken coffee table crushed by one of them.

I press my lips against the bottle and take a swig, praying to every God to bring her back to me.

It's been two days since Elizabeth confessed to sending Ava away. I'm in no mood to be at a family dinner, but my mum called me herself and begged me to come. She missed me. I could never say no to my mum.

I've been a mess.

I haven't even slept in my own bed. Harris found me lying on the floor where I was when Elizabeth left my apartment. He helped me get into the shower for today as he complained about how much I smelt like liquor. He doesn't understand.

He has his Ruth with him. She loves him and would never leave him. And Harris isn't a fool who would cheat on her. Like me.

I begged him to leave me there to rot in my own filth, but he reminded me that I was expected.

Needing another drink, I make my way to my father's liquor cabinet. My father and mum have been pestering me about what has been bothering me. I know my mum is worried about me; she cares for me and just wants to make sure her son is okay. My father, on the other hand, just wants to scold me. It's become his favourite thing over the years. As if he isn't the reason I am the way that I am. He makes his way into the living room, a scowl on his face while he digs his hands into his pockets.

"Boy, enough with the pouting and drinking. I've had it, you worrying your mother." He says with a stern voice—his Australian accent heavy on his tongue. If I could punch him in the face, I would.

I take a sip before answering. "Not now, dad." I'm in no mood for him to test me.

His jaw clenched tightly as he grinds his back teeth the way he always does when he's angry. "You're selfish!" He hisses, shocking me in my place. "Your mother can't stand to see you this way, boy, and you're selfish by not putting her first."

He has some nerve.

"*Jack!*" My mum says in shock as she enters the room with my sister. She looks nervous, but I'm already angry at my foolish father's words.

"What the fuck did you just say, old man?" I ask angrily as I set my drink down. I'm afraid I'll break the cup in my hand.

"*Gabriel!*" My sister says in shock.

"I gave up everything for this family! *Everything*! I had to grow up and be the man of this family because *you* couldn't!" I yell, stepping closer with each word. He isn't backing down; instead, I'm fuelling his anger.

"*Gabriel!*" My mother says nervously.

"Careful." My father warns.

I laugh angrily. "*Why?!* You can't handle the truth, dad? Let's talk about it! You're the reason I'm fucked up!"

He shakes his head. "All this for a girl?! This isn't love, boy. This is some foolish teenage dream you're trying to live out! Grow up!"

"*I DID!*" I yell at the top of my lungs. "I had to grow up because you lost your balls and couldn't! I had to be the man because *YOU* couldn't!"

His fist collides with my face, spraying blood from my lip onto the carpet.

Fucker.

"*JACK WARNER!*" My mum yells, shocked as she makes her way to me, but I shake my head, stopping her in her tracks. I don't want the fucker to take his anger out on my poor mum.

I look at my father, who looks anything but sorry. He seems happy to have hit me. "Maybe, this is why you can't stand the sight of me. When you see me, you see yourself, and when you look in the mirror, you see grandad. You forced me the same way he tried to do with you. The only difference is I loved my family enough and took the job."

"*OUT!*" My father yells as he points at the door. His face turning red. "Get out of my house, boy!"

I want to apologize to my mum, but I know it's not possible. Too many things have been said.

I nod and give him a small smile. "I think you mean *my house*, dad," I say before walking out.

CHAPTER 3

GABRIEL

Nineteen

I'm pacing around my grandad's office as I wait for him to finish his meeting. He always tells me whenever I feel too angry to be around my father to come to him. No one understands more than my grandad. Moving here and leaving...

I run my fingers through my hair as I watch the people below me, living their lives.

I miss her, I really do.

Moving here was the hardest thing. My mum is still sick, and I pray to every God that she makes it through this. I lost...Ava, I can't lose my mum too. Without my grandad, I would have been completely lost. He's taken me under his wing and has helped me through my heartache. He doesn't speak to my father, but he asks me every day how my mother is. He adores my mother and thought my father had picked someone spectacular. But their differences continue to keep them apart.

My grandad has been more of a father to me than my own. Jack Warner only saves his breath for his wife and sometimes his daughter but never me. Ever since my mum got sick, he's distant, almost like the man can't stand the sight of me.

I still don't understand why.

I never did anything but give up everything for my family.

I thought he would be thankful, grateful, and more loving. Instead, he's a jackass.

"What happened now, son?" My grandad asks as he walks in, holding manuscripts in his hands. He throws them onto his desk and sits in his leather chair before turning to face me.

I frown. "I hate him."

He exhales loudly. "Gabriel—

"*No*," I argue. "Dad has pushed me too far, grandad! He looks at me like I'm nothing. I went to visit mum, and he wouldn't even shift his body in my direction!"

He stays quiet as he scratches his beard. "Son, you don't mean that, and you shouldn't mean that. Hating your father isn't right."

I look at him in shock. If there is anyone who should understand my hatred toward my father, it's my grandad. Before my mum got sick, they hadn't spoken since my father was in high school. When my mum got ill, my father swallowed his pride but not to take his place next in line for the family business. Instead, he offered me. He begged my grandad and said Emilia was sick. We needed help.

My grandad said, '*anything for Emilia.*'

Not even for his own son, his own blood.

And yet the old man stands here and tells me not to hate him. "How could you say that? You hate him more than I do."

He shakes his head with a frown. "That's not true, Gabriel. I never said I hated my son."

I sit on the chair on the other side of his desk. "What? But I thought?"

He leans forward. "Gabriel, I *love* my son. It's my son that wants nothing to do with me. Yes, I pushed him hard for years to be the best so he could lead this company. I was hard on him the way my Australian dad was with me. It was all I knew. Then he introduced me to your mother. I loved Emilia the second I met her. She was who your father needed. I had made apart of him tough and cold, but your mother was the one who would soften him. Then she was pregnant with you, and I knew I needed to make things right. I hadn't seen my son in years nor his wife because of this anger we had toward one another. Emilia phoned me the day you were born, and I showed up at the hospital. I had a few moments alone with you and Emilia while your father was asleep on the chair beside her bed. Emilia explained when he woke, that I came to make things right between us, and he shut me down. He said the damage had been done. Your mother was distraught, and so was I, so, she let me see you two kids behind his back."

He sighs heavily as he looks away from me. The sadness in his eyes is something I've never seen before when it comes to him talking about my father. There only used to be anger, disappointment, and coldness.

"You don't understand it now, son, but Emilia is your father's best friend. They were partners in crime, lovers, wife and husband before they were your parents. He has no idea how to act because he's trying to pretend there isn't a possibility where he might have to live in a world where she doesn't. He's lost because if he loses her..." He sighs heavily and looks at the picture on his desk of his wife, my grandmother. "Losing my wife was the hardest thing I have ever been through. She wanted me to make things right with your father a long time ago, but I had too much pride. I thought I would have more time to make things right with him. She wanted more than just phone calls and a Christmas card from her son...then she died. Stroke in her sleep. It was the darkest of my days, and it broke my heart that my son wouldn't let me fulfil his mother's wishes."

I think about Ava and what I felt for her. My father said it was foolish to think I was in love with her. That I was a child who couldn't even begin to comprehend what love meant. He yelled this in my face when I told him I would never forgive him for taking me away.

"Don't be like me and make the same mistake, Gabriel."

I listen, but I can't imagine forgiving my father for doing the same thing he resents his own father for.

If he dies, I don't know If I will survive it. He has been by my side since I stepped foot in Seattle. I'm not ready to take over the company.

I'm only twenty-two.

The old bastard can't leave me.

He can't leave me here to face my father all by myself.

He can't leave me here to deal with my mum's cancer.

She's getting worse, and he's supposed to be there, telling me that she's too strong for this small disease to get her. She belongs down here with my father, with us. I used to believe him, but lately, every time I see her and see how skinny, pale and fragile she is, I stopped believing. How can she recover? I look at my father and see the same look in his eyes that I have. He's worried that he will lose her, which means Isabella and I will lose both parents. Isabella has been a wreck trying to be there for both of them, and my jackass father doesn't give her even the slightest *thank you*. He's too consumed with my mum to appreciate his children. Unlike Isabella, I'm okay with it.

My father hasn't arrived yet, which is no surprise, but my mum promised me they would be here. I'm waiting for the all-clear so I can see that he's still breathing. I need to know he's still with me. We need more time together, we missed out on seventeen years of memories, and we weren't even close to being done.

I still have so much to learn.

"Mr. Warner, your grandfather is awake." A nurse says as he approaches me.

I bolt to my feet and clear my throat. "Can I see him?" I ask.

He gives me a frown. "He should rest, Mr. Warner."

I take out a roll of cash from my pocket and look at the nurse to see him looking at the money like his one true love. "How much for me to see him?" I ask and place the whole roll in his hand.

He looks from the money to me then back to the money.

I'm losing my patience.

"My grandad, please," I demand, and he sticks the roll of money in his lab coat.

"Right this way, Sir." He says and leads me to my grandad's room.

"I'd like privacy, please," I say as I walk into the room, not bothering to look back at him. I'm not asking, and I hope he can tell by my tone.

I hear the door close, but I'm too busy focusing on my grandad's body on a hospital bed. He has wires and machines attached to him, each machine making a loud sound that can't be easy to sleep with.

Maybe, I can pay someone to turn it down for him.

His eyes slowly open, leaving me motionless as I watch him gather his surroundings. When he spots me, he gives me a small smile. "There's my boy." He says with a raspy voice. "How long have you been standing there?"

I make my way to the chair next to his bed and sit. "I just got here, grandad. How are you feeling?"

What a silly question to ask a man who just had a heart attack.

His eyes are glossy, and he gives me a small smile. "*Jack,*" he whispers and reaches to touch my cheek. He lets out a shaky breath. "I've missed you so much, boy."

I want to correct him, but I know my father well enough to know he won't be here to say good-bye. My grandad won't get the closure he needs with his son, so I will give that to him.

"I've missed you too," I mumble.

He gives me a grin. "Look how big you look. Your mother would hardly believe her eyes if she were here." He chuckles. "What's taken you so long to get here?"

I frown. "I-I'm sorry, dad, but I'm here now." I squeeze his hand. "Are you in any pain?"

He shakes his head. "No, of course not. I'm ready for this." He says as he looks up to the ceiling. He looks back at me and jumps. "*Gabriel*, I didn't know you were here."

He no longer sees me as my father.

"What do you mean you're ready for this?" I ask nervously.

He can't die.

He gives me a sympathetic expression. "Gabriel, I was ready to die when my wife died. Why do you think I never remarried? We belong together, and I have lived five years without her. That's enough. I've done my job. I've helped you, and now it's time."

I look at him in disbelief. "I'm not ready. How can you say this?" I ask.

He pats my hand and closes his eyes. "Of course you are. You are *my grandson*, Gabriel, which means you have my strength; you have my work ethic. There is no one I believe in more than you."

I'm glad his eyes are closed. It gives me the privacy I need to wipe away the tears that escaped. I don't want to cry in front of him. Knowing he believes in me fills me with something I can't describe. My father stopped believing in me a long time ago.

The door opens before I can say anything else and it's my mum. She's walking on her own, which sends me soaring toward her to help her walk. She's too weak to be on her own.

Where the fuck is my father?

"Where is he?" I ask.

She kisses my cheek. "Don't, baby boy, not in front of him." She whispers for only me to hear.

"There *she* is," My grandad says and chuckles breathlessly. "The only woman I know who can light a room up with cancer."

I watch my grandad in disbelief, but my mum laughs as we walk closer to his bed. "Says you. You make old age and a heart attack look *too* good."

He laughs as she leans down and kisses his cheek. I have never seen my grandad in this environment. Just like my father, he softens for my mum. I imagine this is the way he was with my grandmother. This is what he's been talking about.

"How are you, darling? You hanging in there?" He asks.

My mum frowns. "I should be asking you that, Simon. We *need* more time."

My grandad looks at me then back to her. "He isn't coming." He's not asking.

She frowns. "You know how Jack is. He's *your* son."

He looks at me, his eyes filled with tears. "At least I made time with my grandson."

"Simon," my mom exasperates. "You still have time."

I want to tell her that he doesn't, but I know my grandad is too honest. He will tell her even if she will pick a fight.

He shakes his head. "No, Emilia, I'm ready to go. My sweetheart has waited long enough for me. You already know she's pissed."

My mum laughs and covers her mouth. She looks at me, wiping her tears away so my grandad doesn't see. She looks back at him and strokes his cheek. "You give her the biggest hug for me and tell her about my babies."

He smiles lovingly at her. "Of course. She misses them; I know she does."

She kisses his cheek one more time and stands, sniffling. He takes my mum's hand and squeezes it.

"You'll tell him I love him." He sounds like he's begging her.

"I always have, and I always will."

My grandad died six hours later with me, my mum, and Isabella by his side. We said our good-byes, and our grandad told us stories of us when we were kids. The times he got to see us, how excited my grandmother used to be. My mum and grandmother used to chat over coffee while watching us play with grandad.

I promised him that I will pour my blood, sweat and tears into this company and that I would make him proud. The last words he said to me were,

"Son, you could run this business into the ground, and I would still be proud of you."

CHAPTER 4

EMILIA WARNER

I stare at my husband in shock as he paces the living room. Isabella went to go clean the kitchen, knowing she can't stand the sight of her father. My husband never used to be this... *cold*. When we met, he had a fire in him, drive and determination, but he was soft, kind, polite, and a gentleman. He still is but only for his dearest Isabella and me. I used to love seeing him melt when our baby girl would smile at him, but then I began to notice the way he looked at Gabriel. It wasn't until I got sick where he stopped showering our boy in affection. He adored Gabriel and vowed when he was born to have a better relationship than he and Simon did.

I, on the other hand, adored Simon. In a way, I didn't expect it but I was frustrated due to their stubbornness. They loved one another just had too much pride.

Sadly, my husband still does and passes it onto my son.

When growing up, things came easy to my boy. He has his father's looks, which meant things would come easy to him. But I wanted him to feel unconditional love. We wanted him to grow up to be whatever he wanted to be.

Then I got sick. I wanted to curse everything on this earth, but I knew I couldn't. My faith and the love for my family were the only things keeping me going. But knowing my son had to leave his childhood behind to be ready to provide for his family filled me with a deep shame. It's Jack and me that are supposed to be working and supporting, not my eighteen-year-old son.

"How could you speak to him that way?" I ask with anger in my voice. We don't fight often, but when it comes to my children, I will fight anyone. "How could you call him selfish when you know he gave up *everything* to provide for us in our time of need."

Jack turns to face me, his face in disbelief. "What he gave up? Emilia, you were sick with cancer, and the boy wants a gold fucking medal."

"*No!*" I shout, which catches him by surprise. I hear silence from the kitchen, and I know Isabella has left. She never liked hearing us fight on the rare occasions we did. She would always hide in the basement until one of us went to get her.

It was usually Gabriel.

"He's waiting for a damn *thank you* or an *I love you* from you, Jack. The boy is looking for approval, something that tells him you know what he did, and you're grateful. Instead, you make him feel small and what he did was for self-gain."

He scoffs and runs his fingers through his hair. "Look at him, Lia! This is all for his self-gain!"

I exhale loudly. "Why can't you see it, Jack? Gabriel was just a child, freshly eighteen; he had no idea how much money this business would give him. All he cared about was saving and being there for his parents."

He kisses his teeth. "Can we drop this? This isn't worth arguing about."

My heart aches.

Hearing him say a fight over our son is not worth it makes me weep as a mother. This man has so many issues with his father he can't fix things with his son. I begged Jack to make things right after his father had a heart attack, but he didn't listen. Simon passed away a few hours later in his sleep, and Jack never got the chance to say what he needed to say to his father. Now, he takes it out on my son. I've stood by blindly because of who my husband is to me. He's still the same boy who let me fall asleep on his lap while studying in the library. He would sit upright against the shelves trying to finish reading whatever chapter he was on but would fall asleep a few minutes after I did.

He's the same boy who would give me a lazy smile as I woke him up in the same library the morning after, with a fresh cup of coffee. Who used to hold my hair back when I had too much to drink even though he told me I needed to pace myself. He's my best friend, my partner, my other half, and he used to be my greatest love until I had Gabriel. There's something about holding your child in your arms that shows you what love is. I thought I couldn't love anything more than I love Jack, but suddenly there was no comparison. My love didn't fade for Jack, he will always have my heart, but my kids have my soul.

I know how delicate life can be and how short time is, which means I can no longer stand by blindly, watching my son fight his father as if they're enemies. Seeing Jack hit my son is something I won't forgive quickly.

"You will never lay your hand on my son again. *Ever*." I threaten, which takes him by surprise.

I have never spoken to him this way.

"Lia, I'm sorry."

I lift my hand. "I'm not the one you need to apologize to, Jack. Your son needs to hear your apology. You're the one who is supposed to protect him, not be the one hurting him." I shake my head as I blink back tears, my voice wavering with each word. "I can't stand by and watch you treat him this way any longer. I won't let him have the same life you did with your father."

He gives me a sad look and goes to reach for me, but I take a step back. I can't let him persuade me. I need to stand my ground, which I usually can't do when he touches me. He has the same effect on me he always has. Fighting or no fighting, he always will.

"You're going to leave me?" He asks.

We have never even thought about divorce. It was never something we had to worry about. The love we have is something I believe is truly one in a million. I want to tell him no, but I think that is what I mean. Gabriel has to come first. He needs a parent on his side; he needs me. I know he does. When I see him, he may be a man. As a young boy, I still see him, who used to fall asleep with my finger in his grasp.

This will be the hardest thing I have ever said to him in all our years of marriage.

I place my hands on his cheeks, cupping his face. "I love you, Jack Warner, so I'm going to tell you right now if I have to choose you or my son... it will *always* be my son."

I turn and leave him standing there with a blank look on his face. I tell myself this is for the best, but I also know I'm going to our bedroom to pack. I know my husband, and I know he loves me, that he doesn't want to lose me.

But his stubbornness will be his destruction.

CHAPTER 5

AVA

"So are you finally going to tell me about him, Bug?" Drew asks as we roast marshmallows over the fire. I've been here for two weeks and still haven't really spoken about Gabriel. My father doesn't even know what happened between us. He knows we broke up, and it wasn't a good breakup either. Now that I know I'm pregnant, I don't think I will tell him. Even though Gabriel hurt me, I don't want anyone to bad-mouth my child's father. This child is apart of both of us, and that means I should protect Gabriel's reputation... *right?*

I told Drew how we broke up and what he did, but I haven't said anything more about him. Talking about the things I like about Gabriel will make it too hard to get over him. I'm trying to be strong because what I feel, this baby now feels, but the emptiness is still there. My heart still hurts every day, all day.

I blow on the marshmallow and pop it in my mouth as he waits for me to answer him. He knows I'm stalling. "I don't know where to start."

"How did you meet him?" He asks and starts to swing his stick, trying to put out the fire on his marshmallow, just like when we were kids. My uncle used to yell at him that he would put someone's eye out.

I remember the library and smile. "In Portland. I was sixteen and working in the library to be away from my mom. He came up to me and helped me put a book on a high shelf that I couldn't reach. I, like every other girl in high school, was madly obsessed with him. He never noticed me, though."

"Until then." My cousin says, and I look at him to see him smiling.

"Yeah, until then."

"Then what?" He asks as he puts the marshmallow in this mouth.

I shrug. "We dated for a year, then he left with no word. He left me pregnant and alone, but then I lost the baby, but you already know that."

My dad told my uncle, who told Drew and my aunt, that we would visit them for a few weeks after my miscarriage. I needed to be around family, and my dad saw that. What was supposed to be a quick visit became a two-month extended stay for me. I got my GED online and helped my family run the farm. My dad stayed for three weeks but had to go back to Portland. He had a business to go back to, but he would fly back whenever I was ready to go home. Even though I felt more like myself, I knew I needed to get back to Portland. I had a dream of going to university and try to make my way into the publishing world. Little did I know at the time I would be finding my way back to Gabriel. "Then I got a job at a publishing company as an assistant only to find out Gabriel is the one who owns the company."

He gasps dramatically.

I roll my eyes at him. "Very funny."

"How did you not know he ran this company, Bug?" He asks, truly curious about how I missed the damn signs.

I shrug. "I don't know. I spent my whole life trying to get away from him and forget the pain he caused me. I truly thought nothing of anything. I made peace with the fact that I wouldn't find him again."

"So, ya'll find one another again and fall madly in love." He says with a teasing tone.

I scowl. "No, it wasn't that simple. I wasn't ready to accept him back in my life because—

"You still loved him." He finishes for me, and before I can argue with him, he continues. "C'mon, Bug, you can say it. I saw you all those years ago and the pain you carried for those months. Love like that doesn't go away, you thought it did, but he was out of sight and out of mind. You didn't want him back in your life because you would realize you never stopped loving him."

He's right.

When I think back to how hard I fought Gabriel's advances even though everything in me screamed for him, I know it's because I would get lost in him. He would consume me and have the power to destroy me. I was afraid if he *did* destroy me, I would just let him and continue to be by his side. I didn't want that for me; I wanted to be stronger than that. I walked away, which I never thought I would, but the heartache I feel reminds me how much I miss him, how much I love him still.

"Yeah," I breathe. "And I did realize it. It ended in nothing but heartache."

He frowns. "That's not true. You have a little bug growin' inside ya."

The doorbell begins to ring from inside the house. "That's probably the pizza." The adults are out at a club in town, leaving Drew and me to fend for ourselves tonight. Which, of course, means fast food.

"The money is on the table!" He says with his mouth full of marshmallows as I make my way into the house. I grab the bills on the table and make my way to the front porch to greet the pizza delivery driver. I step out on the porch, and everything slips away. My breath is knocked out of me as everything below my feet sinks.

There's no way.

"*Tristan*," I whisper with a quiver.

I want to scream, but I can't find my voice. I want to run, but there's no ground. I'm floating in the air. My legs won't cooperate.

"Hi, flower," he whispers, and it makes me flinch. I hate that nickname. "I can't believe I found you."

He looks different from when we dated. His blonde hair is now buzzed and he has grown out his facial hair. His beard is untamed and wild. He's also a lot more muscular than when we dated.

I look around, hoping someone will be here to save me. "What are you doing here, Tristan?" I ask as I finally take one step back, but he steps forward.

I need to be ready to run. I place my hand protectively over my stomach even though he has no idea there's a baby there.

"I just wanted to talk to you." He says and begins to walk toward me.

"*Stop!*" I shout a little too loud, but he listens.

"I'm not going to hurt you, Ava," he says cautiously, but the look in his eyes tells me otherwise. I know that look. He's drunk, and when he's drunk, that means he can't control his temper.

"Tristan, I have a restraining order against you. You know you can get in trouble for being here, and I don't want you in trouble." I have to play this smart. He has to think I mean him no harm, that I'm looking out for him. He doesn't want me to be against him. That's one of the things he always accused me of: betraying him.

"I went to look for you, but you were no longer with *that* guy." He says, and my body covers in goosebumps as I think of Gabriel. Gabriel could have gotten hurt because of me; he still can. Tristan has to believe that Gabriel and I are done for good... *that's the truth, isn't it?*

I shake my head. "I left him; I don't plan on going back to him," I say, hoping he believes me.

He chuckles. "I want to believe you, but you always were a liar. I saw how in love you were with him!"

I tense. "So, you were the one who broke into my apartment?" I ask.

He gives me a puzzled look. "No, no, I didn't break into your apartment."

I search his eyes. He's telling the truth. "Did you send someone?"

He shakes his head and takes one step forward. "Ava, I want to talk to you. Come with me, and let's talk." He reaches for my arm, and I begin to walk backward quickly.

"Don't touch me!" I yell, and I run into something. I look up to see my cousin with a shotgun in his hand. He cocks the gun and aims it right at Tristan.

"Step off my porch before I pull the trigger," Drew says as he nudges with the tip of his shotgun toward the driveway. Tristan gives him a challenging look, and I'm afraid for my cousin, but I know he can handle himself with a weapon.

He's shot things before.

"I don't believe you'd shoot me." Tristan challenges.

Drew takes the shot, and I scream, not expecting him to fire so soon. I cover my ears, and when I open my eyes, I see Tristan on the floor completely fine. He's shocked, however.

"Test me again," Drew says as he reloads and aims at Tristan. "Leave before I call the cops."

Tristan looks at me as he stands. He turns and gets into his car, pulling away then speeding off.

Drew put his shotgun down and embraces me. "Are you okay, Bug? Did he hurt you?" He asks worriedly and pulls away to examine me for any signs of wounds.

I nod. "I'm okay," I whisper.

Everything is telling me to warn Gabriel just in case, but I'm not ready to call him.

"How the fuck did the fucker find you?" He asks angrily.

"I don't know," I mumble and step away from him. I need to be alone. "I'm going to go freshen up."

"Bug," he says, sadly, but I don't stop to listen. I make my way into the house and upstairs to my guest room. I sit on my bed and cover my mouth, letting out a soft sob. I don't want him to hear me cry.

Tristan wasn't the one who broke into my apartment, which means it was someone else trying to hurt me. My apartment was on the top floor, meaning whoever did it did it on purpose. Who could it have been? My mind goes straight to Elizabeth. She is the only other person who would have it out for me other than Scott. This is all too much.

Tristan, Elizabeth, this break-in, Gabriel, and now this baby.

It wasn't supposed to happen this way. I thought when I'd have a child, their father would be right there with me.

My breathing becomes heavier as I try to catch my breath between sobs. The feeling in my stomach comes out of nowhere. I race to the bathroom and discard everything I had eaten today into the toilet. I fall against the tub and hug my knees as I sob.

I hear the door open and see Drew take in the surroundings. He makes his way to me and sits down next to me, wrapping his arms around me. I lay my head on his chest and let myself be comforted for the first time since I got here.

DREW

I would do anything to take away Bug's pain. It's been like that since we were kids. I always wanted a sibling, but my parents divorced, and my step-mom didn't want children, which meant Ava was the closest thing I had.

Don't get me wrong, I was a little upset in the beginning that she wasn't a he, but as she got older, I realized this girl wasn't a typical girl. She wasn't afraid to get her hands dirty on the farm; she was shy with other people, but she spoke her mind and never held her tongue with us. My uncle Ray used to joke that he would have grey hairs by next year because of Bug. If she wasn't challenging that bitch mother of hers, she would be challenging Ray and the women he brought home.

No woman was good enough or her father until Val came along, of course.

Bug quickly became my best friend and I hers. She didn't make many friends due to her being shy and not interested in the usual things kids were—Ava liked milking cows, riding horses and reading books. I always told her to try and party—even wanted to take her to one when she visited Texas—but I quickly learned it was not her scene. By the time I found her, she was reading a book in the backyard while eating a bag of chips.

That was just Bug.

So, when my dad sat me down to tell me that she was having a baby, I laughed my ass off, but when he didn't join in, I knew he wasn't kidding. There was no way our Bug could be pregnant, she was only seventeen, but then she lost it and came to live with us. I was excited, but when I saw her she wasn't my Bug... she was broken.

Grief had consumed her, and it showed.

There were so many nights that I held her like this when she couldn't control her breathing from how hard she was crying. If it wasn't over the baby, it was over the city man. She didn't tell me anything about him back then—we couldn't even mutter his name.

I carry her to her bed and tuck her in, laying down beside her, like I used to when she lived here. She couldn't sleep alone for the longest time, and I had to step up and be her protector, her big brother.

A big brother would do anything to make her feel better, right?

I grab my phone out of my pocket and begin to look for her city man.

CHAPTER 6

GABRIEL

I hold the ice pack against my lip as I pour myself another drink. I should be pissed that the bastard hit me, but I'm more grateful than anything. This makes it easier for me to hate him. What does hurt me was seeing my mum look at my father in a way she never has. She saw him as a monster when he laid his hand on me. Even though I hate my father, that doesn't mean I wanted to change him in my mum's eyes. I know how much she loves him and how high she holds him in her mind.

Seeing Isabella watch in horror as we yelled at one another also broke my heart. She could never stand us fighting. She isn't one for conflict, which is surprising because I've seen her with John.

Man has fucking patience.

My front door opens, causing me to freeze. Isabella walks into my kitchen with a grocery bag. She throws it on the counter as stops to gather her surroundings.

"What the hell happened in here?" She asks.

I look over at the living room to see the broken coffee table and bar stools.

Shit.

I guess I should have cleaned that.

"That's not important. What are you doing here?" I ask and put the ice pack down to take a swig of the rum. I prefer whisky, but I happened to finish all seven bottles I had stored.

She jumps onto the counter and begins to take out what she has in the bag. She pulls out chips, candy, and ice cream. I notice it's the same snacks we enjoyed as kids.

I narrow my eyebrows. "I don't have this body by eating this shit, Belle."

Women like my body, which means discipline and hard work.

She rolls her eyes and picks up the bottle of rum, taking a swig straight from the bottle. "Says the guy who has," she looks over by the sink and counts the liquor bottles out loud. "Twelve empty liquor bottles. Booze isn't good for you either. I figured with dad hitting you, you're going to need your family."

I frown. "I'm fine with dad hitting me."

She gives me a questioning look. "Gabriel, our father punched you right in the face. You can hate him all you want, but I know deep down, it has to hurt. Besides, you're going through a breakup, and this is the first time you've let me in your house."

"I didn't let you in," I argue.

"Hush," she says and waves me off before taking another sip. "We're doing this my way."

I sigh and take the bag of salt and vinegar chips, opening them and putting a handful in my mouth. My lips and the inside of my mouth begin to burn from the strong taste. My sister opens the ice cream pint, and I hand her a spoon, taking one for myself.

"How have you been doing... you know, about Ava."

I try not to flinch at the sound of her name. I haven't told anyone why she left. No one really knows we were together other than my staff and my sister. No one knows why I'm so empty or how empty I really am. I've been telling myself I can continue without her because I've done it before, but this time is different. It was more intense this time. I fell harder than I thought I could.

"She left me because of Elizabeth." I leave out the part where I let Elizabeth blow me before Ava and I had our first date. I know my sister, and she won't forgive me. "She thinks I slept with her. Now, I'm just empty."

She scowls. "So, you're just going to give up on her? You're going to let that bitch Elizabeth win?"

"It's not that simple, Belle. Ava left me for a reason. I don't see her coming back or even wanting to come back."

She reaches for the bag of chips and takes it out of my hand. "Gabriel, she deserves to know the truth. What if that changes everything? I have never seen you this way about anybody, and I won't lose my brother."

She's worried about me when she shouldn't be. I need to be the one taking care of her and watching over her. But my sister is just like our mum, so it's not surprising.

"What if she sends me away?" I ask, afraid.

I've thought about hunting her down, going to any lengths to find her, but I can't handle the rejection.

What if she doesn't even miss me? Has she even thought about me? Does she hate me?

These questions are what stop me from trying to mend what I destroyed.

My phone begins to ring, and I look at the caller I.D, but it reads *unknown caller*.

"Who is it?" Isabella asks as she tries to see my screen.

What if it's Ava?

Keep dreaming.

"I don't know," I mumble.

"Answer!" My sister yells, and I do.

I swipe to answer. "Hello, Gabriel speaking."

"Gimme a second," a whisper says over the phone. There is shuffling and muffled noises coming from the next line. "Hello, is this Gabriel Warner?" He has a southern accent.

"Yes, it is. Who is this?" I ask.

I know nobody with a southern accent.

"Bloody hell. Thank God. Do you know how long it took me to look you up? No wonder, Ava, had no idea you owned the company. For being a rich man, you're a hard man to track down."

What the hell is he talking about?

"You said the name, Ava," I say and my sister gasps.

"Put it on speaker!" She hisses and tries to reach for the phone. I move away and extend my arm to keep her at bay.

"Are you talking about Ava Thompson?" I ask.

He sighs heavily over the phone. "Yes, *city man*, now pay attention. I shouldn't even be calling you because she will kill me."

I can't believe I'm talking to... I stop. Who the fuck am I talking to? "Who is this?" I ask.

"My name is Drew Thompson. I'm Ava's cousin. Listen to me here, boy; you need to get your ass to her ASAP." He says with annoyance in his tone.

"I have no idea where '*here*' is," I say.

I hear Isabella whispering, "Is it Ava?" While eating the chips.

I scowl at her. "Does it sound like, Ava? Shush, Isabella, I'm trying to listen." I scold.

He blows out a breath. "Listen, sadly, I can't tell you where she is. I-I didn't think this all the way through, but you just have to think hard and figure out where she is. She won't forgive me if I tell you, and I'm the only one she has. She needs you even though you fucked up."

The line goes dead, and I look over at Isabella, who was hanging on my every word.

"Well?!" She asks.

"He didn't tell me where she is, but he told me to go look for her," I mumble as I go over our conversation. It hardly made sense, and I still had many more questions. The man hung up too quickly, but he was whispering at first, which meant Ava must have been close by.

"So..." she says and smirks at me. "What are you going to do?" She's smirking because she knows me well. She knows I'm going to go find her.

"I have to go look for her."

She grins. "Yes, yes, you do."

I decided the best way to start was by driving to Portland. Unable to right when Drew called due to the alcohol, I decided getting sleep and starting the day with a clear mind is the best way to go. Isabella drove home first thing in the morning after falling asslep on my couch.

If there is anyone who knows where Ava could be, it would be Ava's mum. They didn't have the best relationship, and I don't even know if they've spoken since she was in high school, but I figured it was worth a try.

It wasn't a peaceful sleep as nightmares tortured me. Drew said Ava needed me, and that's all my dreams were about. Ava was in trouble, calling for me, and I wasn't there to save her. I found her lifeless body in many different places, waking me up in a heavy sweat every time. Harris hasn't been able to find out who broke into her apartment, which means she's still in danger.

What if this person followed her to wherever she went?

I'm hoping her cousin is protecting her.

After three hours on the road, I pull up to her mum's old house and pray to God she still lives here. If she doesn't live here, I'm shit out of luck unless Harris finds something. I knock three times and begin to pace. She's never even met me.

Will she give me her daughter's information?

A good parent wouldn't... right?

The door swings open, and an older woman is standing there who looks precisely like Ava. The same, hair, eyes, face, skin but a tad shorter. There's no mistaking that this is Ava's mum.

"Yes?" She asks.

She has a slight accent I don't recognize.

Ava doesn't have an accent.

"Hi, ma'am, I'm Ava—your daughter's... boyfriend." I lie. "I was hoping you would know where she is?"

She gives me a quizzical look. "Come on in." She says and takes a step back, opening the door for me.

I follow her into her living room, and she takes a seat on the sofa. "How is she? Ava?" She asks.

I sit and clear my throat. "Honestly, I don't know. We had a misunderstanding, and I've been trying to call her to make things right, but she won't answer me."

She smirks. "Sounds like Ava. My daughter isn't very good with handling her emotions." She sighs heavily. "I guess she gets that from me. So, what did she misunderstand?"

I wasn't expecting her to ask me that.

I shift uncomfortably. "Ava thinks I slept with someone I didn't." I'm hoping she doesn't pry anymore.

She frowns. "I cheated on Ava's father. That's the first time she told me she hated me. This is going to be hard for her to look past."

I had no idea.

I shouldn't have done anything with Elizabeth in the first place, but of course, she would leave without a word when she caught Elizabeth naked in my apartment. Her dislike for her mum is strong, and her father's love is vital, which means she would dislike anything that is remotely related to her.

"Ma'am, her cousin Drew called me last night saying that she needs me, but he couldn't tell me where she is. He said he couldn't betray her trust, and I had to find out where she is. You're really my only hope."

She watches me in silence then stands up, walking to a small side table. She takes a notepad and begins to write something down, then tearing the piece of paper. "Here, this is the address of her dad's farm in Fort Worth, Texas. Ava's uncle still works the farm, and we tried to visit once a year. I hardly went, but the times I did go, Ava always used to say she wished she could live there. Knowing her, it's where she is."

I take the slip of paper and examine the address. I fold it and tuck it into my pocket before standing. "Thank you for this. I know it must not be easy to trust a stranger."

"You're not a stranger, Gabriel. I was wondering if I would meet you. I got your letter that you wrote all those years ago." She blows out a small chuckle. "Calling my ex-husband to give him that letter was... awkward, but when I read it, I knew she needed to read it. She deserved to know how you felt."

If only Ava would have listened to her father and read the letter. Instead, she shut him down at the mention of my name, but I understand. I would have been angry as well.

"Thank you for doing that. Given your relationship with Ava, you didn't have to pass on that letter. You could have thrown it out and gone about your day. I'm in your debt." I button my jacket and turn to leave.

"I do miss her." She says, stopping me in my tracks. I turn to see her and see her eyes full of unshed tears. "I made my mistakes, but I want nothing but happiness for her."

I think of my mum, and my heart squeezes for this woman.

"I hope she gives me another chance so I can tell her that."

It's how I'll repay my debt.

CHAPTER 7

AVA

My dad slams the door, and I sigh heavily as I go after him. He's not taking the news well that Tristan showed up here.

"Daddy, please, breathe," I beg as he takes off his cowboy hat.

"I should have been here," he says through his teeth. "I should have been here to kill that fucker!"

I know there's no calming him down right now, especially with my uncle and cousin being angry.

"Ray, you need to calm down. The girl is going through enough." Valerie says as she steps into the porch. She drapes her arm over my shoulders. "You heard Drew; he was there to protect the girl."

My dad runs his fingers through his hair and puts his hat back on. "He's lucky I wasn't here. That fucker." He spits.

"I know, daddy," I mumble and smirk at Valerie, who is rolling her eyes.

"This is serious, Val!" He snarls.

She kisses her teeth. "I know that, Ray! I'm not saying it isn't, but the girl is scared enough without having to worry about her daddy goin' mad!"

He sighs heavily and gives me a sympathetic smile. "I'm sorry, sweetheart, I should've been calm."

I look at Valerie in surprise. I knew she was exactly what my dad needed. "It's alright, daddy, I'm safe. That's all that matters."

He kisses my forehead and strokes my cheek. "You promise me you'll let me know if he ever comes close to you again?"

I nod. "Of course, I will. I did now, didn't I?"

He raises an eyebrow. "Only because you knew Drew wouldn't keep quiet." He says and walks inside.

He has a point.

I got to walk inside, but Valerie grabs my arm. "Wait for a second, darlin'." She says.

Oh no.

"What?" I ask nervously.

"Margi told me everything. When do you plan on letting your father know about you... bearing a child." She finishes in a whisper. I knew my aunt wouldn't be able to keep quiet. If she can't tell my uncle, she goes to the next best thing—her wine buddy Valerie.

"Please, don't tell him," I beg. "I've hardly had time to process this myself."

She frowns. "Darlin', whoever is the daddy deserves to know if he doesn't and knowing that you just found out tells me he doesn't have a damn clue."

She doesn't understand.

"It wasn't a good break up, Val; it's more complicated than that." Like sex clubs, ex's, cheating, break in's and now pregnancy.

She doesn't look impressed. "It does not matter, baby girl; this doesn't mean he has to be your husband. He just has to step up and take care of what's his. You don't deserve to go through this alone."

If I told her everything that happened between Gabriel and me, she would be on my side, yet I say nothing. The betrayal should be enough to bad mouth him. I should want to hurt him the way he hurt me, but what good would that do?

What if this child wants a relationship with Gabriel later in life? My family wouldn't even be able to look at him, especially my dad.

He hurt me, and I'm thinking about his reputation.

I sigh. "I promise, I will let everyone else know when the time is right. There's a lot I need to think about."

She's disappointed in my answer. That much is obvious.

She cups my face. "I know I'm not your mom, but I promise I am here for you with anything that you need."

My heart expands in my chest as tears well up in my eyes. I blame the hormones that come with pregnancy, but I have no idea when all that is even supposed to start. Valerie has been in my life since I began dating Tristan. My dad was doing renovations in her home, and the connection was immediate.

I sniffle, not bothering to hide my emotions. "I know, Val, thank you."

She kisses my cheek and begins to walk into the house.

"Val," I call out.

She stops and turns to face me. "Yes, darlin'?"

I swallow past the lump in my throat. "I consider you more of my mom than my real one."

I need her to know.

She isn't able to have kids. She told my father this pretty early in their relationship. She wanted to make sure he didn't want any more kids, that we would be content with just the two of them... and me. Every birthday, every card she wrote, 'thank you for being the daughter I always wanted.'

It was hard not to instantly fall in love with this woman.

She gives me a warm smile. "Good, 'cause you're my girl."

Drew has been acting weird around me since this morning. After he held and comforted me in the bathroom, I fell asleep. I woke up in my bed and assumed he carried me. When I went to his room, he began to stutter and trip over his words. When I asked him what was wrong, he just laughed and said he had to go tend to the horses. We went downstairs, and that's when he told my dad about Tristan.

He then proceeded to the stables and left me to deal with my angry dad. After Valerie went inside, I decided to go to the stables. Something is making Drew act weird, and I'm going to get to the bottom of it.

I see him in the pen with the other horses and check the stables to see Luna there.

Perfect.

Knowing I can't ride my horse at full speed is disappointing. I set the saddle up, wishing I could just ride Luna the way Drew rides Sunny. Drew has been riding horses since he was an infant, which means he doesn't have to use a saddle. You need great skill, experience, and trust to ride a horse without a saddle. The harness keeps inexperienced riders on the horses and can control them with the reins. Riders like Drew, my uncle, and my dad know how to balance their weight to stay on the horse.

"Ready to go, Luna?" I ask as I brush my palm over her side. I rest my cheek against her, hearing her breathe. "We can't go fast, I know you want to, but we have a baby we need to be gentle with."

I mount Luna and brush her side. "Let's go, girl." I kiss my teeth, and she begins to saunter, her hooves clicking against the dirt. Drew sees me as I get halfway to him, and Sunny starts to speed toward us.

"Should you be on a horse, girl?!" He scolds as Sunny comes to a stop.

He doesn't seem happy.

I roll my eyes. "Margi said it's okay, but, sadly, Luna can't go fast. Trotting only."

I need to ask him what's bothering him again before he can change the subject. "What is going on with you? You're keeping your distance from me."

He frowns and looks down at Sunny. "Ava, you need to drop this. I already told you nothing was wrong."

"Look at me," I command. He's lying through his teeth. "Tell me now, or I go."

He sighs heavily as he makes eye contact with me. "I called him."

Oh my god.

"You did what?" I ask through my teeth.

How could he?! Who does he think he is to call Gabriel?

If Drew told Gabriel where I am, that means nothing is stopping him from coming to find me. I'm not ready to see him; I'm not prepared to tell him. I look at my flat stomach and don't even believe there's a baby in there, and I stare at the ultrasound picture every night. Now, I may have to tell Gabriel a lot faster than I planned. I didn't even know if I wanted to tell him.

Luna begins to whine, bringing me back to reality. Animals can sense distress. I pet her side. "I'm okay," I whisper and look at Drew, who is gnawing on his bottom lip.

"I'm waiting, Drew."

"I didn't tell him where you were. I just called."

I scowl. "What was the point of calling then?"

"You can't do this alone." He argues.

He has some nerve.

"That's my decision to make, not yours." I turn Luna and make my way to the house.

I have to act fast.

He doesn't know Gabriel the way I do. He let me get away once, and I know he won't do it again. Especially now that Drew has called him.

I make my way into the house calmly so I don't worry my dad. I don't need anyone asking questions. I go upstairs and into the guest bedroom where I'm staying. I throw my suitcase on my bed and begin to throw everything inside.

"Where are you going, bug?" Drew asks.

"Anywhere," I say as I make my way into the bathroom. Of course, he followed me. He does as he pleases, and it's aggravating.

"Ava, we both know you can't leave. Where are you going to go?" He asks, and I stop.

He's right.

Where will I go?

I look down at my stomach and sigh heavily. It's no longer just me; it's this baby too. I have no money, no job, no home, nothing to my name except what's right here. What kind of mother would I be if I didn't have a plan? I know he will come to find me, but I'm hoping I have more time. I'm hoping he will give me the chance to figure out where I go from here. I need to find another job and begin saving for what this child will bring. I'm going to have to bust my ass to provide for this child on my own. Nor do I want anyone's help.

"What if he's already on his way?" I ask and turn to face Drew.

He's leaning against my doorframe with his arms crossed over his chest. "I'll lock the door." He shrugs.

I smirk.

"C'mon, bug, I didn't tell him where we live. How could he find you this quickly?" He asks and walks into my bedroom, then begins to empty my poorly packed suitcase. "You're overreacting."

I scowl. "This doesn't mean you're forgiven."

He stops. "Or we could be even since I scared Tristan off?" He asks, hopeful.

Damn it.

I roll my eyes. "Fine."

I spit in my hand and stick it out for him. He was the one who taught me this in the first place. He spits in his hand and shakes mine.

"See, bug, you can't hate me. I'm too damn lovable." He winks and exits my bedroom.

CHAPTER 8

GABRIEL

It's morning when I arrive in Texas. I was hoping
sleep would come on the plane, but anxiety got the best
of me. I haven't been this nervous for anything in a very
long time. Spending two days flying to get here isn't
helping. Scenario after scenario run through my head,
but only one is sticking. The scenario where she sends
me away because she doesn't love me anymore. I tell
myself that I can handle it; I'm a grown-ass man who is
CEO of a successful company.

Ah, fuck.

I know I'm shit out of luck.

I can't seem to control my emotions where Ava is
concerned. I called Drew back to let him know I got a
flight out to Texas. He had been shocked that it took me
less than 24 hours to find out where he lives. He warned
me that Ava tried to bolt when he confessed that he

called me. It made me more grateful to leave so soon. I can't let her run away again. I have to fight for her.

I need to prove myself.

I told him to pick me up from the airport and make a really good fucking excuse on why he's gone. He can't make it obvious, or she'll be gone before I even pull into the driveway. After claiming my bag from the belt, I see if I can spot someone who may look like Ava... but a guy...

This is going to be impossible.

Then I spot a man wearing a plaid button-down, ratty jeans, cowboy boots and a cowboy hat.

No fucking way this guy is for me.

He's carrying a sign that says "Rich City Man."
Jesus.

I make my way to him, and he looks at me in pure shock. "You must be Drew," I say when I'm close enough. I stick my hand out of him to shake. "I'm... rich, city man."

He shakes my hand. "Of course you are." He mumbles. "Bug, left a ton of shit out when she told me about you."

Bug?

"*Bug?*" I ask.

He clears his throat. "Ah, shit. I always forget not to call her that around other people. She hates it. Bug is Ava. My uncle gave her that nickname when she was little, and it kind of stuck." He reaches for my bag. "Let me get that for you."

He doesn't give me a chance to respond before his hands are already taking my luggage.

Southern hospitality, I suppose.

"Thanks," I mumbled, not really sure where to go from here. I planned to beg for her forgiveness, but now that I'm here, all I want to do is go back home. She wants nothing to do with me, she's made that clear, yet here I am, racing toward rejection.

I follow him out of the airport in silence. I'm glad he doesn't pester. I need time to think about what to say to her. She's going to be angry when she sees me; I know that much. She's going to tell me I had to right to come after her, that I should have just left her alone so she can move on.

"What's on your mind?" He asks as we drive.

I hardly remember even getting in the car. "How is she?" I ask. If she sends me away, I at least need to know she's okay. I need to know that she's been happy and she will be satisfied here.

He takes a beat then sighs. "She was rough when she first got here, but it's been getting better. Not because I think she's moving on, but I think she's trying to convince herself that she can live without you."

His words pierce me profoundly, but I deserve it. She should forget me. "I'm not sure what she's told you..."

He shakes his head. "It's none of my business what happened between y'all."

I frown. "I love her." I'm not sure why I'm telling him. Maybe, I need him to believe me?

He chuckles under his breath. "You found her in under twenty-four-fucking-hours. You're either batshit crazy or in love."

I sigh as I run my fingers through my hair. "What's the difference?"

He laughs loudly.

"My dad said that she's in the barn, so it's safe pulling into the house," Drew says as he finishes parking. He turns off the engine and looks at me. "You ready, partner?"

I nod.

It's now or never.

We step out of his truck—which is magnificent—and he leads me around the farmhouse. I'm definitely not in Seattle anymore. The land the house sits on goes for miles with crops, barns, pens, and animals. I see horses in the distance, and someone is on a horse with them. The smell of manure is strong, along with the fucking bugs. I slap my hand against my neck, and Drew looks at me with amusement.

"Welcome, to Texas." He grins. He stops when we're about halfway and takes his hat off to run his hand through his long hair.

"It's all you now, partner. She's going to know I brought you here, which means I don't want to be anywhere near her." He nods, then puts his hat back on. "Good luck."

He pats my shoulder and makes his way back to, what looks like, the main house. I can feel my heart pounding against my chest as if it's going to rip through. I keep pushing through the anxiety as I make my way to the barn but stop when I see a woman on the horse in a horse pen. I begin to make my way closer, and her silhouette becomes more apparent.

I know it's her the second I see her black hair trailing down her back. She's making noises with her mouth, and the dark brown horse she's on response almost instantly. I make my way to the railing and lean against it, watching her in an element I never thought I would see her in. She's wearing a dark brown leather cowboy hat, a green plaid shirt that's tucked into her dark jeans, with dark brown cowboy boots. Today is about winning her back; I know that, but I'm still a man and seeing her in this outfit is the hottest thing I've ever fucking seen.

I had no idea she could even ride a horse.

I feel out of place in my casual jeans and t-shirt.

The horse begins to turn, and that's when her eyes meet mine. Her face falls as she blinks quickly to really see if I'm standing before her.

She kisses her teeth, and the horse begins to stroll out of the pen. I stand up straight and wait for her to approach me, praying she doesn't take off on the horse. It would take me way too long to catch up to her. She stops and climbs off the horse, then ties it to the post. She pets the horse before turning to face me.

"What are you doing here, Gabriel?" She asks, annoyed.

Okay, not the tone I was hoping for.

"When I found out this is where you might have gone, I needed to see for myself." I want to touch her, but I know if I move closer to her, she will begin to bolt. "Ava, there are some things I need to explain."

She shakes her head. "I've heard and seen enough, Gabriel, thanks." She turns.

Fuck.

"I didn't sleep with Elizabeth!" I shout. This isn't how I wanted to say this, but I know the stubborn woman won't sit down and discuss this over a cup of tea. She has her mind made up, which means blurting this is the only way to tell her.

She turns on her heels and marches toward me, her hips swaying.

Shit, Gabriel, focus on her, not her fucking body.

She pushes my chest hard, catching me by surprise. "Don't you dare fucking lie to me!" She yells. "I saw her!"

She begins to push me again while grunting, and I watch her sadly. I continue to let her hit me, knowing she needs to do this. She thinks I fucked that dreadful woman right after I left her place that day; she has every right to be angry with me. Right now, I wish I could wring Elizabeth's neck. Seeing her like this proves how much pain she's been in because of this lie.

"Why are you here?!" She yells as she begins to punch me. "Why can't you leave me alone?! Why can't you let me move on?!"

I try to grab her arms, but she begins to move them faster and hit harder. "*Ava,*" I say between my teeth as she begins to tear. "Ava, stop."

I grab her arms, and she tries to free herself. "I hate you!" She yells as she continues to push and pull her arms free.

"*Ava,*" I say tiredly and grab her, pinning her against the railing of the pen. It hurts too badly to hear these words come from her.

"*Enough,*" I demand. This is not how I wanted this to go; I was hoping we could talk. I had no idea she would begin to hit me. "I came here to tell you I didn't sleep with her. When I left your apartment that day after leaving that voicemail, I went to the gym to work out my anger. I wasn't ready to go home because I knew I would break everything in my sight. I didn't shower at the gym because it wasn't my plan to even go there. I got home and went straight to the shower. When I finished, I came down and found Elizabeth naked in my apartment, but I sent her away. I *never* slept with her, Ava, and I *never* will. I fucked up, angel, I know that, but I'm here to beg you to forgive me. This past month and five days have been hell without you, and I can't do it anymore. I can't drink myself numb."

She isn't looking me in the eyes; instead, her eyes are on my lips. "What happened to you?" She asks in a whisper.

She is catching me by surprise left, right and centre.

"I got in a little argument with my father." I frown.

She meets my eyes. "He *hit* you?" She asks, shocked.

This is not what I thought she would say after I said all that, but at least she's speaking to me. "Yes," I mumble.

The last thing I want to be talking about is my father hitting me.

"You didn't sleep with her?" She asks.

I shake my head. "No. I...I hurt you once already, Ava, with that woman I wasn't going to do it again." I need her to know. "I haven't touched or looked at a single woman. I've hardly left my apartment wondering if you were even alive."

She lets her head hang. "Gabriel, we can't do this." She whispers.

"Angel, don't say that...please." I know it's not fair to beg her. I know it's not fair to beg for a second chance.

"*Ava?*" A woman says from behind us. Ava shoots up straight, and I let her arms go, turning around to see who interrupted us.

"Oh, uh, Aunt Margi, this is *Gabriel*." She says, putting emphasis on my name. I give her a confused expression before looking at Aunt Margi. She has strawberry blonde hair and is wearing the same kind of outfit that Ava is wearing. She seems to be about in her mid to late forties. Her bright blue eyes shine when they spot me. With no shame, her eyes begin to scan my body quickly, causing a slight blush to touch her cheeks.

I give her an award-winning smile that I usually give to women when I need to charm them. "Hi, ma'am, nice to meet you. By the sound of it, I'm guessing you already know about me."

I wonder what Ava has told her.

She puts her hand in mine. "Nice to meet you, darlin'. And believe me, there's a *lot* my niece left out." She gives Ava a look as if I'm not standing right here.

I clear my throat to hide my chuckle. "As her boyfriend, I would *love* to hear what she's told you."

"You're *not* my boyfriend." She says bitterly.

"*Ava.*" Margi scolds and pats my shoulder. "I was just coming to get Ava for lunch if you'd like to join us."

I grin and look at Ava, who is scowling at her aunt. "Well, that's why I flew here."

She grins. "Great." She hooks her arm with mine, and I know I've charmed her. "C'mon, girl, we can't wait on you forever!" Margi calls out to Ava, who curses under her breath as she follows us.

We enter the house, and all eyes are on me. There's Drew sitting on the couch with a beer in his hand, sitting next to a man I don't recognize. Walking from the kitchen and into the living room is Ava's father. He looks much older than when we were in high school but still recognizable. He stops when he spots me with Aunt Margi on my arm.

"Margi, wanna tell me why the hell you have some big ass man on your arm?" The man I don't recognize says as he stands.

"Dev, please, this is Gabriel. He came all this way to see Ava." She says, and Ava walks into the house but doesn't stop to participate. She grabs Drew's hand and pulls him off the couch, ignoring his protests. You can tell that the cousins are close.

"Hey," Devon says, but they don't stop. I watch them go up the stairs, and the last thing we hear is a door slam close with a lot of force.

Drew was right; she would kill him.

"Nice to meet you, sir; I hope I'm not intruding," I say politely as I stick my hand out for him to shake. I can feel Ava's father's eyes on me. I'm praying to God he doesn't know because he wouldn't let me close to Ava again.

Devon puts his hand in mine. "Nice to meet you, kid. You, Bug's, boyfriend?" He asks.

"I'll get back to you on that," I say, and he chuckles. I look over at Stephen, who is scowling at me.

"Mr. Thompson, nice to see you again." I haven't seen the man in a decade. I'm sure he isn't my biggest fan.

"Gabriel," He says. "Margi, Devon, can you two give us the room?"

He's asking, but the look on his face says it all, *do as I say*. They're quick to leave.

"What are you doing here? Last time I checked, my daughter wanted nowhere near you." I knew trying to win over this man would be a challenge, but I'm not going down quickly.

"I know, and she has every right to hate me. I've done things that make me completely unworthy of her but believe me when I say I love your daughter more than I have loved anything in this world. I came here to apologize and beg her to take me back, but if she really is truly happy without me, I promise you, I will leave her no matter how much it pains me." I walk closer to him and stick out my hand for him. "You don't have to like me because Lord knows I can't stand the sight of myself lately, but that won't stop me from trying to win her back."

He looks at my hand then back at me. "She likes it here, and she wants to stay." He says.

She's never mentioned that she wants to live in Texas. I know being part of the writing world is her dream, but if this is also her dream, I will do anything to give it to her. "Then looks like this is where I stay too."

His eyebrow arched slightly. "You would give up that fancy company?" He's surprised.

I nod. "It means nothing to me where she's concerned."

He smiles and places his hand in mine. "Good."

CHAPTER 9

AVA

I'm panting as I bang my hand against the bathroom door. I can't believe he brought Gabriel here when he promised me he wouldn't get more involved! He told me not to pack, knowing damn well he would pick Gabriel up from the fucking airport. If I wasn't pregnant, I would have bolted with Luna, leaving him behind, knowing he won't be able to catch me. This pregnancy is already stopping me from doing things, and the hormone change is making me pissed off with it all.

I kick the door. "Open up, you scaredy-cat!" I yell through the door. I dragged Drew up here to kill him, but the idiot ran into the bathroom and locked it.

"You're pregnant," he whispers, unclearly. His lips are against the door, so I can hear him better. "You shouldn't be overworking yourself."

"You're the one riling me up!" I yell.

Stress is the one thing I should be avoiding, but with the men in my life, that's going to be impossible. The door unlocks, and he opens the door slowly. I roll my eyes and make my way to the bed, sitting down. How am I supposed to go down there and face him? Of course, my aunt took one look at him, and like all the other women that meet him, she melted completely.

"Bug, what is the problem, hm? Why are you fighting this?" He asks as he sits down next to me.

"Why are you pushing us together?" I ask.

That is what has been confusing me the most. Shouldn't Drew be protecting me from this?

He shrugs. "I know you love Texas, Bug, but I also know that this wasn't your dream. The little girl who would leave books laying all over the damn place wanted to be an editor. She wants to be a publisher, making someone's dreams come true. He is who you belong with, in Seattle—and I know he'll take care of you."

I laugh. "How can you possibly know that?" I ask in disbelief.

"I saw the look in his eyes, Bug." He says seriously as if that means anything. "Answer me this: why are you trying to fight this? I know you miss him even though you've stopped crying. I see it all over your face, Bug; something in you has changed. You're not yourself, and I don't think you will be until you're back with him. There's nothing to be ashamed of for taking him back.

He's the father of your child, and you guys deserve a chance at making things work. I saw this same thing ten years ago and I can't see it again. Besides, Tristan is out there, and I can't be there to always protect you. I need to make sure you're safe."

I think of Tristan and what that means for this child and me. What if he finds me again and I'm showing more? Will that make him crazy knowing Gabriel is the father of my child? Will he stalk me even more? Would he try to hurt me? Worse, would he try to harm my baby or Gabriel? I haven't felt myself since I left Gabriel. That empty pit in my chest grows and grows no matter what I do.

This isn't how I wanted my time being pregnant to be. I was hoping I would be married, first of all, but I imagined my husband and me falling in love with this child every day. Discussing names in bed, laughing as we paint the nursery because we can't paint for shit. Picking out clothes even though we swore we would wait until after the baby shower. I just pictured happiness, and so far, it has been fear and sadness.

We make our way downstairs, and Gabriel is already seated with a beer in his hand and in deep discussion with my dad and uncle. My aunt is serving them as if he belongs at that table. Drew continues to walk into the kitchen to be seated, but I stand back and watch for a few seconds. I enjoy the sight of Gabriel, who looks like he doesn't belong at all but still putting effort into bonding with my family. I place my hand on my stomach as I begin to feel butterflies. I picture our child running around when we visit for holidays. I would be helping Margi and Valerie in the kitchen while Gabriel catches up with my dad. Drew and my uncle are watching some game after my uncle tried to assist in the kitchen but managed to burn something in the first few seconds.

Gabriel looks up as he laughs and spots me over everyone. He stops laughing and gives me a small smile. It's almost shy. He nods, gesturing for me to come to him. I take a deep breath and enter the kitchen. Valerie moves to stand behind Gabriel and looks at me with wide eyes.

'*WOW*,' she mouths and begins to fan herself.

I roll my eyes and begin to laugh, gaining the attention of the men. Valerie walks away quickly, leaving me to explain what's so funny. Gabriel is giving me an amused smirk.

"Sorry," I mumble. "Didn't know laughing was against the rules." I turn and walk over to my aunt and stepmom.

"Please, don't drool all over my... *ex-boyfriend*," I mumble and scowl at the two women who are blushing like school girls. I don't need this right now. I take the food to the dinner table and sit down right beside Gabriel.

Great.

Everyone begins to fill their plate once we're all seated, and the awkward silence has already started. My stomach growls loudly, and I feel Gabriel's eyes on me. My morning sickness started today, leaving breakfast out of my daily schedule now. I noticed I have to wait until I'm starving before this baby will let me keep food down.

It's torture, really.

"You okay?" He asks me, and he places his hand on my knee. Goosebumps begin to cover my skin as it heats up intensely. It feels like my skin is on fire. I have to cross my legs to stop the sudden ache between my legs.

Woah.

I look at him to see if he's noticed, but he hasn't. Thank God. He hardly touched me, and I felt like I was going to explode.

I nod, swallowing hard. "Yes," I say, my throat suddenly dry. I reach for my water and drink the whole glass as if I haven't had water in days.

I'm flustered.

What the hell is happening?

"Slow down, girl; there's more water." My dad scolds me as I wipe the water that's on my chin.

I clear my throat and take a quick peek at Gabriel, who is smirking but looking down at his food. "Sorry," I mumble.

I can't believe he's even at this table.

"So, Gabriel, I noticed you have an accent," Valerie says with a gleam in her eyes.

This woman can't contain herself.

"So, do *you*, Val." I point out.

"Yes, girl, but ours are borin' compared to his. He's Australian." She informs me like I'm not the one who dated him.

Gabriel chuckles. "It's okay, Ava; I find it flattering that you like my accent. A lot of people tend to confuse it with the English accent."

"Oh, no, yours is *much* sexier," Margi says, and I drop my utensils.

"*MARGI!*" Devon says, shocked, and Drew begins to laugh.

"Oh my god," I mumble and bury my face in my hands. This isn't happening. My family isn't embarrassing me—a twenty-seven-year-old—in front of her ex-boyfriend. This is all a dream.

Gabriel begins to chuckle and touches my thigh, causing me to gasp and clench my thigh together. Everyone is too busy reacting to my aunt's inappropriate comment to pay Gabriel and me any mind right now. He looks down at his hand that is on my thigh. The tips of his fingers are being squeezed by my thighs. I unclench, and his eyes meet mine. They're hungry and dark. My stomach squeezes tightly in anticipation.

I have never felt this...overwhelmed before.

"Settle down." My dad says and looks at Gabriel. "Sorry about that, son."

SON?!

What the hell? When did that happen?!

I look at him in disbelief. "I can't believe this," I say as anger begins to build up.

"*Ava,*" my aunt says as a warning, but I ignore her.

"I have been heartbroken for weeks because of this man, and he's all charmed you straight up his—

"Ava," Valerie says. "Your emotions aren't the best right now, so why don't you try and calm down."

I clench my jaw as everyone watches me. "*Fine,*" I say between my teeth and walk away, needing the safety my bedroom offers. I throw myself on my bed and scream into the pillow.

That was a wild rollercoaster of emotions in such a short period. I had never been so awkward, turned on, embarrassed, and angry. Now, all I can think about is how good it would feel to cry.

Jesus.

I sit up and run my fingers through my hair. If it only gets worse as pregnancy goes on, I'm screwed. There's a slight knock at my door, and it open slowly. Gabriel steps into the room and closes the door behind him.

"Ava, what the hell was that?" He asks, confused. I want to ask him what he means, but I know he's referring to my thigh clenching and me gasping at his touch. I can't tell him it's hormones because I'm not ready to tell him about the baby. I have no idea if I'm going to take him back or not. Everything is happening too quickly.

I shake my head. "I don't know." I lie and stand up. I can't think when he's this close to me and a bed. "I'm sorry. I'm not feeling myself today."

He frowns and steps slowly toward me. I back up until I'm against the wall with nowhere else to go. He stops a foot away. "Ava, if me being here isn't what you want, you can tell me, and I will leave. Even though it will fucking kill me, angel, I will walk out that door." He fills the space between us and lifts his hand to touch my cheek. I let out a shaky breath as I try to hold in a moan that wants to escape from the contact. "Just tell me what you want."

His hand slides down to my neck, and I let my head drop against the wall, moaning softly from the sensation. My skin begins to heat up again as goosebumps appear. My body is screaming for him, and my mind is having a hard time fighting off that desire. My body is taking over, and I have no choice in submitting myself to him.

His hands make way to my shirt's buttons and begin to slowly unbutton until the tops of my breasts are visible. I feel his lips press against my neck and make their way down to my breasts.

"*Please,*" I whisper, my hand going into his hair. I never thought I would be okay with this happening in my uncle's house. But right now, all I'm thinking about is having Gabriel all over me.

"Please, what?" He breathes and begins to kiss under my ear.

"Please, don't stop," I mumble, unashamed. I want him to know how badly I want him right now. I unbutton my jeans until they're slightly loose and grab his hand, pushing it down my jeans and panties.

"*Ava.*" He says, shocked and groans when his fingers slide through my folds, feeling how wet I already am. "*Fuck.*" He curses as I wrap my arms around his neck and hitch my leg around his waist to lift myself slightly. I begin to ride his fingers, not bothering to be ashamed. He slides his finger in me and groans against my neck. "You look hot as fuck in this outfit, angel."

I whimper at his words. He takes his fingers out and sets me down on my feet. He unbuttons my shirt quickly, letting it fall open.

"You're my personal cowgirl, and I'm a caveman about it, baby." He pulls down my bra, pushing my breasts up. I gasp from the tenderness but don't stop him. I'm craving his mouth on my nipples. He leans down, and his tongue brushes against my already hard nipple before taking it in his mouth and sucking softly.

I slap my hand over my mouth, trying to keep my screaming at bay. Everything is so intense now my body can hardly handle it. My legs begin to shake as I already feel that familiar climbing feeling I've come to love. I push him away and back him up until he falls onto the bed. I take him out of his jeans and wrap my mouth around his tip, taking him slowly until he hits the back of my throat.

"*Oh fuck,*" he moans softly as he lets his head drop between his shoulders. I continue to work my mouth over him until he's dripping wet. I stand and take my jeans off along with my panties and then reach for my hat resting on my pillow. I put it on, and his eyes darken.

"Take off your bra but leave the shirt on." He demands, and I do as he says before straddling him. "I've died and gone to fucking heaven." He says as he cups my breasts.

I smirk. "Not yet, baby," I whisper.

I lean down and press my lips against his for the first time in a month; I relish in the feeling, my body coming finally coming to life. My libido falls into a puddle with a relaxing sigh. My anxiety falling away as calming butterflies fill my stomach. His mouth worships mine slowly, and I savour the feeling of his tongue brushing against mine. I bite his lip softly, pulling a moan from deep in his chest.

I position him at my entrance and slowly sink down, gasping with every inch of his length. He groans and squeezes my ass. Once I've taken him completely, I begin to move up and down with intensity. My libido isn't here for slow lovemaking. It's hungry and wants to devour. It needs to be tamed, and I know Gabriel is the only one who can do it.

"Shit, Ava," He groans quietly and digs his nails into my ass, causing me to moan. The pain is needed a lot more, too, which I wasn't expecting. I never let a man spank me until Gabriel. "Ride me fast, angel; I want to watch you get off."

He leans back on his shoulder, and I do exactly that. I begin to rub my clit, but he swats my hand away. "You focus on riding me." He demands and with the pad of his thumb he begins to rub my clit in circular motions.

My head falls back as I gasp from the sensation. He's deep inside me, yet I need more. I want to feel him everywhere. I need my fill of Gabriel. I move off my knees and rest my feet on the bed, perching myself higher. I begin to move harder and faster on his cock as I place my hands on his chest, scratching and clawing over his shirt.

"Just like that, Ava, ride me until you explode." He says. His hair is a mess, his lips red and swollen from our kiss; his muscles flexing under the shirt that's clinging to his sweaty body; his eyes are dark and full of lust. His dirty words go straight to my clit, and my body begins to shake.

"There we go." He mumbles and grabs, me flipping me onto my front. He slaps my ass hard as he straddles me from behind and sinks back into me, deeper this time. I claw at the bed, and he doesn't give me time to catch my breath before he's pounding forward, taking out my breath with every blow. I can feel his mouth by my ear.

"Come for me, angel, like the dirty girl that you are." He whispers, and just like a bomb, I explode, muffling my sounds into my mattress.

"Fuck, Ava." He groans through his teeth, and his body shakes over top of mine as he empties himself inside me. He collapses to the side, and we're both panting. He looks at me in shock, and I begin to giggle.

He grins and begins to laugh with me.

I sigh and grin at him.

His eyes soften for me. "I missed you."

I bite my lip as I think about what to say. Do I tell him that I haven't missed him even though we just had sex? I would be lying through my teeth. We both missed one another, and at this moment, I'm okay with that.

"I missed you too."

CHAPTER 10

AVA

As the sexual fog begins to clear, I wonder what the fuck I was thinking? I jumped on him and didn't even stop to ask if he wanted this. I stand and quickly begin to put my clothes back on.

"Ava." He says sternly.

I don't turn to face him as I button my jeans then begin to button my shirt. I don't know what came over me. I felt the same burning desire for him, but it was intensified. Everything in my body was singing, my skin burning, needing him to touch me. My body missed him and didn't care that he broke my heart or that my mind was telling me this wasn't a good idea.

Clearly, he missed me just as much.

If this is how it's going to be the whole pregnancy, I won't stand a chance. I'll need to be with Gabriel just for him to ease this new, unexpected urge.

"I'm sorry, I shouldn't have attacked you that way," I say with embarrassment. I can't believe I put on my cowboy hat before riding him. I can't believe I rode his fingers with no shame.

I make my way to the bathroom and begin to wash my face. My body is still cooling down, and it doesn't help to have him close by.

"Why are you apologizing? I wanted it just as bad." He says from behind me. I grab a towel and begin to dry my face. I turn to face him to see him fully clothed. His hair is a complete mess but still looks so yummy.

"That shouldn't have happened," I mumble.

He scowls. "Are we really going back to this? Do we need to fucking sing together again for you to realize how you feel for me?" He approaches me and cups my face. I get lost in his green eyes that have a hint of yellow around his pupils. "Give me a second chance to prove myself. I know I don't deserve to ask this of you, but I'm begging, baby. I will never hurt you again."

I sigh. "I can't have that woman in our lives." I hate that I'm going to make him choose.

He shakes his head. "Trust me, you don't have to worry about her. She told me that she sent you away by lying to you that we slept together. That's what made me want to come after you... well, Isabella convinced me."

My heart squeezes at the mention of Isabella. "How is she?" I ask, sadly.

His eyes soften. "She's good. Worried about you."

I feel like shit.

"I should have said something," I mumble.

"Don't. You had every right to leave the way you did. No one is upset with you. Everyone should be upset with me." His face falls. "I'm sorry."

"Shh," I whisper, knowing I don't need to hear him apologize anymore. I don't know if it's the baby, but I feel more connected to him, more attached. I'm drawn to him more than ever. I want to tell him about the baby, but I need to see where this goes first. I need to make sure I'm putting this child first. If anything were to go wrong, I need to be able to leave swiftly and quickly.

I need to trust him a little more before I give him the chance to hurt the both of us.

There's a knock at the door, startling us. "Time to feed the horses, girl." My uncle says through my bedroom door.

I wonder how Gabriel would be working the farm. "How long are you staying for?" I ask.

I don't know where we go from here, but I'm not quite ready to leave Texas. I love the farm life.

Am I supposed to follow Gabriel when he goes back to Seattle?

The realization that I have no idea what I'm going to do is dawning on me. I have to develop a plan and find a job to provide for this child... and a new place to live.

"However long you want me here." He says, and I smile.

I forgot how sweet he is with words.

"Then you better follow me. It's time to feed the horses." I can't help but grin when he gives me a nervous expression. I don't think this man has had to work hard labour a day in his life.

When we went downstairs, my aunt and lovely stepmother went shopping for clothes for Gabriel. Gabriel hushed me and laughed, thanking them for the sweet gesture. They had also taken in his luggage and left it by my bedroom door. I just pray they didn't hear us...*canoodling.*

He sent me off to the field and said he would be there as soon as he finished dressing into his new clothes. I would love to see him on a horse. I think my whole family would.

"Bug, he is the hottest thing I have ever seen," Margi says as Valerie and I stand in the barn. I don't know what has gotten into my aunt.

"And Australian," Val says as if that multiplies his attractiveness.

I roll my eyes. "Are you two going to embarrass me more today?" I ask. They have no shame. "Enough with the compliments. That man already knows how attractive he is; he doesn't need y'all filling his ego more."

"Did you tell him?" Val asks with a disapproving tone.

I sigh and brush Luna. "*No…*" I say sadly.

"Why?" Margi asks. "He came all the way here for you, Bug; he deserves to know."

I know she's right, but fear takes the ladder. "I know; I just want to make sure he… that he can love and accept the both of us. I don't want my child to come second." Or myself.

Val and Margi exchange a look. "We understand that," Val says with sympathy. "C'mon, let's get Luna out of the barn."

We begin to walk out to the men, and I stop when I see Gabriel walking toward us in his new attire.

You have got to be kidding me.

He's wearing a dark brown leather cowboy hat, a denim button-up that hugs his sexy, muscular arms. He's rolled up the sleeves like he usually does, exposing the tattoos on his arms. I could write poetry about his strong arms. He's wearing dark wash denim jeans that I can tell are hanging low on his hips. If I were to lift his plaid shirt, I know I would see that delicious *V-shape—focus, Ava*—and black cowboy boots.

He's even hotter in this than a suit.

Val was not joking around, clearly. She wanted to see if this man would actually put on this outfit.

I can hear the women whispering between themselves, but I can't bother to look away from my

God walking before me. I never imagined him this way because it seemed very out of his comfort zone, but the ruggedness he gets from his dad makes him fit into this role easily.

"Australian cowboy," I say when he's close enough with a slight smirk.

He tips his hat to me, and I hate that I can feel myself blush. "*Your* Australian cowboy." He leans down with no shame and gives me a swift kiss, leaving me wanting. He smells different. His purely fresh scent smells divine. "Now, what're we doing?"

"Well, we just fed the horses. Now, you're going to ride one." I say with a grin.

He narrows his eyes. "*Pardon?*"

I giggle. "You're going to ride the horse. Well, *my* horse."

"Uh," I hear Drew say from the pen. "Bug, have we forgotten that Luna only lets you, daddy-o, and Ray ride her?"

It's true.

Luna only trusts me, my uncle and my dad. They never understood why but I did. It's all about my connection. Riding a horse is more than transportation. It's companionship, and Luna is picky when it comes down to it. But I wanted to see how she did with Gabriel. It's not like she will hurt him. She just gets a little skittish.

"You want me to ride a horse that's picky with its riders?" He asks in disbelief.

I roll my eyes. "You'll be fine," I say as I lace my fingers with his, pulling him toward Luna, who my dad is petting and feeding an apple. She stuck with my daddy and uncle because they were the ones that helped birth her. At least that's what they say.

"It's a connection you won't understand until you do it yourself." My uncle used to say.

My dad moves aside with a smirk, and everyone watches to see what my picky horse will do. I let his hand go when I'm close to Luna and pet her. She neighs when Gabriel gets close.

"Be good," I whisper as I kiss her. "He's a good one, I promise."

I gesture with my hand for him to move closer. "C'mon, *city boy*." I tease, and he rolls his eyes. He approaches her, and she begins to move her head a bit, but he doesn't stop. He reaches his hand out and slowly makes his way to pet her. She begins to show distress, but he places his hand on her head and the other on her side, brushing her lightly.

"Holy shit," he whispers and chuckles as he looks at me, his eyes filled with joy and amazement.

I grin. "Cool, isn't it?"

My dad begins to walk him through how to mount the horse and how to use the reins. Drew is on Sunny next to Luna, waiting for Gabriel to saddle, and he will take him through the trails.

Gabriel whispers something to Luna and mounts her swiftly. Val and Margi begin to applaud along with my uncle, who is on his own horse—*Spirit*.

I shake my head in disbelief. *She's gentle with him*. He gives me a cocky grin and winks at me. "I have a way with ladies."

I roll my eyes, and before I know it, they're off. Luna begins to saunter in between Sunny and Spirit. When they are a few feet away, all three horses start to sprint, and I shake my head in shock. He shouldn't be sprinting as a beginner, but knowing my cousin, he challenged him and knowing Gabriel, he doesn't say no to a challenge.

When Gabriel returned from riding, all three of the men were laughing. He had the biggest grin on his face and couldn't stop talking about how magical it was to be on a horse. He wished he had known about this sooner. I couldn't stop smiling as I watched him talk on and on as if I didn't know about any of this. It made my heart swell. I've never felt more ready to tell him about this baby, but I know it's hormones mixing with love and lust.

I have to make sure I'm thinking clearly.

We're all sitting by the fire, my family telling Gabriel way too personal stories about me growing up, but I let them because Gabriel brightens with each story. Music is playing in the background as we roast marshmallows, and I couldn't think of a better day in my life... except finding out about this baby. A song I recognize begins to play, and I can't stop the gasp from escaping. I'm not one for country music, but I know being here in Texas that's unacceptable. However, I do love Carrie Underwood and this song.

"I love this song," I say and begin to sway with Gabriel's arm draped around my shoulder. He grabs my stick and places it on the ground along with his. I watch him, waiting for him to tell me what's going on. He takes the blanket off our shoulders and stands. Everyone's eyes are on him, but he doesn't care.

"May I have this dance?" He asks as he sticks his hand out for me to take.

I look at his hand then up to him with a smile. "How can I say no?" I place my hand in his, and he pulls me against him. I hear Val and Margi sigh in admiration, and I know my uncle is rolling his eyes. Gabriel is showing them up without even meaning to. This is just who he is. He begins to sway with me, dancing around the fire to Carrie Underwood, singing beautifully just for us.

"I love you for being here," I whisper out of nowhere as I look up at him.

He's still wearing his hat. "Wherever you are, angel, is where I belong too."

CHAPTER 11

GABRIEL

I didn't know how I was going to persuade her to come back to Seattle with me. I see how much she loves it here in Texas, and I don't want to take it away, but I have a job to get back to. I meant it when I told her father I would leave my world if she wanted, but she hasn't told me so yet. Knowing Ava, she won't like me to. I would have to receive a miracle for her to go down without a fight.

Besides, I know she belongs in the world of publishing. She's always been passionate about it even in high school. I want to tell her that I haven't replaced her position that she hardly got to be in, but she will fight with me. I need to come up with a plan she won't argue with.

She fell asleep pretty quickly after we finished dancing and came to bed. We showered together—which was nearly impossible in the tiny shower—and I massaged her feet before she fell asleep. Now, here I lay next to her, trying to figure out how to get her home with me, where she belongs.

My phone begins to vibrate against the nightstand, and I read Harris's name light across my phone. I sneak into the bathroom.

"Harris, what's going on? It's midnight in Seattle." I mumble quietly.

"Warner, I need you back here asap." He says with concern laced in his voice. "Somethings happened."

Fear creeps over me. "What happened?"

"Your mother and father got into it, and she phoned me to pick her up and bring her here. I would have called you, but she begged me not to. When we got back, I found Elizabeth here, and she destroyed the place...and took two bottles of pills. I got a call from the hospital; she's fine."

I sit on the edge of the tub and run my fingers through my hair, tugging slightly. I can't believe this is happening. I thought I would be leaving with Ava. "Shit. Okay, book me the next flight to Seattle. I don't care what time. Text me the details." I hang up.

What was Elizabeth thinking?

I didn't know she was one for suicide. I want to say I don't care for her, that this doesn't bother me, but it's not the case. She was my friend, and although she tried to ruin my relationship with Ava, it doesn't mean I want bad things for her. I need to help her in any way I can.

She shouldn't have to worry about paying for the help she needs.

Then there are my parents. I have never seen them fight to the point where my mum decides to pack up and leave. I had never seen two people so in love with one another. Whatever my father did *has* to be terrible. I need to go back and check on her.

I exit the bathroom and make my way to the bed. I hate to wake her, but I need her to know I need to leave. I refuse to leave without an explanation. I stroke her hair softly and gently kiss her lips; I graze my lips against her cheeks and eyes; that's when she begins to stir. Her hand lazily searches for me until they find my hair. Her nails scratch softly against my scalp and start to stroke my hair back. I've never had a woman play with my hair before; it's...*different*. It feels nice, which I wasn't expecting.

"Angel," I whisper, and her eyes begin to flutter open slowly.

"Hmm." She mumbles softly.

I smile. "Let me see those beautiful eyes," I whisper and kiss her cheek.

Her eyes open, but they're swollen from lack of sleep. She smiles lazily at me. "What's going on?" She asks with a raspy voice.

"I'm sorry to wake you, but I didn't want to leave without an explanation." Her eyes widen, and the sleep leaves her when I mention *leaving*. "My mum was going through something with my foolish father and went to stay at my home, only to find Elizabeth overdosed in my apartment after trashing it. I *need* to go back."

I hate that I need to leave her. I hate that I have to clean up my father's mess. Once again, I'm dropping what's important to me to help my family. My mum, I would do anything for but my father, he's a burden to me.

"What?" She asks, confused and runs her fingers through her hair. "Is Elizabeth okay? Is your mom okay?" She is distraught for them. What surprises me is her worry for Elizabeth. She can't stand her, last time I checked.

"Elizabeth almost ruined us, and you're concerned for her?" I ask, confused.

She scoffs. "Gabriel, yes, she's nasty, but that doesn't mean I want the woman to *die*. Of course, I want her to be okay. She needs help, not ridicule."

I'm astonished by this woman.

I kiss her swiftly. "I wish I didn't have to go." I wish you would come with me is what I really want to say.

She bites her bottom lip and is silent for a moment. "I can't let you go alone." She says softly and strokes my cheek with her palm. "When do you have to go?"

"Harris is trying to get me a flight out as soon as possible. The airport is far; I need to get a move on."

She throws the blanket off her and stands from the bed, beginning to stretch. Then she throws her suitcase on the bed, causing me to move, so I don't get hit.

"What are you doing?" I ask with amusement.

She rubs her eyes tiredly. "Packing. Knowing Harris, he's going to call you in a few minutes because he found you a flight. We need to get ready."

My heart swells in my chest—something I don't often experience, especially with women I'm sleeping with—but I welcome the feeling. I suppose this is what it feels like to be cared for and loved unconditionally by someone who doesn't *have* to love you. She can have whomever she pleases, and yet she chooses me.

"You're coming with me?" I'm genuinely shocked that I didn't have to beg.

She narrows her eyebrows. "Didn't you hear me? I said I can't let you go alone, meaning I'm coming with you. If something is happening with your father, somebody has to be there to stop him from hitting you."

She's worried about me, genuinely concerned for me. *I love you* is on the tip of my tongue, but I'm not sure if I'm allowed to say it yet. I have never been so unsure and cautious in a relationship. I told Elizabeth what I wanted, and if she disapproved, then that was her issue. But when it comes to Ava, I want to be everything she needs me to be. Suddenly, my wants don't matter as much as they used to. I would do anything to make this one girl smile.

What is she doing to me?

"You're going to stop my father from hitting me again?" I ask with a teasing smirk. The man isn't afraid of me, let alone little Ava.

She gives me a determined expression. "If it comes down to it." She isn't joking.

I stand and do the only thing I can think of. I cup her face and kiss her softly. No urgency, no wild hunger, no tongue. Just two young—*but not really*—kids truly in love with one another.

Ava couldn't leave without saying good-bye to her family, even if it meant waking them all up at three in the morning. Her uncle was least excited about it because, and I repeat, *"Damn it, girl, don't you know I gotta be up in two hours"*. But he still said goodbye to his only niece when the truck was packed. Her father insisted on taking us to the airport, wanting to see Ava off. I didn't argue with the man. Harris found us a flight at seven a.m. so we needed to get a move on. It would be quicker than prepping my jet.

Ray wanted to stay until we took off, but Ava's argued with him, telling him to go back home and sleep. I wanted to interject, saying that she would be safe and perfectly fine with me. I can protect her just fine.

Jesus, Gabriel, relax.

They embrace tightly, and I see his eyes begin to water. I haven't had that in a long time. The second I turned eighteen, it's as if all the love my father had for me vanished without a trace. There was no distancing slowly; there was no reason—*that I know of*—just bitterness. I had a great relationship with my father growing up and adored the man dearly. The same way Ava loves her father. I can see it when she speaks about him; I can see it when they're together; they are one another's best friend. They know they can rely on one another, which is something I didn't miss—*until now*. I look away and reach for my phone as it begins to vibrate. It's Isabella.

"What's wrong?" I ask, knowing well that it's too late for her to be calling.

"Mum, left, dad." She says in a harsh whisper.

I know this.

"Harris called me and told me she came to stay the night at my place."

Why is she calling me to tell me this?

"No, Gabe, she *left* him." She says in a more serious matter. "She packed her things. She isn't just staying for the night. I don't know when or if she plans to go back."

I'm shocked.

Knowing that they had a fight big enough to send her to my house for a night was surprising enough, but this...this is truly something I never saw coming. The love they have for one another is something you only see in movies or read in novels...until I found Ava, of course. Finding her proved that kind of love is possible and more. I'm consumed by her.

Why would she leave my father?

What did he do that would send her away?

I want to guess an affair, but I know my father hasn't bothered looking at another woman in his time with my mum. As a child, he always used to tell me that his eyes have already found what they've been looking for. There's no need to look at any other woman because they simply don't compare to *Emilia*.

"I don't understand," I mutter as I run my fingers through my hair. "What the fuck did he do to her?"

She sighs heavily. "I have no idea. Harris brought her here, and she was too upset to talk after finding Elizabeth the way she did." I hear her mutter something to someone in the background. It must be John. "She wants to see you first thing when you arrive in Seattle."

I look at Ava to see her still saying her good-byes. Her father is wiping tears from her face. "Okay... I'm coming back with Ava. We still have some things to discuss; I'm hoping we will have it sorted before I'm due at your apartment. Keep me updated, okay?"

"You got her back," she says, and I know she's grinning over the phone, trying to contain her excitement. If this wasn't such a difficult situation, I know my sister would be yelling questions over the phone. She isn't very patient.

I smile from the satisfaction, knowing I got Ava back. "I did, but I will explain later. I have to go." I hang up.

Ray makes his way to me and isn't shaking my hand like I assumed he would; he embraces me tightly. I look at Ava over my shoulder, but she isn't watching; she's wiping her tears with a tissue. I wonder if she's always this emotional saying good-bye to her father.

I hesitate to put my arms around the man as I try to remember the last time anyone but my mum and sister has hugged me.

"I don't want to pick her up again in the same conditions as I did the last time," he says sadly, and guilt fills me. I'm the reason he saw her so broken. "Take care of her for me, please."

"Of course," I mumble and pull away. "I'll protect her with my life."

After a four-hour flight, we are finally at the penthouse. Harris collected us at the airport, where Ava gave him a hug, something I had never seen before. The women I slept with hardly ever spoke to my staff. Never Harris but sometimes his wife. Usually, to bark food or drink orders. Let alone would any of those women hug Harris after time apart. Elizabeth didn't even like him.

Harris looked at me in shock, not knowing if it's appropriate to hug her in return. When I gave him a nod of approval, he patted her back awkwardly, causing me to laugh.

Poor man.

We didn't discuss if Ava would be living with me like she was supposed to before she left. I didn't want to pressure her or push her past her limits. I want her to decide that she wants to live with me...and to work for me. That's something that is going to take very good convincing. Maybe, I should withhold sex again...it was wrong, but my God, was it the best and hottest sex we have had yet.

When we enter the penthouse, it isn't the mess that Harris described. It's been cleaned up, even the mess I left behind before I left. Ruth deserves a raise; I need to keep that in mind.

"You should get some rest. I know we slept on the plane, but it wasn't enough. I have to go meet my mum at Isabella's." I place my suitcase down and turn to see Ava scowling.

"You're not a very good listener, Warner. I told you I'm not letting you go through this alone." She says and walks past me into the kitchen. She begins to tinker with the coffee maker. "I'll make us coffee for the road."

She really is refusing to let me go through this alone. I don't deserve this, and I have no clue why she's this kind to me.

So I decide to ask. "Ava, why are you doing this?"

She turns, holding the coffee filters. "Why am I doing what?" She scrunches up her nose in confusion.

"Why are you treating me this well when I don't deserve it? You won't let me go through my family drama alone; you left Texas to come here with me." I shake my head. "I don't understand."

She frowns deeply. "Gabriel, do you not understand unconditional love?" She asks sadly. "Yes, you made a mistake and hurt me, but I decided to forgive you, which means moving past it. It must not be easy to go through all this alone, especially since the age of eighteen—but you don't have you go through anything alone anymore. You have me."

I make my way to her and grab hold of her hips, lifting her to sit on the counter. I don't care if Harris is still lingering. I need to kiss my girl. I lean in and kiss her softly, but she meets me with hunger. Her hands go directly into my hair, tugging and pulling me closer. I step between her legs and run my hands up her thighs. We're getting carried away, but she's controlling this kiss now, and she's desperate. She's hungry for me, and my body is having a hard time not responding. It's begging me to bend her over this counter and take her.

I have to remember my mum is waiting for me.

I pull away slowly and rest my forehead against hers. The kiss was short, but we're panting as if we ran a marathon. I don't know what's gotten into her. First, the way she acted in Texas at the dinner table, the way she was when we were having—*very unexpected*—sex in her bedroom; now this. She seems more needy, desperate; her body becomes weak when I touch her. Not that I'm complaining.

"I love you." She whispers, catching me by surprise.

I swallow past the lump in my throat. "And I, you, angel."

Someone clears their throat, and I know it's Ruth. I pull away, catching Ava's cheeks turning red from embarrassment. I turn to Ruth and flash her a charming smile.

"Good-morning, Ruth."

She gives me a disapproving frown. She has caught me with many women...in many different situations. "Boy, did I not tell you no more of this in the kitchen?" She walks past me and hits me with a towel rag before smiling at Ava. "Good morning, dear. Coffee?" She takes the filters out of Ava's hands.

Ava smiles softly. "Morning, Ruth, yes, please." She says before sliding off the counter. "I'm going to get changed." She takes her suitcase and makes her way to the stairs.

"I see we're done being a sulk," Ruth says with her back to me once Ava is entirely upstairs.

She hates it when I drink.

"I'm sorry for worrying you," I mumble, ashamed.

She turns to face me. "No more fucking about, boy. I love you dearly and can't keep seeing you make the same mistakes. If you want the girl, stick with *just* her."

I try to ignore the hurt in my chest, but it's hard. Ruth seems to be the only one who can call me on my shit ever since my grandad passed. "I know. I won't hurt her again. She's the one I want for the rest of my life."

She gives me an approving smile. "Good, now freshen up. Your mother is expecting you. I'll have the coffee's ready."

I sigh and prepare myself to fix another family mess.

CHAPTER 12

AVA

He hasn't said much since we got in the car. He asked me if I wanted to collect breakfast on our way to Isabella's, but I refused. I can't eat yet without getting sick. Trying to remain quiet while throwing up in the bathroom was a challenge. I know he was speaking with Ruth and probably wouldn't have heard me, but I didn't want to take any chances. Soon, it's going to get too complicated to try and hide this baby. He is going to find out sooner or later. I want him to be excited, to be thrilled we made something so beautiful together. Something in me tells me that isn't going to be the case.

I watch him staring out the window as our song—*the song we sang together*—plays through the car sound system. His hand is laced with mine, his thumb rubbing small circles into my skin. I want to ask him if he's okay, but I can't. I don't know how to help if something *is* wrong. I meant it when I told him I would be there to

stop his father from hitting him again. It makes me sick
to my stomach knowing a parent can do that to their
child, no matter what age. I could never see my dad
hitting me—*girl or not.* There has to be someone in the
room that cares about this man, that will look out for
him and protect him. I think he's so used to being the
one who protects that no one even stops to think if *he*
needs it. I know he's strong and tough, but that doesn't
mean he has to fight every battle independently. I'll be
there to hold him up just in case he needs me.

"Ready?" I ask as we step off the elevator.

He squeezes my hand. "Let's find out what my
bastard of a father has done now."

I'm not used to hearing someone talk about their dad
this way. I wonder if they had the same relationship my
mother and I have. Did they always resent one another,
or did it happen out of nowhere?

He pushes past the front door and sighs. "I have to
talk to her about leaving this door unlocked." He
mumbles distastefully.

I'm sure if John is home, she would be perfectly safe,
but I keep that to myself.

We make our way into the apartment, and I'm
reminded of its exquisiteness. He pulls me down the hall
quickly, and in the kitchen are John, Isabella and their
mum. Isabella is the first one to spot us and runs up the
small steps to greet me. Her arms wrap around me,
tightly and I hug her in return.

"You bloody woman. I've missed you." She says and pulls away. "You still look amazing."

I grin. "You do too, Isabella."

"C'mon," Gabriel says to Isabella. He's clearly inpatient and wants to find out what is going on. He pushes past her, and Isabella rolls her eyes behind his back. She links arms with me, and we take the small step leading to her kitchen.

"Mrs. Warner, it's good to see you again," I say politely. I wish it were under better terms than this.

She gives me a soft smile as she holds a hot mug in her hands. "It's good to see you, dear. I see my son couldn't wait for you to come on your own."

I look at Gabriel, who is speaking with John quietly. "Looks like it." I don't know what else to say.

"Mum," Gabriel says worriedly and kisses her cheek. "What's going on? Why are you here and not at home."

She sighs. "Gabriel, sit." She demands, and he does as she says, taking the chair next to where I'm standing. I lace his hand with mine, and he squeezes it in appreciation.

Her eyes fill with sadness before she speaks. "I have stood by for too long and let him mistreat you. I made excuses for him because of how much I love him, and I remember how he was when you were little. He adored you, Gabriel, and you came to adore him as well."

I frown, knowing that young Gabriel adored his dad just to have it taken away with no explanation. He didn't ask for this, and it must have pained him to see his dad pull away.

"When he hit you...it was the last straw. I should have gone after you to make sure you were okay, but I knew I had to talk with him. I told him that I could no longer be with him—*even though it would kill me*—if he didn't fix things with you. You are my son," she says, her voice is raw with emotion as she reaches her hand out across the breakfast bar to take Gabriel's hand. "You will always come first to me, even above my husband. You have done so much for us, sweetheart, and I can't thank you enough for it."

Gabriel's eyes are sad as he squeezes his mother's hand. I can see how much it pains her to be away from her husband, but she's willing to throw it all away for her son. I place my hands on my stomach protectively. She will choose her children every time. Gabriel can see how much it hurts her as well.

"Mum, I can't let you be miserable because of me. We have our differences, but I know much you love him. You've said it yourself; he's your soul mate."

She shakes her head. "No," she says sadly and takes Isabella's hand. "You two are my soulmates. You two are my whole world and the reason why I fought so hard."

I look to John, who has his arm wrapped around Isabella with his lips against her head. He's not speaking or even reacting; he is the rock Isabella needs to lean

on. I look back at Gabriel and wish I could do anything.
I would give anything for him to feel the love he needs.

Gabriel sighs. "I will talk with, dad." He says. "I will
try and make things right."

I'm shocked but angry at the same time. It should be
his dad coming to make things right, not Gabriel. But
I've come to see that he will do anything for his mom.
He truly cares for her in a way I've never seen before.
He's gentle for the women in his family.

She shakes her head. "That's not your job to do,
Gabriel. He needs to make things right." She's not going
to sway on this; I know it. If she was willing to leave the
man she's madly in love with, then she won't bend.

"Then let me allow him to make it right." He frowns.
"I said some hurtful things too, mum. I should
apologize."

A tear escapes. "I can't let you do that." She says and
says nothing more. She leaves the kitchen swiftly, letting
a small sob escaped. My heart aches for her.

Gabriels rubs his temples. "Call dad, tell the fucker
we need to have a family dinner whether he wants it or
not." He spits, and Isabella frowns.

"Must you call him that?" She asks.

John looks at Gabriel worriedly, and I feel him tense
beside me. "You're defending him?" He asks, appalled.

"*Gabe,*" John warns.

Isabella holds her hand up. "He is still our father."

Gabriel laughs, but there is no joy or amusement. "Maybe, to you, but last time I checked, he's the guy who punched me in the face."

I touch Gabriel's shoulder. There's no need for him to fight with his sister. It's not her fault either. "Gabriel," I whisper and stroke his back.

His body relaxes, and he looks down at me with sad eyes. He's embarrassed by his behaviour. I know he doesn't speak to Isabella this way.

"I'm sorry," he says on a sigh. "Just please call him. I'm going to check on, mum." He kisses my cheek softly and leaves us to attend to her.

Out of nowhere, my stomach begins to twist and turn. I can feel the bile rising. "Bathroom?" That is the only thing I say. I'm afraid if I keep speaking, I'll vomit.

"Upstairs, first door on the left," John says, and I scurry toward the stairs. I need to be quick. I've come to discover that this baby will not wait for me to be near a toilet. I find it quickly and dart for the bathroom, emptying nothing but stomach bile and the two sips of coffee I had. Why does any woman get pregnant knowing that morning sickness is a thing? I've only had it for a few days, but it has felt like a lifetime. I miss breakfast and being able to eat what I choose. Whatever the baby doesn't like is immediately thrown up. I was fine in Texas. Everything my aunt made in that kitchen, the baby loved dearly. Thank goodness.

"How long are you going to make me sick for, hmm?" I ask as I rub my stomach. "If you keep at this, people are going to find out, and I'm not ready for that."

I stand and begin to freshen up. I open the bathroom door, and Isabella is leaning against the wall. She has her arms crossed over her chest as a small *v* appears between her eyebrows from scowling.

"Are you pregnant?" She asks.

Shit.

"What are you talking about?"

She scoffs. "You think I'm stupid? You went from being perfectly okay to basically running to the bathroom. Then I hear you throwing up and talking to nobody."

I can't lie to her, nor do I want to. I thought I would have reservations about her finding out, but I'm more relieved than anything. I have people who know back in Texas but nobody here to speak to about any of it. I want someone I can trust, and I know I can trust Isabella.

I sigh. "I am," I admit.

Her face instantly brightens as a grin spreads across her face. "I can't believe it!" She yells, and I run to her, slapping my hand over her mouth. Her eyebrows narrow in confusion.

"Gabriel doesn't know," I whisper.

I move my hand slowly, and she looks at me in disbelief. "What do you mean he doesn't know?" She asks in a harsh whisper. "Why doesn't he know?"

"We broke up, Isabella. I wasn't counting on him to come after me in Texas. I thought I would raise this baby on my own, but now it's looking different. I'm not ready to tell him... I don't trust him enough yet."

She bites her bottom lip. "But you will tell him?" She asks.

I nod. "I will when I know he won't hurt me again. I have to think about this baby too."

"Damn it," she mutters under her breath. "Okay, okay. I will keep it a secret. I'm really going to be an aunt?"

I grin. "Yeah."

She grins and wraps her arms around me. "I'm so excited."

Her excitement is infectious.

We left shortly after Gabriel had finished speaking with his mom. Isabella called her dad, and he wanted to see all of them tonight. Meaning, Gabriel and I had to rush home to—*hopefully*—nap, shower, and make our way to his parent's home. This time together. When I think back to the last time I was there, it seems ages ago. Gabriel and I have come so far so fast since then.

The car ride was silent as he rested his hand on my thigh. Even on this sombre occasion, my hormones can't seem to control themselves. At this point, I can't separate my baby hormones and the regular lust I feel for Gabriel. Either way, all I can think about is tearing his clothes off and having him inside me. It's when he squeezes my thigh softly that my body can't help itself. I'm instantly wet between my thighs, and I let a soft moan escape my lips. My eyes snap immediately to Gabriel to find him watching where his hand is. His eyes slowly meet mine, and there's confusion in them. I've never been like this. Yes, this man can bring me to my knees—*pregnant or not*—but it's different now. I'm more needy, desperate, and greedy for him. My body has no shame in reacting out loud. If I weren't pregnant, I would control myself until we were in the privacy of his home.

He says nothing because Harris is still in the front seat and can hear us. His hand slowly squeezes again, my breath hitching in response, my cheeks warming slightly.

Control yourself, Ava; this man is going through shit.

He doesn't make it easy, however. His hand begins to slowly make its way up my thigh. He stops right before touching my sex, and my libido can't take it. It's begging for him to feel me, to pleasure me. She doesn't care who is in the car. My thighs squeeze together tightly in anticipation.

His eyes darken and his mouth agape. He brings his lips close to my ear. "Are you turned on, angel?" He whispers, his lips brushing against my ear, causing goosebumps to appear.

I try to stifle a moan, barely getting through it. "Yes," I whisper and turn my head to kiss him, but he senses what I'm about to do, pulling away with a sly smirk. He keeps his hand in place, driving me absolutely wild with need. He knows he's teasing me. He's so close and yet so far. I need him, and I'm not above begging.

I've never been more grateful as we pull into the underground parking garage. Gabriel is the first to get out, holding the door open for me. I step out, and I feel him press his front against me. His lips touch my neck as his hand rubs my ass.

"You're so bad right now I don't know whether to encourage it or spank the shit out of you." He whispers. I notice Harris walking forward toward the elevator, but he could turn around any second.

"Both," I say breathlessly. "Please."

He smacks my ass lightly and closes the car door with force. "Move. You got me so turned on I can't even think straight." He says with a clipped tone. "I need you upstairs."

We walk hand in hand, but he stops before we board the elevator. "Harris, Ruth has already taken off. Go enjoy the rest of your night with her."

He isn't asking.

Harris gives him a confused look. "Are you sure, Warner?"

Gabriel nods. "Yeah," says coolly. "Ava and I should be fine for the rest of the night."

Harris nods and exits the elevator. He nods his head to me as he passes us. Warner."

"Bye, Harris." I give him a small wave as Gabriel is already pulling me into the empty elevator. He hits the penthouse button hard and turns to face me once again, his eyes hooded with lust.

"I don't know what's gotten into you lately, angel, but I'm excited about it." I didn't think he would be so observant of my behaviour. I have to be more subtle from now on—even though I don't think I can be. When he touches me, my body ignites and is ready for him, no matter the context.

His hands grip my hips and slowly make their way to my ass, squeezing with no shame. I feel his cock harden immediately as he presses it against my lower belly; I let my head fall back against the wall and let out a shaky, breathless moan. His lips graze against my neck, the tip of his tongue following. He pulls away and blows softly.

"Gabriel." I breathe.

"Yes?" He mumbles and begins to suck softly on my skin.

I'm so turned on; it's uncomfortable. I need him inside me, and I don't think I can wait until we're in the privacy of his penthouse.

"I need you, please." My libido is begging for him, panting heavily as she waits for the pleasure Gabriel brings us.

I can feel his smirk against my skin. "So, greedy." He mumbles and begins to kiss slowly toward my ear. My body is on fire; I can feel his touch ringing through every vein, muscle, and inch of my skin.

I can't wait any longer; I'm too hungry for him. I push him off of me. He looks at me with a puzzled expression. I don't hesitate; I strut to him, wrapping my legs around his waist—his hands resting on my ass, holding me up—I smash my lips against his. Our tongues immediately intertwine. Our kiss is hungry and impatient, my hands tugging his hair. He backs me up until my back hits the wall.

I can't begin to explain how he makes me feel. How I thought I could live without this passion, this intensity—that used to scare me, but now I crave it—I was fooling myself. I feel alive when I'm with him. The way he touches me makes me feel loved, cherished but most importantly, desired.

The elevator arrives at our floor with a ding, but we don't stop kissing. He pulls me away from the wall and walks toward the front door leading to his penthouse. His hand fiddles with the doorknob as he bites my bottom lip. His mouth moves to my neck and begins to bite and suck softly. He pushes past the door, slamming it closed with his foot and proceeds to walk.

He sets me down on the kitchen island, pulling away from me to take off his shirt. We're supposed to be using this time to catch up on sleep before dinner. At this rate, we'll hardly have time to shower.

I grab my t-shirt, ripping it off me, unhooking my bra and whipping it in a random direction. His eyes drop straight to my breasts that are tender. Thinking about his tongue licking my sensitive nipples causes them to pucker. His eyes flare with desire. He pushes my breasts upward, and his mouth covers my nipple. His tongue swirling and flicking across the sensitive nub; my legs are shaking as I gasp for air. The pleasure is so intense I can hardly see, I can hardly think. My body wants more, but at the same time, it's begging for him to stop this torture. It needs him harder but softer at the same time; it's driving me crazy. I claw at his back, and he groans loudly.

I'm frantic now. I'm hungry, and my body is done waiting; my libido begging to be fucked hard.

"Gabriel," I gasp as he moves between each nipple. "I need you now."

"Let's go upstairs." He says and moves to pick me up, but I shake my head.

"No, I want you here. I need you to take me hard, please; I need it." I sound desperate, but I am. The ache and dampness between my legs are only getting worse with each throb. He could easily slide deep inside me—I'm burning at the thought.

"*Fuck*." He says through his teeth and helps me off the counter. He drops to his knees, taking my jeans and panties with them. I step out of them, kicking them off to the side. He slides his fingers through my folds. His head snaps up to look at me.

"You're soaking wet, Ava." He says breathlessly.

This shouldn't come as a surprise. Gabriel is incredibly sexy. How can I not be soaking wet? His alpha-male presence is enough to make any woman fall to their knees before him.

"Yes, now fuck me." My libido is losing her patience.

He curses under his breath and turns me around, bending me over the breakfast island. His palm connects with my behind—*very hard*—causing me to cry out in pleasure and pain. The excitement that courses through me when he spanks me causes the ache between my legs to intensify.

"I've missed this ass, angel." He says through his teeth as he smacks his cock against my behind. "There's nothing sexier than seeing it in the air for me." His palms slap my behind two more times before sliding into me slowly on a loud groan.

"It's been too long since I've had this pussy." He says while grinding his hips.

I welcome the cold sensation from the countertop against my hot cheek. I'm sweating and overheating.

"Gabriel, please, I need it hard. I need it rough." I beg with no shame.

I hear him let out a shaky breath. My words are affecting him. *Oh, how the tables have turned.* "Hold on, angel. You will let me know if it is too much, understand?"

He's speaking through his teeth as if it causes him pain to be still for this long when I'm throbbing around him.

He spanks me hard, impatient for my answer.

"I understand!" I cry out as my toes curl in pleasure.

"Good girl." He places one hand on my hip, and the other grabs hold of my shoulder. Without warning, he begins to pound violently.

"*Fuck!*" I scream as I'm sent forward on the counter. I clench around him, loving the intense, forceful movements. "Don't stop!"

A deep growl rips from deep in his chest, and he begins to go harder, faster; every time he inserts himself back into me, he grinds slowly so I can feel how deep he is. My legs are beginning to shake, but I'm not ready to orgasm—I'm not prepared for this to be over. His hand leaves my hip, and he grabs hold of my hair, pulling— with both hands—my body upright. He brings his mouth to my ear as I cry out from the intensity of the position. I can feel him deep in my stomach; I have never had someone so deep.

"You're the sexiest thing I have ever seen," he whispers in my ear and pinches my nipple in between his fingers. "I love how desperate you are for me. It makes me fucking crazy."

I grind against him with need. He's taking his time; he's teasing me and torturing me. He smirks against my skin and spanks me, the loud slap echoing in the quiet apartment. My libido is telling me to take over, wanting the orgasm I had denied her earlier. I lean forward until he falls out of me and turns before he can reposition himself. I push him, walking him toward the couch, shoving him to sit. He licks his lips as he watches my body,

"Stop." He commands in a severe tone. A tone that says not to challenge his word. He leans back, throwing his arms over the back of the sofa. He's not ashamed of his naked body or of his rigid erection that continues to throb with want. I want it too, but he's depriving me. My libido won't be able to behave for much longer. "Touch yourself." He shows no sign of amusement or teasing. He means it.

My libido purrs with pleasure.

I slide my hand down my front—his eyes following—until I reach my sex. I begin to slowly rub circles over my clit. I let a soft moan escape, my other hand going to my nipple. He didn't ask me to, but I know he'll be pleased with my decision. My legs twitch and buckle.

"Enough." He says, and I stop, opening my eyes to see him squeezing his rock solid length in his hand. "Do you want it?" He asks.

My eyes are locked on his hand that's pleasure himself. "Yes," I whisper.

I was never the type of woman to crave a man's penis. Yes, it did the trick, but none of these men could even make me orgasm. It was really just for the ache to settle. Did I give blowjobs often? Only when I was drunk, really. But when it comes to Gabriel, I crave him and crave giving him pleasure. There's something powerful and sexual about seeing this man come undone just from my mouth. Seeing my alpha God submit to me and only me makes me hotter than I can describe.

I can't believe I was settling for the sex I had in the past. I should have waited for this mind-blowing pleasure that comes with Gabriel Warner.

He strokes it. "What do you want to do to it?" He groans.

"I want to suck on it, Sir."

His jaw clenches at the unexpected name.

He likes it.

"I'm not stopping you."

I don't wait for further instruction and make my way to him, stopping when I'm between his legs and dropping to my knees before him. My mouth waters for him—something else I wasn't expecting, nor have I ever experienced with other men.

I wrap my hand around the base of his thick length and wrap my lips around the tip, never breaking eye contact. His eyes flare with intensity, his mouth agape, his hand in my hair following—*not forcing*—my rhythm. He lets me take control when it comes to sucking his cock. My tongue is lapping over his length as I bob my head up and down—taking him deep into my throat before paying attention to his tip.

"Fuck, Ava." He groans as he tries to refrain from his hips bucking. He doesn't want to force himself on me— *alpha or no alpha*—he would never want to hurt me. He knows he has to let me control this. "Get up."

I let his length fall with *pop* and straddle him without direction. I position him and sink down as hard as I can, sending his head dying back, shouting a curse. His hands are on my behind, his nails digging into my skin, but I welcome it.

"Just like that, angel, I love the way you ride me." He says through his teeth.

He brings my nipple into his mouth, sucking, licking and biting softly. That's when my vision begins to blur; I clench around him as I throw my head back. I cry out his name and shake violently on top of him as my orgasm rips through me. My movements have stopped, but he continues to hold my hips while he drives into me.

"*AVA!*" He shouts as he wraps his arms around me.

CHAPTER 13

GABRIEL

I was not planning to have sex with her. After I spoke to my mum and convinced her to talk to my father—we left so Ava could take a nap. Anxiety would keep me from sleeping, but I would lay there with her until she dozed off. I was anxious on the car ride home, thinking of how I would approach my father. My mum won't forgive him until he makes amends with me, but I know him too well. He couldn't even say good-bye to his father on his death bed. Yet, I need him to make things right, so my mum goes back to being happy.

Then out of nowhere, I had squeezed her thigh softly —I'm not sure why, maybe, to ease my nerves—and she let out a soft moan. If I wasn't so perceptive when it comes to Ava, I wouldn't have noticed. Her cheeks became flushed, goosebumps appearing on her skin; then her thighs squeezed together. That's when I realized she's turned on. Our sex life has been quick-paced even when we were in high school, but this was...different. First, the way she attacked me back in Texas and now this.

She's insatiable.

We showered quickly—and separately because I knew I wouldn't resist her body—then made our way to my mum's. I was anxious, and she could tell. Her hands were on me the entire drive here. I wanted to watch her watching me but, sadly, my eyes needed to remain on the road. However, she didn't seem nervous—as if she isn't attending a dinner with a dysfunctional family—she seemed determined, assertive more than anything. She truly meant it when she said she is coming to protect me. It isn't sitting right with her knowing my father hit me. Would it sit right with anyone?

"Are you ready?" She asks as we pull into the driveway. Her hand rests on top of mine that is still clutching the steering wheel tightly.

I look at her and see a slight frown on her face. I hate seeing her frown. "I am. Let's go." I exit first and make my way to her side of the car, opening her door. I lace my hand with hers. "Did I tell you how beautiful you look?"

I know for a fact I have told her. I've probably told her how beautiful she is more than a handful amount of times today alone. She's wearing a cream thin long sleeve shirt—that hugs her gorgeous body—tucked into her dark denim jeans. Her hair is tied up in a ponytail even though I argued with her. I love her hair when it's flowing down in endless dark waves. I would rather have her naked in my apartment than have to deal with this nonsense.

We enter the home, and I inhale sharply, welcoming the smell of my mum's food. Our household was more American than anything—especially the food due to my mum being American. All my dad had left of Australia was his accent. It seemed like he didn't want anything to do with his culture because of my grandad.

Soft Jazz music is playing in the background. I'm surprised by my mum's comfort in cooking here even though she isn't a fan of my father. Walking into the dining room, I see Isabella sitting next to John at the piano. He's fiddling with the keys as she instructs him on each note. She's been trying to teach John the piano for years and has failed. He isn't the type to be patient enough to learn piano.

"Isabella can play as well?" Ava asks in awe.

I look down at my girl, who is paying attention to my sister and her husband. "Yes, she learned before I did. I came to love it more, however. She learned just to learn."

She scoffs and looks up at me. "Of course she did."

I smirk at her disbelief that my young sister would learn the piano just for fun then do anything else a young person would do.

Way to sound old, Warner.

"John, when are you going to give up?" I ask with a grin, catching their attention.

He groans as he looks at us over his shoulder. "I gave up a long time ago. It's my wife that doesn't want me to give up."

Isabella stands and makes her way to us, embracing Ava tightly. My sister has never been shy. She doesn't care if Ava and I are back on good terms or not.

She embraces me next, and I kiss the top of her head. I can feel Ava's eyes on me. Usually, women don't get to see this side of me. Elizabeth did, but she didn't care for Isabella for it to affect her. She didn't swoon, but when I catch Ava's eyes, I see they're soft and warm. She enjoys seeing me this way, clearly.

"Where's dad?" I ask.

Isabella frowns. "He's upstairs. Mum sent him up there so she could cook in peace." My father may be stubborn, but he bends and breaks for my mum. If it were I that tried to send him up there, he would have yelled and fought, and told me he's a grown-ass man, and you can't tell him what to do in his home. I can see my mum sending him upstairs and him going willingly. He's probably grateful that she's just home.

I scowl. "The..." I stop. I know Isabella doesn't like it when I call him names. "Why don't you go get him? I'm going to say hi to mum."

Ava's hand drops from mine as I begin to walk toward the kitchen; I turn to look at her. She gives me a small smile. "You go say hi. I'll be here." She reassures me. She doesn't want to intrude; that much is clear.

I see my mum setting the table and begin to help her like I did as a boy. I can feel her eyes on me; I know she's sad. What I would do to fix things for her. My father is selfish. He forgets that she's been through enough—cancer, the loss of my grandad whom she loved, and now this. I'm not worth this. I know how happy my father makes her, and knowing I'm the reason they are apart slices my heart deeply.

"Gabriel," she whispers sadly. She's hesitant about this, I think, for the same reason that I am. She knows how stubborn he can be. She knows she will get hurt because it would take a miracle for my father to treat me the way he used to. I want to tell her that I don't want it, that I'm okay without it. It's enough to know that he loves her and Isabella. That's all that matters to me. I've been fine without it for a decade. I think of Ava and the joy she brings me, the way she makes my heart swell in my chest with love. Her love is enough for me. She's my everything. "I won't forgive him if he continues to treat you this way."

She's firm in her decision.

I frown. "Mum, I'm not worth this." She needs to know. Someone has to tell her—someone other than my father. "I'm a grown man. I don't need my father's love or approval."

She puts the napkins down and comes to me, cupping my face in her small hands. "Don't you dare tell me that you are not worth it. I won't hear you talk about yourself that way."

She disregards my comment of not needing my father because it doesn't matter to her. She—*as a parent*—needs my father to love me. She needs him to be the man he used to be. She's doing this for both of us.

I hear my father and sister coming down the stairs, and my first instinct is to run to Ava's aide. My father tends to be cruel to the women I see. My mum's shoulders are tense, meaning she knows he's close. I've never hated myself more than I do now. I'm the cause of all this. A part of me wishes I had stayed in Texas. Maybe, if I had thrown this life away, everything would have been okay. My mum doesn't deserve this suffering.

"Let's eat!" My mum calls out, and John walks into the dining room with his arm draped over Ava's shoulder. Usually, I wouldn't want any man to touch her, but I know John is harmless. His eyes have always been for Isabella. No one can change that. They're staring at his phone, and when she looks up at me, my heart expands in my chest. She gives me a soft smile, and it gives me the strength to face what's ahead for tonight.

We're seated at the table—my father at the head and my mum at the other. They aren't giving one another the looks they usually do. There isn't a day that goes by that they don't give one another a loving glance. I used to find it sickening. I didn't understand how she loved him so much, but I remembered that she fell in love with him at a different time.

Ava has one hand on my knee as she uses the other to eat my mum's food. He hasn't said a word that I knew would happen. I know he's still fuming over my comment about this being my home.

I know I'm going to have to be the one to begin this discussion. I clear my throat. "Dad, I want to apologize for how I behaved the other day." Ava's body stiffens beside me. I take a quick glance at her to see her jaw tense and clenched as she stares down at her food. She doesn't like that I'm the one who has to apologize. "I was out of line."

"*Gabriel*." My mum mumbles.

My dad clears his throat. "Thank you." He says, and I hear John sigh under his breath.

"Are you not going to apologize?" My mum asks as she scowls at her husband.

His jaw clenches as he looks at her. "Why would I?"

I laugh once in disbelief. "You've got to be kidding me." I try to ignore my heart sinking into my stomach. I knew this was going to happen, and yet I'm still disappointed.

"Gabriel," Isabella says as a warning, but it's too late.

"Jack, you hit our son. You seem to forget that he's *your* boy too. I told you I wouldn't stay here if you remained this way." Her voice breaks from the sadness.

I clench my fists.

My father hits the table with his fist. "Emilia, this is absurd. You belong here with me. This isn't worth it."

Instead of his words hurting me, I watch my mother's face as it cripples in despair. She closes her eyes and winces at his words like they cut through her.

Unable to help myself, I throw back the rest of my whisky and stand, pushing myself away from the table. "How long are you going to be selfish?!" I yell, causing Isabella and Ava to jump—spotting them in the corner of my eye. Ava has heard me yell but never like this. I know my face is red, I know the veins in my neck are bulging, but I don't stop. "This woman has been through enough! Or have you forgotten, old man, that she had fucking cancer!" My body begins to shake. My fists are clenched so hard my nails are digging into my palms. His face matches mine, but I don't fear him. Not since I was a kid.

"You claim to love her, and yet you sit here acting like a fucking child who can't even mutter a sincere apology!"

That is what causes him to break. Me questioning his love for Emilia is something he won't tolerate. Especially not from me. He stands so quickly his chair falls back, and this time I'm ready to hit him in return. He clenches his fists and begins to charge toward me. Everything moves so quickly I don't even know what's happening. I hear my mum shouting along with Isabella. I hear something smash against a plate, a chair falling. Then in a blink of an eye, Ava's body is in front of mine. My father stops in his tracks, breathing heavily from the rage. Everyone stops what they're doing. I look at her in shock; the urge to throw her behind me to protect her is strong. But...she's protecting me...

"*Enough*." She says through her teeth. Her hands are clenched, her body rigid in place. She doesn't flinch or shows any sign of fear of my angry father. "I won't let you hit him, and I know he won't let you hurt me. Shame on you for speaking to your child like he's garbage. I feel sorry for you." She shakes her head and looks at me with a soft expression, then to my father cold as ice. "You will never get to know the amazing man that he is."

She doesn't wait for him to speak. She takes my hand and gives me a small smile. "Thank you for having us." She says without looking at my family, then leads me out of the dining room. She doesn't stop to see anyone's reaction or wait to see if my father will come after us. She keeps walking until we're out of the house. I can hear footsteps coming after us, but it doesn't phase her. She opens the passenger door for me, gesturing for me to enter. I want to ask her what she's thinking, what she's doing. Once I'm in, she enters herself then speeds away with no hesitation.

"Ava," I say softly, but she shakes her head. Her knuckles are turning white from her tight grip on the wheel. I place my hand over hers. "What's wrong?"

She scoffs. "What's wrong?! Were you not paying attention in there?! He-he treated you like shit!" She yells angrily. "I couldn't stand there and let him talk about you that way."

She's angry for me. In her eyes, she *had* to rescue me. She needed to avenge me. Just like that, the air shifts between us, but she doesn't notice. How could she? I want to remember this moment forever because I've come to the realization that I'm going to marry this woman. I don't want to wait years; there's no point. If life has taught me anything, it's that it is too short. You can plan everything perfectly, but sometimes thing's don't work out. We never planned on my mum getting sick; we never planned on my grandad having a heart attack. We thought we had all this time. I want her to have my last name with a giant ring on her finger to accompany it.

She truly loves me unconditionally and wants to protect me just as much as I want to protect her. She will speak up for me even though I can do it on my own. She does it just so I know I'm not alone. I curse myself for ever hurting this woman who is too perfect for me. I don't deserve her, but as long as she wants me, I will be the man she needs me to be.

"You stepped in front of me," I say in disbelief. What if my father hadn't stopped?

She gives me a quick glance. "I told you I wouldn't let him hit you again. I don't want you to listen to him. You're worth...*everything*."

The heaviness in my chest is unexpected. I swallow past the lump in my throat, looking out the window. I'm overcome with emotion, knowing she thinks so highly after what I've done to her. I deserve hell and a miserable life, but in her eyes, I don't. In her eyes, I still deserve the best.

And that alone...makes me want to cry.

Sleep didn't come easy for me. Thoughts raced in my mind of my mum, the company, Ava, proposing, finding a new editor, finding Ava a new home—*if she doesn't want to stay with me*—my father, and my grandad. It's times like this where I need his advice. If he knew that my father hit me, he would have raced to him. He would have demanded an explanation on why my grandmother's only grandson is bruised. I look at the empty bottle of whisky that was full almost two hours ago. I hated to leave Ava alone in the bed just to drink, but I needed to... numb the heavy ache in my chest.

"You're going to drink yourself dumb, boy; how many times have I told you?" I hear my grandad's voice in my head. It's so clear; it's like he's here. I open my eyes and look out at the sky as I sit on the balcony. The stars seem so dim compared to the city lights. In Texas, the stars seemed almost too big, too bright.

"Gabriel," his voice says, and I look to the other side of the balcony to see him sitting on the other chair. I must be fucking plastered.

"Grandad?" I mumble.

His mouth forms a straight line. "What's going on?"

I frown. "I don't know," I answer honestly. "I'm...hurting."

He sighs heavily. "Don't let my son convince you that you're nothing, my boy. He's angry, I see it. He's angry at himself for so many things, and he's taking it out on the wrong person."

"Why must you defend him?" I snarl.

He stands and leans against the railing of the balcony. "You'll understand soon. When you're a father."

I wouldn't say *soon*. I'm not even sure Ava wants children. Yes, I got her pregnant a decade ago, but she's different now.

I stand next to him, admiring the view with him. "How's grandmother?" I ask.

He gives me a soft smile. "She misses you, boy."

My heart clenches. "I miss her too," I whisper. "I miss you as well, grandad." I need him to know that. I need him to know I wasn't ready to say good-bye.

He looks at me and places his palm against my cheek. "I miss you too, boy, but I'm watching, and I'm still proud of you. More than you know."

"Gabriel?" Ava's soft voice interrupts. Suddenly, he's gone. I turn to face her. She's wearing one of my shirts and nothing else. My mouth waters at the sight of her. "What are you doing out here?"

Her eyes zone in on the empty bottle I'm holding. "I couldn't sleep," I mumble and place the bottle down on the patio table. "Needed some air."

She closes the sliding door and sits on the lounge chair. "Do you want to talk about it?" She asks.

I frown and sit down with her. "No, I'm okay." I lie.

She leans back and spreads her legs, gesturing for me to lay in between them. Usually, it would be the other way around, and I would be the one holding her. I lay my head against her chest, and she begins to stroke my hair. We're silent, but I hear her mouth part as if she's about to say something, but it doesn't come. I can hear the cogs in her mind going at light speed.

"Is there something you want to ask?" I mumble and bury my face into her breasts. I love her breasts.

"Did he always treat you this way?" She asks softly with a tad of anxiety.

I stiffen as I recall how my father used to be with me. "No," I mumble. "We used to be close." The lump in my throat grows bigger. I want to tell her how much I loved him. I looked up to my father, and as a child, I wanted to be just like him. I wanted to love a woman the way he loves my mum. I want to tell her that my granddad showered me in the love I needed from my father. But I'm afraid if I open my mouth, the crying will begin.

"Oh," She whispers sadly.

She's hurting for me. I can hear her heart change in rhythm as she inhaled a sharp breath. As if the pain went straight to her chest.

She presses her lips against my head. "I love you more than you will ever know, Gabriel Warner. I will love you so much that you won't feel the pain your father causes you. All you'll feel is me."

I close my eyes as the tears I've been holding back—*I don't know how long for*—begin to fall down my cheeks. I hide my face in her chest as a sob rips through me. She doesn't judge me or think less of me. Instead, she wraps her arms and legs around me, shielding me from the world. She brings her lips close to my ear and begins to sing our song. Her lovely voice eases the ache in my chest.

CHAPTER 14

AVA

My heart aches for my alpha male God—who could never admit that it hurts him not to have his dad's love. Running to Gabriel's aid was all instinct. Out of nowhere, I threw myself in front of him when I saw the look on his dad's face. He didn't see Gabriel as his son. I knew Gabriel could defend himself. His father's build nowhere near Gabriel's muscular, tall stature. I just couldn't stand the thought of sitting there watching Gabriel be treated this way. Someone had to save him.

He cried himself to sleep as we sat outside. I brushed his hair as I held him, singing to him over and over again. Remembering when he asked me why I never sang in front of him—it was the only thing I could think to do. I woke him shortly after when I could no longer feel my legs and took him to bed. He was very intoxicated, which made it a lot harder. I undressed him then myself before crawling into bed with him. I laid my head on his chest, and his arm wrapped around me, protectively, keeping me close. His breathing slows, and I look up at him to see his mouth parted.

"You're going to be a great dad," I whisper. "I know it."

I woke up before Gabriel. This morning was different; I woke up with determination and a sense of security. I saw a side of Gabriel I didn't think I would see —that I didn't even know was there. I wanted to tell him about our baby, and I've never been more sure. I want to find a creative way to tell him, so I'm going to need Isabella's help. We should also talk about where the baby and I are going to live. He's going to want me to live here, but...how safe can a baby be here? Too many people have access. Elizabeth is unstable. I'd like to move somewhere safer, and I could never ask him to leave his penthouse. Just because we have this baby doesn't mean we have to move in together.

You know he asked you to move in way before this baby.

I ignore the voice in my head. I slowly climb out of bed and make my way to his closet to get fresh clothes. I don't know if Ruth will be here today, but I shouldn't be naked just in case. I would tell her that I want to make breakfast for Gabriel myself. I would give her the day off...if I have that power. I look through different pairs of shorts until I find one with a drawstring. I grab a shirt, accidentally pulling one of his suit jackets down as well.

Damn.

I go to pick it up, spotting a card on the floor. It doesn't look like a credit card or a business card. It's all black. I pick it up and turn it around to see two words in blue.

White Collar.

I remember him explaining he was part of a sex club called *White Collar*. This is the card to get in. I'm appalled thinking about Gabriel at a sex club, but my libido is awake at the thought.

What would it be like to have Gabriel take me to that club?

I dampen at the thought. I shouldn't like it. I don't want to like it...but my body is excited at the thought of being with him in *that* club. I wouldn't drink, but I know I would be high off just his presence. I'm curious to see what intrigued him to join in the first place.

How have I never heard of this club or seen it?

I begin to wonder if he misses it. If he joined this club, it means they have what he is interested in. I try to imagine what it would look like, but I can't.

I decide to take it with me. My stomach begins to roll and squeeze with discomfort. "Oh no," I mumble and run to the bathroom, making sure to close the door before getting sick in the toilet. I rest my head in my hands as I take deep breaths while my stomach rolls again in pain. I need to look up how long morning sickness usually lasts. I'm hoping it won't be much longer; praying, really.

After flushing, washing my face and brushing my teeth, I tiptoe out to see Gabriel still peacefully sleeping. His arm draped across his face as he snores.

I make my way downstairs and see that no one is there. Maybe, we do have the house to ourselves. "Okay, baby, no throwing up. We aren't eating; we're just cooking for your dad." I don't believe the baby even has ears yet, but it feels right speaking to him or her.

I begin to fry bacon and scramble eggs. I find a remote on the counter and point in the air, pressing the play button. Soft piano music begins to flow through the house. I begin to brew coffee, inhaling sharply. I miss coffee. I have to set up an appointment with a doctor for my next ultrasound; I will ask her if I'm allowed to drink coffee. It didn't even occur to me to ask my aunt. I also make a mental note to order parenting books the second I tell Gabriel. We have a lot to learn and a lot to prepare for.

I'm terrified of what his reaction may be. Isabella was thrilled, but I'm not sure how Gabriel feels about children. Is he ready to be a dad? Did he see it in his plan? Did he see it in his plan *so soon?* We may be moving at the speed of light, but that doesn't mean he wants to skip that far, that fast.

"Is my angel making me breakfast?" Gabriel's hoarse voice fills the room.

I turn and see his muscular, defined torso. He's only wearing tight, white boxer briefs that hug his thick thighs—my mouth waters at the sight of him. I missed the view of his tattoos. I wonder if he will get more if I asked.

"I am." I grin. "I assume Ruth has the day off, and my man needs to eat."

He smirks lazily as he sits down on the bar stools—which I've noticed are different from the last time I was here. "Well, aren't I lucky?" He rests his chin in his hands, his elbows propped on the counter. "I want to thank you for last night." Shame is in his voice with a hint of embarrassment.

I frown at his tone. He should never be embarrassed to show his emotions in front of me. I make my way to him, cupping his face in my hands. "You never have to thank me for being there for you, Gabriel. That's what lovers do."

His eyebrows narrow as he takes in my words. He's not used to having a woman care for him who isn't his family or Ruth. I loathe Elizabeth. Even though the woman is in the hospital, I can't stand knowing she used him for money and status.

He kisses me swiftly then hits my behind lightly. "Don't burn my breakfast, angel." He says in a teasing tone. Sensitive Gabriel is gone now.

I roll my eyes and make my way back to the stove. My mind is going crazy, wondering how to bring up the White Collar . I have my libido's attention. "So," I mumble with my back to him. This makes it easier. "I wanted to know about that club you told me about. *White Collar*."

I hear him inhale sharply, then his throat clearing. *I've taken him by surprise.*

"Ava, I'm not telling you about that club." He says with aggravation. I turn to see him scowling. "I would never taint your mind that way."

My libido sags in her chair with disappointment—but what takes me by surprise is the disappointment I feel. I'm almost heartbroken that he's not interested in taking me there. Does he not want me in that sense? My ego is bruised, but I decide to let it go...*for now.*

"May *I* ask you something now?" He asks softly. He regrets the way he spoke.

I turn my back to him again and put the bacon on a plate I lined with a paper towel. "I suppose."

"Will you move back in with me?" He asks nervously. I freeze.

I didn't know how long it would take us to get back here; get back to us living together. I assumed I would live on my own until the baby came, but I know him.

The second I tell him, he will demand I move in with him so he can be there hovering over me—making sure I'm safe. It would make my list of *to-do's* go a lot faster if I just move in now rather than in a few months. Besides, I don't have a job, which means I don't have any money for down payments.

If I'm honest with myself, I want to live with him. I want to be in this fantasy with him where he is happy about this baby. Where he talks to my stomach and buys things, he sees when he's out and about. I want to have that family life that I never got to have.

"Okay," I say with a smile as I place the scrambled eggs onto a plate. I don't turn to face him, knowing he will come to me, to kiss me.

His hands are on my hips, turning me around. He kisses me hard. His tongue brushing against mine, making me want more of him. He pulls away and touches his nose against mine. "Now, work for me again," he whispers casually.

I tense and pull my head back, away from him. "What?" I ask in shock.

He can't be serious. I don't deserve to work at that company. I've done so much damage; I haven't earned my position.

He sighs heavily. "Please, Ava, I think we both knew I would ask this of you. I still need an editor. More than anything, I need my mind back in the business, and I can't do that if I'm constantly wondering if you're safe.

Tristan is out there somewhere, and we still haven't found out who broke into your apartment. Having you work with me—as partners and lovers—will make it a lot easier to focus on work."

Damn him for trying to guilt me.

If I wasn't firm in my decision, he would have got me.

I shake my head. "I can't, Gabriel. You're just giving it to me because we're lovers." I refuse for Elizabeth to be correct. I don't want to be sleeping my way to the top.

He frowns. "I'm insulted that you still think that. Ava, you're bright, hard-working, dedicated, loyal, and everything I look for when it comes to an employee. You proved yourself in that board meeting, and you know it as well. Everyone was impressed with your intelligence. As was I. I'm still blown away by you every day."

I want to believe him but doubt clouds my mind... until... a light bulbs go off in my head. My libido is tapping her fingers slowly with a sultry smirk. She's thrilled with my idea.

"I *will* say yes," I say, causing his eyes to brighten. Oh, he is not going to like this. "On one condition: you take me to the White Collar ."

His eyes widen in shock. "What is your fascination with this club?" He asks through his teeth. "Why do you want me to take you to the place where I fucked other women?" He spits.

I flinch at his words as the images fill my brain. As silly as it sounds, that is precisely why I want him to take me there. When I think about that club, I just want to see him and me making passionate love. When he passes by that club, I want him to only think of me—not how much he misses his old life. "I won't budge on this, Gabriel. I want you to show me the things you enjoy." I run my hands over his bare chest. "I want to know that type of pleasure with you."

His eyes darken, and I know I've got him. He wants to see me that way too. It heals the earlier damage to my ego. "And you'll work with me again?" I notice he doesn't like to say that I would be working *for* him.

I nod while biting my lip.

"Don't do that." He breathes and runs his fingers through his hair. My mouth drops at the sight of his arm flexing. His thumb pulls my lip free. "When?"

My libido jumps with excitement. "Tonight." Before I tell him I'm pregnant, and he begins to treat me with kid gloves.

His jaw is tight. "Okay." He agrees and sticks his hand out for me to shake. "Deal."

I grin and shake his hand. "Deal."

He exhales loudly. "I can't believe this is happening."

My libido couldn't be happier, and neither could I.

"There's something else you're not going to like." He mumbles.

I frown.

"I'm going to go visit Elizabeth today." He says nervously, gauging my reaction. He has every right to be nervous. I wouldn't wish death upon the woman, but that doesn't change the fact that I hate her. I want to yell at him for even wanting to see her, but how can I? Before we found one another again, this was his version of love. She was his dearest friend and *wife* at one point. Even though it's a hard pill to swallow, I must be okay with it. He wouldn't be the person I fell in love with if he didn't visit her.

"Send her my good wishes," I say and kiss him softly. "Now, sit and eat."

He gives me a wide grin before digging in.

Gabriel going to visit Elizabeth left me time to go out shopping for something to surprise Gabriel with. I didn't just want to announce that I'm pregnant. I wanted something he could open. Something he could cherish forever. Then I would find lingerie for tonight. I don't know what to expect in this club, but I just picture rooms upon rooms where people have dormant sex. Or only a giant bed in the middle of the room for group sex. would Gabriel be interested in having sex with a crowd of people? Has he ever? He said he slept with four women simultaneously—which hurts every time I think of it—but is that the most at one time?

After driving to multiple stores, my last stop is Barnes and Noble. After rummaging through the store, I decided on an onesie that reads *coming soon* and a travel mug that reads *Best Dad*. I figured it was cute enough. Nothing else really caught my eye. I bought a gift box and got them to wrap it—rolling and tucking the onesie into the travel mug. I will find the right time to give this to him. When he isn't so hurt about his own father. When we get through tonight.

Now, lingerie time. Usually, I wouldn't want anything too daring or too...out of my comfort zone, but I know my body will change dramatically. I'm going to wish I appreciated how my body looks now. That leaves me with one option, embrace my body and find something wholly sexy and sultry. Something that would wow him; bring him to his knees. It took five boutiques to find the one. It a 3-piece black and red lace set. The bra hangs low—leaving the top of my breasts very exposed—with a thin strap crisscrossing. The strappy thong—leaves my ass exposed—is attached to the waist garter belt. The garter belt is linked to the black lace stocking I bought to match. I saw beautiful dark red velvet heels and knew I needed to get them. Wanting the lingerie to be the main attraction, I decided to keep the outfit for tonight simple. I'm not sure what to expect with this club or dress code, but I figured a dress would do. I chose a thin strap black silk—*very tight*—dress.

Nerves are starting to get the best of me as I take the cab back to Gabriel's. What if he doesn't enjoy himself? What if I don't enjoy myself? My libido is excited for this, but what if I can't actually handle what this club is about. Will people try to join us... will he want that? I know he won't want to scare me, but that doesn't mean he doesn't want them.

Don't do this to yourself, Ava. You want this with him; he will like it too.

I won't let nerves get the best of me. I want to be the sexy temptress that can bring her alpha god to his knees.

CHAPTER 15

GABRIEL

Tulips are Elizabeth's favourite. That I remembered. The anger and betrayal were still very much present, but I knew I had to see her. I still worry for her deeply. I cared for her; I used to think I cared for her the same way I did Ava. I was wrong. If the past few days taught me anything, it's that Ava is the only woman to truly love me. Elizabeth tolerated me so she wouldn't lose what I brought to the table. She used me, but I didn't blame her. She was damaged. I understood that.

However, at this moment, I wish I didn't want to visit her. Ava caught me by surprise by bringing up *White Collar* this morning. I hadn't thought about the club since I confessed to her that I was apart of it. It no longer interested me now that I had Ava. There was hardly any privacy in this club which meant Ava's beautiful body could be seen by someone else. The thought makes me want to murder someone. The genuine shocking part was her begging to be apart of that life. She wanted to know a different world of pleasure and only wanted *me* to take her there. She knew that I wanted her to work with me badly; that's the only reason she used it as her bargaining chip.

Smart woman.

A pain in my ass but very intelligent.

I'm nervous about bringing her to the same place where I have slept with multiple women—most of them at the same time. We would have to agree to some ground rules. I need to know what she is uncomfortable with; her limits, turn-offs, and turn on's. We would need to come up with a safe word; I would make sure it's burned in her brain. The last thing I need is her forgetting the safe word, not that I wouldn't stop if she yelled the word stop. Anxiety fills me. I try to remember every word that could mean stop.

Enough, no, no more, stop, I can't.

I've never been this nervous. I never had to worry about the women I slept with at the club. They were members longer than I've been. They all had the experience, and most of them didn't even have limits; they were open to anything. I've only had one woman tell me to stop with her safe word. I imagine Ava will be the second.

Enough of this for now. Right now is about Elizabeth.

I step into her private hospital room and see her sitting on the bed, eating a bowl of soup. Her eyes widen when she sees me. The blue eyes that I loved so much—because they were far from Ava's—but now don't compare to my angel's chocolate brown eyes.

"Gabriel," she mutters under her breath. "I didn't think you would come to see me."

Neither did I.

I set the vase of tulips down beside her bed. "You're in the hospital, Elizabeth. Of course, I would be here."

She gives me a small smile. "Thank you for the private suite."

I sit in the chair next to her bed. "Anytime," I sigh heavily. "What were you thinking?"

She could be dead right now. She's fortunate.

She frowns guiltily. "I know...I'm sorry. I was so upset after our fight over what I did. I wasn't thinking."

I lean forward and run my hand over my face. "Never scare me like that again."

"So, you forgive me?" Her voice is quiet; shy.

I look at her, and all I remember is what she confessed to doing. Was it her plan all along to get in between Ava and me? I can't hold *just* her accountable; I made mistakes too. I didn't have to let Elizabeth give me that blowjob.

Do I forgive her?

I suppose I do.

I nod.

She says in relief. "Good, I don't want to lose you." She reaches for my hand, taking it in hers.

I frown as I watch our hands laced together. I wait for the feeling I get when Ava touches me or even when she looks at me, but it doesn't come. Not even slightly.

"Elizabeth, that doesn't mean I can have you in my life." It hurts me to tell her this. It was easier to do this with anger and alcohol in my system.

Her face falls. "She's back."

I sigh. "Yes, and she won't forgive you for what you've done. She was worried about you, but that doesn't mean she wants you around, understandingly so."

She scoffs and pulls her hand away. "It's not about what she wants, Gabriel; it's about you."

"She *is* what *I* want. I will do anything to make her happy because I love her, Elizabeth. I will protect her, no matter who it is." I stand. This was a mistake.

"She's made you weak." She hisses in disgust.

I freeze. "That's where you're wrong. With Ava beside me, I can do anything."

I walk out without another word and prepare myself for tonight's events.

Ava had messaged me to eat before I came home. She had stopped somewhere and got something to eat before coming home. I felt uncomfortable with her leaving the house without Harris or myself. Tristan is still out there, and even though he isn't in the country it doesn't mean I'm not worried.

But there are bigger things to worry about. Tonight I would be taking Ava to White Collar and introducing her to what I used to enjoy.

"Ava!" I call out as I make my way into the kitchen. I need a drink. I pour myself a glass of whisky, downing it almost instantly.

"Coming!" She calls out from upstairs. I should get changed. I don't want layers of a suit to get in the way. I may just go for jeans and a simple long sleeve. I would see how Ava is dressed before I make my decision. I hear her heels against the floor as she makes her way downstairs—while I pour myself another glass. I lift the glass to my mouth and stop when I see her step off the stairs. She's wearing a black silk dress that hugs her wide hips. Her breasts look phenomenal, as do her legs —which are accompanied by lovely red heels. I want to see her in just those heels and nothing else. Her black lush hair is curled into endless waves.

"A goddess," I mutter under my breath. There's no way someone can be this beautiful. She has to be an angel, a goddess from Greek mythology.

She eyes my alcohol, her face falling in concern. "How was Elizabeth?" She asks.

I can hardly focus on her question with her looking this good, but my girl is worried. "Not as well as I was hoping, but she's just fine." Too fine. You would think almost dying would change her.

She walks toward me—my eyes never leaving her figure—then proceeds to cup my face. "I'm sorry about your friend." She's being genuine. It truly upsets her. I don't want to think about this right now.

"You look mouthwatering," I say, hoping to change the subject.

Her cheeks flush slightly. "Thank you…" She takes a deep breath. "You should wait to see what's underneath."

I twitch in anticipation. "What's underneath?" My voice is hoarse already.

She smirks. "That would ruin the surprise."

I want to grab her and take her to the club right now if that means I get to see what's underneath. "Would you like a glass of wine before we leave?" She just needs something to calm her nerves.

She tenses. "No, I already had a few glasses while I was getting ready." She doesn't meet my eyes.

I wonder why that would make her tense up?

"Let me get changed, and we will go." I kiss her swiftly and make my way upstairs. I'm hoping there will be something I can say to change her mind, but I know her well enough that she will be too stubborn. She wants a peek of the sexual life she's never known. I wasn't expecting her to be interested. I was expecting her to be repulsed and angry. She's taking me by surprise lately. I throw on a plain white v-neck t-shirt—*I know she will want to see my tattoos*—and blue jeans. I stare at myself in the mirror and shake my head with embarrassment.

"Stop being nervous," I scold myself. "You're a grown-ass man, and you're letting one woman shake you."

She isn't just any woman. My subconscious says. *This is the woman you want to marry and spend the rest of your life with.*

"Breathe," I whisper and fix my hair one last time before taking my—*faux*—leather jacket, then heading back down to my girl.

She's pacing the living room and stops when she sees me. Her eyes flare with desire as she drinks me in from head to toe. "It's not fair that you look this good with little effort."

Little effort?

I had to bust my ass for this body.

But I'll take her compliment even though I'm not used to the way *she* does it. Her praise carries more... adoration and love. All those other women just feel lust.

I give her my charming smile that usually makes women swoon. The only difference is, I'm swooning in return. "Are you ready?"

She swallows hard. *So, she is nervous.* "Yes." She breathes and bites her lip. "Will...will others try to join us?"

I tense, my jaw clenching hard enough I'm sure she can hear my teeth grinding. "*Never,*" I hiss. "I won't even let anyone *see* you." I can't imagine the anger I would feel if someone tried to join us.

She frowns. "Well, I don't want anyone seeing *you*."

My anger fades, and I smirk. "If no one sees you, angel, then no one will be seeing me."

She nods. "Good," she says and reaches for my hand. "Let's go."

"Gabriel," Shawn—*the bodyguard*—says with a nod. Ava tenses beside me when he says my first name. I suppose she had no idea how frequently I came here. Everyone knows everyone in this club.

I flash him my card—that Ava later gave me in the car ride here, and we step into the long hallway. We walk through the blue velvet curtain and step into the main floor of the two-story club. There are two bars, a dance floor, booths—*like any other bar*—but on the far side of the wall close to the dance floor, there are blue velvet plush circle sofas. Individual nets are surrounding each sofa. There are six of them where couples can begin...*foreplay*. Sex isn't allowed down here, but that doesn't mean you can't get very close. Most couples do, but if you're caught having sex on the first floor, there are repercussions. Membership is revoked for a week;

the second strike is a month; third, your membership is taken away. Veronica is usually good at giving chances unless it's violence or sex that wasn't consented to. She will not tolerate any monsters in her club.

The upstairs is where all the rooms are and where all the sex happens. There is one large standard room for groups and ten individual rooms furnished with different whips, restraints, ties, handcuffs; you can even place an order for additional toys and vibrators. Knowing that Ava will see all this in a few minutes makes me want to grab her and run. I need to protect her, not taint her. But I know she will take back her side of the deal; she won't come work with me.

Just focus on how this benefits her.

"Would you like a drink?" I ask her over the music. Her eyes are scanning over everything.

She shakes her head, taking me by surprise. "No, I think I would like to keep a clear head." She looks up at me with wide innocent eyes.

Her God is turning out to be the devil who is tainting the angel. Maybe, this is my punishment. Perhaps this is what I deserve for treating women the way that I do or my punishment for cheating on her. Suddenly, I remember the line from Tess of the D'Urbervilles. *'I agree to the conditions, Angel; because you know best what my punishment ought to be; only...only don't make it more than I can bear!'*

I look down at my angel and her nervous expression. I hope this isn't more than I can bear.

"Let me show you around." I take her elbow and walk her over to the netted sofa beds. Anyone can watch here; that's truly the whole purpose. To seduce whomever you'd like, then move upstairs to finish what you started.

"Are they all having sex?" She asks nervously as we walk down the aisle between the sofas. The first sofa has two women—both blondes and in excellent shape. The smaller one has the other's nipple in her mouth. The girl being pleasured is crying out with no shame. I look away and down at Ava who's cheeks are bright red.

"No, they aren't allowed to have sex down here. It's one of the rules. It's too public down here—not that it bothers anyone here, really. This is where the foreplay usually begins, or new members come here first before going upstairs. Baby steps." I find it amusing that they joined this club but need to take *"baby steps"*.

She looks away from the two women and looks to the right of us to see two men and two women—fully clothed—but each of them taking turns to kiss one another; more of the tamer things you can see here. We walk forward, and she stops to see a man-eating out a woman. The woman's brown hair is sticking to her forehead as she props herself up on her elbows. Her nipples are pierced. She has tattoos covering most of her body. I place my hand at the small of her back and guide her to continue. I don't need her to see the half-naked man. There's no need to let jealousy get the best of me if it doesn't have to.

There are three women and one man making out, and two men together. She swallows hard as she looks up at me. "Where do they have sex?" Her voice hoarse with...desire, I presume.

"Upstairs. Would you like me to show you?"

She nods, and I begin to lead her to the stairs. She watches every single person dancing, drinking, and socializing. Her face is flushed, along with her chest. Her breathing is heavier than when we walked in, telling me two things: she's either turned on or very nervous.

We take the stairs, and my whole body tenses as I see Veronica walking down the steps with two younger-looking men. All three of them look pleased. She gives me a sly smirk and stops, ignoring Ava, who is to my right. She wraps her hand around the nape of my neck, kissing my two cheeks.

"Gabriel, I've missed you." She says and finally looks to Ava, who is scowling. "Oh, I'm sorry, I didn't see that you brought someone."

I clear my throat and wrap my arm around Ava's tense shoulders. "Vee, this is my girlfriend, Ava. Ava, this is the owner of the club."

Ava isn't relaxing into me like she usually would.

She's pissed.

Ava gives her a very tight smile while shaking her hand.

Vee gives her a grin. "Is this the reason you've been gone? The girls have been missing you, especially Elizabeth."

I clench my jaw and give her a tight nod. "I'm going to finish the tour for Ava." I push Ava lightly, and she begins to walk up the stairs. Vee's face falls with confusion. She's met Elizabeth, she's had sex with Elizabeth and me when we were married, so it isn't her fault that she assumed Ava and I live the same lifestyle. Ava, however, won't be understanding. Which is also not her fault.

I stop her at the top of the stairs, and she refuses to meet my eye. "Angel," I whisper sadly and lift her chin so she meets my gaze. "I'm sorry you had to hear that. We can go home now." I'm praying she wants to go home.

She scowls and shakes her head. "No, I want to be here. I want to do this." She says with determination.

I sigh heavily.

Great.

"We should talk about this." I argue.

"No," she says through her teeth. "Please, let's not let this ruin what we want to do."

I don't know if I would say *we...*

Don't act like you aren't excited that you have her here.

"Lets go." I take her hand and lead her to the room I reserved for tonight. You get a better view of the first floor from the second. Ava's eyes are glued to the sofa bed's on the first floor—clearly amazed at the different points of view. You can really see everything that's going on.

"Are you ready, angel?" I ask as we approach the room.

"Yes." She breathes.

I push open the door, and we step inside. The rooms are a dark red—almost burgundy. In the middle of the room is a king-sized bed with navy blue silk sheets. There's a wooden *x* with wrist and ankle cuffs at each end on the far left wall. There are ceiling restraints near the bed—that I would usually use if I wanted to fuck the woman in the air with her legs wrapped around my waist.

Each bedpost has restraints attached to them. The right wall is covered with different whips, paddles; ropes; straps and different bondage bars. There's even a small bar stocked with alcohol and other beverages.

Ava looks around and walks over to the bed. "I was expecting white walls." She says in genuine confusion.

I smirk, holding back a chuckle. "That's a fair assumption."

She walks over to the right wall and goes to touch a whip but stops.

"It's clean." I say, knowing what she's thinking.

She looks at me in surprise. "How did you know?"

I shrug. "It seems like something *you* would be concerned about." I walk over to the bar and grab myself a glass, filling it with ice then whisky. "They disinfect everything in here after every use. Veronica is very serious when it comes to the cleanliness of her business and the professionalism."

She nods and takes down a leather flogger. "You whipped women?" She asks breathlessly.

I swallow hard. "They wanted me to, Ava." It almost feels wrong to call her that in here. An angel shouldn't be in here with me.

"Did..." she bites her bottom lip. "Do any of them whip you?"

Many did, yes, mostly Elizabeth.

"Yes." I nod. "However, most of them preferred me in the alpha role."

She frowns. "I don't like the thought of them hitting you."

I understand why she thinks of it as '*hitting*'.

"They had my consent, Ava, it pleased them, and they know it pleased me as well. Don't you enjoy it when I spank you?" I twitch at the thought.

She looks at the flogger then back at me with wide eyes. "Yes, I do, but your hand is a huge difference from *this*."

I walk over to her while finishing the rest of my drink and set the empty cup on the counter where there are hand and ankle cuffs. I know we won't be using this tonight; it can be painful. I grab the flogger and lightly hit her covered ass with it. She winces slightly from surprise.

"Did that hurt?" I ask, knowing there's no way it could.

She shakes her head.

I nod. "I wouldn't hit you any harder than that."

She bites her lips and looks at me with a flushed face. "What if I want you too?" She says breathlessly.

My eyes widen. *But she just said...*

"You don't mean that."

She swallows hard. "Surprisingly, I do." She doesn't believe she's asked for it either. Good, I'm glad she can manage to surprise herself.

"Ava, before we do anything, we should talk ground rules." I place the flogger back on the wall and begin to remove my jacket. "First rule: I thought of giving us a safe word—which is a normal thing when taking someone in the club—but *we* don't need one. When things become too much—*and they will*—you say stop, and I will."

She nods. "You will do the same." She demands.

I'm taken back. Safe words are usually meant for women to make them feel comfortable, so they trust and have a sense of security. Not once has a woman ever reminded me to use a safe word or been concerned that anything we may do may be too much for *me*. I suppose they don't think a man would be uncomfortable or feel unsafe. To be completely honest, neither did I.

"Thank you." I say tightly as my chest warms with admiration. I didn't think I could love this woman more, but as always, she takes me by surprise. "Second: is there anything you're uncomfortable with?" I begin to take off my shoes, and she mirrors my movements—taking off her own.

"Like what?" She asks doubtfully.

I think. I can't imagine her ever performing anything other than vaginal. "Do you enjoy anal play?" I ask bluntly. There can be no shyness in here. I need to know everything, so I make sure I stay within her limits. This is important.

Her eyes bulge in shock, her cheeks a dark crimson. "*No*, no, I don't." She says nervously.

I nod. "I assumed."

I'm entirely okay with that.

"Other than that...I trust you, Gabriel. You don't have to be nervous." She says and makes her way to me. Her hands rest on my arms. "I want this...I want you."

Trust her. She wants this. There's nothing wrong with her wanting this from you.

I take her hand and sit on the edge of the bed. I remember what she said in the apartment, and I can't take it any longer. "I want to see what's under the dress." I let go of her hand and give her a nod of encouragement. I grab the remote on the bedside table

—where I know the toys I specifically requested will be —and dim the lights, pressing the music button. A slow instrumental begins to play through the sound system with a deep bass. Each sultry song was handpicked specially for each room. She looks nervous as she reaches for the straps of her dress, pulling it slowly down her arms until the tops of her breasts are exposed. I see a thin black strap going across her olive-tone skin. The nerves seem to leave her when she catches my eyes. I know what they must look like because I see it in her own eyes. The way they flash with desire just for me— and mine just for her. She continues to pull it down until it pools to her feet.

"*Fuck*." I groan.

I'm instantly hard, and she hasn't even fucking touched me yet. My body is screaming at me to take things faster than I had planned, and I'm about to give in to that temptation. The waist garter hugs her waist perfectly, causing her hips to flare out more. Her garters attached to her very revealing panties.

"Turn around." I croak, knowing when she does, it will be my undoing. My caveman instincts will take over when I see her ass. She turns slowly—in those glorious heels; that I plan to leave on for most of the night—and I let out another groan. The garter straps look like they're cutting into the delicate skin. I stand and drop to my knees behind her. My fingers trail up her legs, leaving goosebumps on her skin. I tuck a finger under the strap and see a mark. "This beautiful outfit is hurting my most prized possession...well, *second*." She's the first. I kiss over the marked area, causing her to gasp softly. I ran my tongue over it and then moved to the other strap, repeating the same thing I did to the other mark.

"What's your first?" She whispers.

I caress her ass before standing, pressing my front to her back so she can feel my erection. "*You*, angel," I whisper, then kiss under her ear.

She shivers. "I think that's crazy." She whispers.

I frown. My hands run up her stomach, and she stiffens slightly then relaxes as my hands go to her breasts. "Why?" I ask, confused.

"You're too...I'm not beautiful enough for you."

My heart restricts in my chest. She truly doesn't see herself. She doesn't see her beauty, elegance; sexiness; intelligence. She thinks she can't compare to Elizabeth or the other women I've taken here in this club—but she doesn't see that no one will compare to her. I'm not worthy of her—I don't think any man will be. If I didn't believe in God before, I did when I saw Ava. Something all-powerful had to be the reason why she existed. There's a reason why I call her angel because, in another world, she would have been. Instead, He made her human and left her on this earth for me to find her. At first, I used to think it was to punish her—which would punish me in the end—the ultimate karma for something I had not done yet. Now, I wonder if she were sent here to save me. To show me what real love is; to soften my cold, bitter soul and heart.

I brush her hair to the side to expose her shoulder. "How very lovable her face was to him. Yet there was nothing ethereal about it; all was real vitality, real warmth, real incarnation. And it was in her mouth that this culminated." I whisper into her ear. "Eyes almost as deep and speaking he had seen before, and cheeks perhaps as fair; brows as arched, a chin and throat almost as shapely; her mouth he had seen nothing to equal on the face of the earth. To a young man with the least fire in him, that little upward lift in the middle of her red top lip was distracting, infatuating, maddening."

"Tess of the D'Urbervilles." She whispers, recognizing Thomas Hardy's brilliant work.

"You are a work of art, Ava. An angel that was sent down to save me; to rid of the darkness." I mumble and pull down the cups of her bra. I brush my thumbs over her already hard nipples. She lets out a shaky breath. I turn us to the left, so we're facing a mirror. Her face is flushed, my fingers working over her nipples. Her mouth is hanging open, and her head rolls back onto my shoulder—her eyes closing. "Open your eyes, angel, look at how beautiful you are."

She slowly opens her eyes, but her gaze is hooded. My right-hand slides down her front, sliding underneath her panties. Her hips buck in excitement. I smirk as I watch her through the mirror. "So, needy." I tease and brush the pad of my finger over her clit.

"Ah," she hisses in pleasure as she throws her head back.

"*Open*." I demand and remove my finger until she obeys.

They slowly open again, and I smile. "Good girl." I praise and begin to circle my finger over her clit.

"*Oh god*," She mumbles and hooks her arm around my neck, her nails digging into my skin. She gasps and bucks her hips, her head falling back.

"Someone isn't good at listening." I scold and pull away. I stand in front of her and begin to remove her—*incredible*—lingerie. Her hands run up my chest, lifting my shirt as she goes. I pull it over my head, and she goes for my jeans, but I grab her hands. "I'm in charge, angel." I lift her causing her to squeal as I lay her on the bed. I cover her body with my own and take her mouth. Our tongues clashing as she wraps her legs around my hips, her heels—*deliciously*—digging into my lower back. I grind my hips against her, pressing my erection against her centre. She moans softly against my mouth. My hands pin hers above her head then I begin to cuff them as we kiss. When I have the one cuff against her wrist, she pulls away and looks up to see her right arm restrained. I do the same to the left and smile.

"I want you still, angel." I kiss her swiftly. I leave her and begin to cuff her ankles. "Lift your head." I go to the bedside table and take out the silk blindfold. I cover her eyes, tying the blindfold tightly.

"Relax." I demand, and she lets her head fall against the bed. She begins to squirm, and I grin in delight. This is getting her excited; she isn't afraid.

I grab the vibrating wand I requested and turn it on. She jumps at the sound of the loud vibration. She's moving her head, trying to find where the sound is coming from. I walk to the end of the bed, resting on my knees in between her spread legs. I run the wand up her leg.

"*AH!*" She gasps in surprise, her leg jolting but hardly moving. I place it on the inside of her thigh. "Fuck." She hisses.

Her hips buck wildly. I'm close to her sex, and she can't handle the suspense. "Get ready for intense pleasure, angel."

CHAPTER 16

AVA

He presses the vibration against my sex, causing my head to throwback on a cry. I pull against the restraint, the cuffs cutting into my skin. I can't move, and that makes the pleasure ten times more intense. Not being able to see makes it almost unbearable. I don't know what he's planning, what he's going to use against me. I'm sweating already as my toes curl from the intense pleasure. The vibration intensifies as his tongue circles around my clit.

"*FUCK!*" I cry out. I thrash my head as my body begins to shake. It has never felt something like this. I never used toys before. I always thought about it and made plans to pick up a few handy devices, but I never got around to it.

God, was I ever missing out.

Just as quick as it came, the vibration is gone, and so is his mouth. "No," I whine in discomfort and pull against the restraints again. I need to pull him to me; I need him closer. The bed dips, and then I don't feel him anymore. "Gabriel?"

"Don't worry, angel, I'm here." He says, his voice far off in a distant corner of the room. "I'm just going to make this a little more fun."

There is teasing and some warning in his voice.

My libido is panting in anticipation. She's on her knees—submitting, begging for Gabriel. She wants everything he's going to give, and so do I.

The bed dips again, and his body covers mine. I search for him, wanting his mouth against mine, but he doesn't give in. I gasp sharply as I feel a stinging cold sensation against my hot, sweaty skin. It trails down the centre of my chest then moves to my breasts, circling around my nipple.

"Ah." I gasp, arching my back. It's painful and pleasurable. I want him to stop, but at the same time, I want more. I will scream for more, plead if I have to. The cold moves to my stomach and almost melts away.

It's ice.

Then out of nowhere, my nipples are being pinched hard. It shoots pleasure straight to my clit, overpowering the pain.

"Oh my god." I groan and throw my head back.

The vibration is back and is on my clit, torturing me endlessly. "Fuck, Gabriel." I moan. My legs begin to shake, my body climbing higher and higher. I'm tugging and pulling against the restraints as I gasp for air. My body is overheating; I can feel everything; I hear every sound while I can't focus on anything but the pleasure. The slight sting is actually intensifying the pleasure. I want more; I need less.

More, more, more. My libido begs.

"I'm going to come!" I scream, and without hesitation, the orgasm rips through me. I'm crying out incoherent words as my body shakes rigidly as he keeps the wand against my clit, and the clamps on my nipples squeezing deliciously.

The vibration stops, and the clamps are slowly taken off. I hear shuffling and feel a wet cloth touch my forehead, wiping the sweat.

"I could watch you orgasm all day, Ava." His voice is hoarse. It comforts me to know this is affecting him too. His lips kiss mine softly. "I'm not done yet."

My wrists and ankles are set free then I'm flipped onto my stomach. My ankles are cuffed again but with something different. He used handcuffs before, but this feels more like a soft material like leather. My hands, however, are kept free.

"Keep yourself up." He orders. "Open your mouth."

I do as he says, and something small, cold and round is shoved into my mouth. There are multiple small balls that my tongue swirls around. *"Enough."* He demands, and I let the balls free. He leaves me, and the bed dips from behind me. I tense up. Those better not be going in my ass.

"Relax," he whispers. "I know your hard limits; I wouldn't betray you." My body relaxes slightly. I feel the same circular shape at my entrance, and it slowly pushed inside—the wetness from my orgasm making it slick. I gasp at the sensation. He gives me little time to savour the intense feeling before another is slowly sliding in me, then another. I gasp as each one enters me slowly. The vibration is back and moving between my legs—as I rest on my knees—then presses against my entrance.

"Ah!" I cry out, my legs shaking, my hips bucking wildly. I can feel every ball moving inside me, rubbing against every inch of my walls. Sweat begins to bead down my face, and he's only just started this. The vibrator slowly moves to my clit where he applies a little more pressure. "*YES!*" I call out.

I'm clawing at the sheets—struggling to keep myself up—as I feel another orgasm so close. My libido is thrashing on the bed, knowing this orgasm will be more powerful than the last. Will I be able to take it? His body shifts more to one side, and I'm about to beg him not to stop when I feel the sting across my behind. It wasn't his hand. I'm sent forward on a moan as the balls move intensely inside me. The vibration is almost unbearable against my clit, but I never want it to end.

"Do you think we can get you to come this way?" He asks.

If I had the strength to roll my eyes, I would. "Yes." I breathe. I cry out as the whip hits my behind again.

"*Fuck*." I hiss through my teeth. My arms begin to give out as my body is getting ready to shoot through the sky. He whips me three more times, one after the other.

"Come for me, Ava." He demands.

"Gabriel!" I scream as everything goes more black than it was already. My arms give out, and I fall forward —leaving my behind in the air—my legs trembling vigorously. My hands fist into the sheets as if to keep me from flying off this bed. I cry out again when the balls are slowly pulled out of me, keeping my orgasm rippling through me for even longer.

"Get ready to come again." He promises, and he fills me deeply.

"Oh my god!" I yell and clench around his length.

He runs his hands over my behind and the curve of my back. His hands leaving a burning sensation. His hand fists in my hair, his hips moving back until it's just his tip left inside me. "I love it when you scream my name." He says, referring to himself as the '*god*' I called out for. He thrusts into me hard, setting a punishing rhythm. He pulls out so torturously slow, then thrusts so hard and deep it goes straight to my clit. I'm sent rocking forward with each thrust, causing my hard nipples to brush against the soft silk sheets—giving me more pleasure. My body is finally coming down from that orgasm just to get strapped back in the rollercoaster. It's climbing higher and higher to the top for the fall, whether I'm ready for it or not.

"You're dripping fucking wet, Ava." He hisses and grinds his hips against me. "Knowing I do this to you drives me fucking crazy."

He drives me crazy when he does this to me.

I'm throbbing around him, and I gasp—my heels digging into the bed—as I feel the orgasm about to rip through me. It's not possible to orgasm this many times in a row—no human can possibly endure this intensity, this overwhelming pleasure. He tugs my hair harder, and instead of it hurting, the pain goes straight to my sex as pleasure.

"I'm—*gasp*—fuck. I'm going to—*moan*—come!" I cry out, and his hand slaps against my ass cheek.

"Come with me, Ava." He breathes.

I do as he says and scream into the sheets as time stops all around me, and there's only Gabriel and Ava.

My body collapses in exhaustion. I try to bring my breathing back to normal and hear through the ringing in my ears. If sex is like this for everyone, how does anyone get anything done? His body weight leaves the bed. My ankles are set free, and the blindfold is taken off. It takes a few minutes to gain the focus in my vision back. I turn my head to the other side of see him sitting

on the bed holding a glass of water and—what must be
—the same damp towel he used to wipe my sweat from
earlier.

"You need to drink." He says with a soft tone. It's
different from the one he was using during all this. I
narrow my eyebrows as I try to rid of the thoughts that
will ruin what we just did. He must do this with every
woman he took in these rooms.

I take the cup and sip lightly. I don't have my full
strength yet. My arms and legs feel like Jell-O. I try to
give him the cup, but he shakes his head.

"Drink more; you need more." He says worriedly, and
I roll my eyes. I drink half the glass before he finally
takes it, setting it on the small console table next to the
bed. I'm almost shy now that the heat of the moment is
over. He saw me in a way that no other has. I
feel...exposed...vulnerable.

"Are you okay?" He asks with worry.

Even though I'm feeling shy, I'm also thoroughly
pleased. My libido is spent as she pants, lifeless on the
bed. I should be worried or scared of how much I
enjoyed myself today, but I'm not. I can give him this—
he doesn't have to give up this part of his life—and I
want to provide him with this. My libido, alone, wants
our sex to be this way constantly.

"I'm thoroughly fucked." I mumble, and his eyes
widen in surprise. A slow smile creeps across his face,
and he begins to laugh. I smile at the sight of him

clutching his stomach as he laughs at my honesty. That truly is how I'm feeling.

Why wouldn't I be okay? If we didn't work out, I would have to be a crabby old woman living in an apartment with all kinds of pets, knowing I will never have anything this powerful. He is the only one who can make me feel this good; this beautiful; this loved; this cherished.

"This is why I love you." He says when he catches his breath. He lays down next to me, not bothering to cover himself up—not that he has to. His body belongs to a DemiGod from another world.

"That was...*amazing*, Gabriel." I whisper shyly. I know I'm blushing.

He frowns slightly. "I was scared I was going to hurt you." Worry is laced in his voice. I can see that bringing me here was a lot for him. I need him to know that I wanted this.

"You would never hurt me, Gabriel." I rest my hand on his cheek. "You're not some monster that others have led you to believe."

I want to protect him from anyone that makes him feel less of himself. Even if that means protecting him from his own father.

"After all I've done, how can you still see good in me?" He asks, perplexed.

My heart constricts for the young boy I met—the young boy who lost his father's affection for no reason.

No one—*but maybe his mother*—has made him feel loved. He has ego, pride, and confidence but is missing everything else in between.

"Because you're still the same boy in high school who used to stay with me when my dad would go out of town. You'd stay and watch over me; protect me." I stroke his cheek with my thumb. "You're human, you make mistakes, and that's okay. It doesn't mean you're damned."

He breathes out a soft chuckle. "You make my..." he exhales loudly, trailing off. His eyebrows narrow as if he's struggling to come up with the words. "In vain have I struggled. It will not do. My feelings will not be repressed. You must allow me to tell you how ardently I admire and love you."

"*Mr. Darcy,*" I whisper with a smile. *Pride and Prejudice* was the first book I got him to read. I had read the story repeatedly in high school, and when Gabriel told me he had only read two or three novels in his seventeen years, I knew I had to get him to read it. It was hard at first, but then one day, when I was working late in the library, he surprised me with a small dinner. We sat on the carpet against the bookshelves, his head in my lap as I read him the story. What I wasn't expecting was for him to fall in love with the story. I'm guessing years in the publishing industry have gotten him to memorize his favourite quotes from Jane Austen's outstanding work.

I've come to discover from what he quoted earlier and now that it must be easier for him to express himself through other's words than his own. If I didn't love novels as much as I do and the great works of Thomas Hardy and Jane Austen, I would probably complain that he can't use his own words or thoughts. But quoting these words goes straight to my heart.

"Her heart did whisper that he had done it for her." I say softly and press my lips against his.

CHAPTER 17

AVA

After work today.

That is when I plan to tell him. I asked Ruth if she could prepare a steak dinner for tonight—*mine fully cooked*—and a nice bottle of wine. Sadly, I can't drink, but Gabriel should be able to for both of us. The gift is in my bag. Even though I know he can't see it or even know that it's there—I'm moving tensely, which is making it more obvious. He gives me weird glances every once in a while, but I brush them off. I'm afraid if I speak, I will blurt it out.

"I have a meeting across town. Harris is going to drive me since I have to be on conference calls on the trip there. I'm going to let you choose one of my cars to take." He says as we step off the elevator to his private parking garage. I look at each car in awe.

I stop at the matte black Ferrari. He laughs under his breath. "Absolutely not." He says with a smirk.

I frown. "But you just said."

He buttons his black suit jacket. "Yes, but not my 488 Pista."

I roll my eyes. "Then which one?" I ask. It will be easier if he just tells me what I'm allowed to drive.

He scans all six cars and goes to the small shack where a safe is. He inputs numbers and sets keys into my hand. "The Rolls."

I look down at the keys then at him with a grin. "Really?" I never imagined myself driving a car this beautiful.

He nods. "Yes, but please, be safe and make it to work alive."

I squeal in delight and unlock the car. "I can't believe I get to drive this," I mumble in awe as I get in, running my hands over the leather steering wheel.

"Only because I know you're nervous about today." He says, leaning down.

Last night after getting home from the club, we discussed my first day back on Monday. I would be officially an editor, which meant finding my own assistant. I can't keep taking Lydia away from Gabriel. He'd be lost without her, his words not mine. I thought of Isabella because she's the only one I trusted. I'm not sure if she wants to be a secretary forever, but I want her by my side. I want her to travel the world with me as my best friend, the aunt of my baby. I just have to ask her first.

I sigh. "Are you sure I'm the one for this?" I ask with doubt. "I'm afraid I'm going to fail you."

His faced falls. He cups my face, bringing his lips close to mine. "You could never fail me, Ava. You were made for success, for great things. I believe in you...*you could...*" His eyes are sad. "*...run this business into the ground, and I would still be proud of you.*" His voice breaks slightly before his lips press against mine. I wonder what has him emotional.

"Have a good day at work. I'm one short phone call away." He mumbles and kisses my forehead. "I love you."

"I love you too," I say before he closes the door and gives me a wink, then walks away to his Escalade where Harris is waiting. The car roars to life, and I can't help but squeal in excitement.

I'm in a goddamn Rolls Royce that belongs to my handsome baby daddy who believes in me.

I step off the elevator; Isabella is sitting on the edge of her desk with a small gift in her hand. She turns her head and grins, her eyes dancing with glee. "I'm so excited your back. Is Gabriel with you?" She asks worriedly.

I shake my head. "He had meetings out of the office," I say as we embrace.

"Great," she squeals. "Open this." She shoves the gift into my hand. It's a cute yellow gift wrap with a white bow.

"What's this for?" I ask, confused.

"For the baby!" She says excitedly, and I throw my hand over her mouth—*again*. This woman is not good at discretion.

"You need to be quiet. I'm telling Gabriel tonight after work. No need for anyone to overhear us and beat me to the punch." I whisper and drop my hand. "You didn't have to get me anything."

I feel guilty knowing Isabella knows before Gabriel, and now she's giving me gifts before him too. If I hadn't decided to tell him today when I woke up, I would have decided at this moment.

"That is my niece or nephew in there, and they deserve to be spoiled." She says quietly. "Now, open."

I can't lie that I'm excited about the gift.

I take off the bow carefully—so I don't leave a trace of evidence—and open the small box to see a pair of baby shoes and a small gift card for five hundred dollars to *Pottery Barn Baby*. My mouth drops open as my eyes widen.

"Isabella," I hiss. "*One thousand dollars?*"

Who the hell gives someone a one thousand dollar gift card? Isn't fifty dollars the max?

She scoffs and rolls her eyes. "I wanted to give you more, but John told me you'd be appalled. Clearly, my husband was right."

MORE?!

"Isabella, I can't accept this," I say and take the card, handing it to her.

She scowls. "Giving it back would be an insult. This isn't about you. This is about that *baby* and me—*the aunt*—loving that baby."

I feel guilty for wanting to take this away from the baby. I sigh heavily. *"Fine.* Thank you." I embrace her, and she squeezes me tightly.

"Thank you for accepting."

I smirk. "I'm only accepting because I have a...proposition." I pull away.

"What?" She asks apprehensively.

"Now that this is officially my role, I need an assistant. I don't like that word, actually, so I'll call it a *business partner.* I want you to be that—if you want, of course."

Her nose scrunches up. "You want me to be your business partner?"

I nod. "There's no one I trust more to be by my side. I don't have any friends, and soon we will be family when the baby comes. I don't know if you want to stay behind that desk or even like it, but I feel like you should be doing more. I want you to read manuscripts with me, attend business meetings, and travel when I need to. We need more women in charge and more women in this business. If you like it—*who knows*—maybe you can be an editor."

She has a poker face, but her eyes gleam with possibilities. She's envisioning what I'm describing and is liking what she sees. "You really want *me*?" She also in disbelief.

I grin. "Yes, now can you accept already so we can work on finding a new secretary for this floor?"

She grins and throws her arms around me. "I would love to." She mumbles in my hair.

"Great. Let's get started. Lydia should have everything we need for today already on my desk." I pull away and begin to walk toward my office. On the door is a plaque that reads: *Ava Thompson: Editor.*

Gabriel works fast, clearly.

The rest of the day goes by in a blur. Gabriel was out of the office the entire workday, and I'm grateful for it. It gave Isabella and me space and time to get organized. I haven't been here in almost two months which meant there would be hardly any time for breaks. I know that if Gabriel was in the building, I wouldn't have been able to focus; I would have wanted to see him—which probably would have led to sex. I was grateful that

Isabella already knew how our systems and computers worked. It saved us time to get through manuscripts. We spoke about the baby and my ideas for names—*which I had none of*—or hoping for one specific sex more than the other. I told her how I would tell Gabriel, and she agreed it was the best way to go. She doesn't believe her brother would have liked anything extravagant or public. It made me smile, knowing I knew him well enough. Gabriel had called me once at lunch, but it had been cut short when something unexpected happened. He gave me a quick good-bye and hung up before I could say I love you in return.

After that phone call, I noticed a text from him but didn't have any time to answer. We had to schedule meetings with specific authors that I should have met if I hadn't gone running. By five-fifteen, Isabella and I are walking to our cars in the underground parking.

"I can't believe he let you drive his Rolls Royce." She says in disbelief after telling her that he let me pick any car—*not really*—to take to work.

"I wanted the Ferrari." I sigh.

She laughs. "The day he lets you drive that car is the day pigs fly."

I laugh with her. As we pass two cars away from ours, the headlights of a grey car turn on, the engine softly purring. The windows are tinted, but I don't think much of it. There are a lot of people that work in this building.

"Will you tell me everything that happens?" She asks, referring to me telling Gabriel the news.

I smile. "I already said I would."

"Just making sure." She unlocks her car and blows me a kiss. "Good luck. I'll see you tomorrow."

"I'll see you!" I call out before getting into the car, attaching my phone via Bluetooth, then pull out of the garage as I dial Gabriel's number. I haven't answered his text and don't want him to worry.

I look in my review mirror and see the grey car behind me now. I pull onto the busy street, heading toward the apartment. After three rings, I hear him on the other end.

"Ava," he says in a clipped tone.

That can't be good. "What's wrong?" I ask immediately. I'm hoping nothing will ruin tonight.

"Why didn't you tell me Tristan showed up when you were in Texas?" He asks. Anger is seeping into his tone.

Fuck.

I had completely forgotten to tell him about Tristan. I had forgotten about it myself when Gabriel had shown up. He took me by surprise, and then my mind was only on him and the baby. Then Elizabeth has almost overdosed while his parents were—*and maybe still are*—on the verge of divorce. I know it should have been the first thing I told him, along with the pregnancy.

A honk brings me out of my thoughts, and I look in my mirror, spotting the same grey car right behind me.

He isn't tailgating me, but I know I've made multiple turns for him to be coincidentally following me.

"*Ava*." Gabriel says, reminding me that he's still on the line.

"Yes, I'm sorry. It happened right when you showed up at my uncle's ranch. It had completely escaped my mind."

He exhales loudly. I can see him rubbing his temples in distress. "That's no excuse, Ava; I need to know where he is at all times. I need to know when he contacts you."

I scowl as I make two random right turns, the grey car still following me. "How did you know about that?" I ask. An alarm begins to slowly go off in my mind, but I decide to take two more random turns to see if he follows me. I'll go onto the highway if I have to.

"Harris, looked him up. I'm keeping tabs on him, Ava; don't seem so surprised. I wish you would have told me, however."

When I take the exit onto the highway, I begin to speed up into the fast lane. In a blink of an eye, I see the same car speeding behind me.

I'm being followed.

Anxiety prickles at my scalp. "Gabriel," I say, my voice breaking in fear. "I'm being followed."

"*What?* How do you know?" He asks with urgency.

"The same grey car has been following me since I left work. I took random turns and got on the highway to see if he would follow me. He still is." I put more pressure on the accelerant, and he follows my lead.

He refuses to lose me.

"We're tracking the car and your phone, baby, just keep driving. Dodge, speed, I don't care what you have to do. Lose him." He's trying to remain calm, but I can hear the fear in his voice. The sign telling me to only go one-twenty zips by in a blur as I begin to go one-sixty. "What's happening, Ava. Talk to me."

"He's still following me. I'm going one-sixty, but he's right on my trail." I grip the steering wheel while telling myself not to cry, not to break. I think of my child that deserves a chance at life. I will do anything and fight anyone to keep him or her alive.

"Faster, baby." He isn't asking.

I go up to one-seventy, and I see his car begin to slow. "He's slowing down."

Gabriel sighs in relief. "Good, take the next exit and come home—

I scream as my body is sent foreword, my forehead hitting off the steering wheel causing my ears to ring. Out of nowhere the car hit the back of mine. I'm trying to regain focus as I hear the engine roaring from how fast I'm going with the car ramming from behind and my foot still on the acceleration. My buddy is screaming at me to regain focus but the pain that is shutting through my in unbearable.

Your child, Ava. You have to focus for your child.

I blink through the tears and my vision being to clear and focus then I begin o hear Gabriel screaming through the speaker phone.

"*AVA!*" Gabriel yells over the phone in pure panic.

I begin to speed up so his car is no longer against mine but Im unable to move into a different lane. "He hit me!" I say with fear as I look in my review mirror to see him speeding up again to hit the back of my car. "Gabriel!" I scream, not knowing what else to do.

He smashes into my car again, whipping my body forward. I take one arm and wrap it protectively around my stomach, hoping to shield it enough. I make sure my head doesn't hit the steering wheel again, knowing it will probably cause me to pass out. I look in the review mirror again and see that my forehead is in fact bleeding.

Shit.

"*HARRIS FASTER!*" He roars over the phone. "You're doing great, Ava." He reassures me.

At this moment, I want to blurt that he's going to be a father. I want to tell him how much I love him and how much he deserves love. But I don't because if I *do*, that means I'm accepting the possibility of not surviving this. I hold this all in, praying that I can tell him when this is all over, and we will live happily ever after. He will be the amazing father that our child deserves. I will watch him drool over our daughter in pure awe, or watch him cherish and protect his son the way he would have wanted from his own father. We're old and grey, but we still look at one another like we did in that library. We will always burn for one another in a way that annoys people, but we won't care. Because what we have is *heaven*. What we have is earth-shattering.

He rams into the back of the car again, and I swerve into the middle lane. "I switched lanes. He can't get in."

He exhales loudly. "Good. Keep going."

The SUV in the lane next to me swerves, crashing into the side of the car.

"*Shit!*" I yell as I try to keep control of the car.

"What's happening, Ava!" He's panicking again.

"There's someone helping! In a blue SUV!"

The SUV hits my side again, sending me into the previous lane I was in with the grey car. My head smacked against the glass, my ears ringing as I try to regain my focus. Everything is spinning, but I blink through it, my vision became clear.

Cars drive to avoid me, they're honking with urgency, but the mystery driver doesn't care. It's his goal to hurt or kill me, and he won't stop until it's done. Tears begin to roll down my cheek. I see him speeding up again as the SUV has me pinned against the median that's separating the traffic. I have nowhere to go.

"Gabriel," I mumble, knowing I don't have a lot of time.

"Yes," He breathes, basically panting. I know if the roles were reversed, I would feel broken, knowing I can hear him but can't get to him to save him.

"I love you." I blurt quickly as I see him speeding up.

"*Don't.*" He begs.

"Say it back, baby." I beg softly.

"*Ava—*

"*Gabriel,* I shall do one thing in this life—that is to love you and long for you and keep wanting you till I die."

I hear sniffling. "You must allow me to tell you how ardently I admire and love you."

He hits me again, and the wheel goes out of control. The SUV pulls to the right, leaving me space for the car to spin out of control. The brakes are out as I slam on them as hard as possible, but the grey car is sending me ahead with great speed. I don't know how many things or cars I crash into. I wrap my arms around my stomach and pray to every God there is that they protect and keep Gabriel—*and our baby*—safe.

CHAPTER 18

GABRIEL

I'm pacing back and forth in the waiting room. I thought I knew pain; I truly did. My mother had cancer; losing Ava the first time, losing my father's love; losing my grandmother and grandad; losing a child I didn't know I had ten years ago; then losing Ava again. These experiences can't compare to the pain I felt hearing her cry over the phone with fear. I felt hopeless, powerless as she cried out my name. I couldn't save her; I couldn't protect her, and if she...*I can't even think it*. She has to make it because I can't be alive in a world where she isn't. We need more time. We need more time to be in love, to get married, have children. We are supposed to grow old together. She can't leave me here on my own.

I rest my forehead against the wall and let the sob rip through me—that I've been holding back since the phone call. I will never forgive myself. I let her down. I never should have left her to defend herself. She should

have told me about Tristan. If this was him, I will kill
him with my bare hands. There are no second chances
for demons.

I had been angry with her before the accident. Harris
had finally located Tristan after realizing someone in
Canada was using his name. Someone he must have
paid off, so he could be off the radar. When Harris came
to me to tell me that he found out Tristan had flown to
Texas to see Ava—*and succeeded*—I had lost it. I wanted
to drive to the office to scream and spank her all at
once. Harris told me to calm down, so I sent Ava a text
saying, *'we need to speak about a few important things
tonight'*.

I wasn't counting on her to call me, hoping she
would wait until we were face to face. Then the worst
thing happened.

"Gabriel." I recognize my mum's voice any day. I look
up to see her standing there with tears in her eyes. She
opens her arms for me, and I walk into them. She
engulfs me—as much as she can with her small arms—
and strokes my back as I cry against her. "She will be
okay. I promise you."

I want to ask her how she can be so confident.
Maybe, this is my actual punishment. Perhaps, the
universe or God or whomever wanted me to believe I
could have the angel. They wanted me to think that I
deserved love and could have had a chance of feeling it
for the rest of my life.

I also want to tell her I won't be able to survive if she doesn't. But I know better. I could never break my mum's heart that way, even in my times of devastation.

I'm numb, cold, and dark. I genuinely feel soulless. She was my light, keeping the darkness at bay. She's my laughter, my smile...she's the warmth that I feel deep in my chest when she looks at me with those deep brown eyes. When she looks at me and tells me she loves me, I feel like I can do anything. That nothing can hurt me.

"Mr. Warner?" A male voice says, and I see the doctor standing there, but I can't move. My mum pulls away but continues to hold my hand.

"Yes." She answers for me. He looks from me to my mum.

"She lost some blood and hit her head pretty badly, but apart from that and a few bruises, she is perfectly okay. It's a miracle; when my team saw her vehicle's condition, we didn't think she would make it. The baby is also in stable condition. When she wakes up, she's going to need to take things easy. Avoid stress."

It's hard to hear anything after he said she was 'okay'. My body is coming to life from the news. The one thing keeping me breathing is alive. She's fine. My angel lives on to bring light into my life.

But when he says the word 'baby' it becomes harder to breathe. It's feel like someone dumped ice water down my back.

"I'm sorry, what did you just *say*?" My mum asks in shock.

Good, she heard it too. I thought the pain of what I may have lost is causing me to go crazy.

"Did you say, *baby*?" I ask in disbelief.

I think I'm going to pass out.

He smirks. "Yes, sir, a baby. Your wife is pregnant."

"Holy shit." I mutter and fall into a seat. I run my fingers through my hair and look at my mum, who is covering her mouth. Her eyes meet mine, and they are filled with unshed tears.

"You're having a baby." She says it like a question, but I know she is just trying to wrap her head around it.

My body is in shock. All I can wonder is, did Ava know about the baby? If she did, why didn't she tell me? I blink, more tears falling down my cheeks.

"I'm going to have a baby." I mumble and chuckle in shock. She sits down next to me, wrapping her arms around me.

She sobs softly. "I'm so happy for you, my boy."

I let myself cry in relief, shock, sadness, and now happiness, knowing the love of my life is carrying our child.

My little sunflower.

It's been two days since the doctor told us she was fine...and two days since he told me I was going to be a father. The pride and joy that swelled in my chest took me by surprise. I didn't think I was ready for a child yet, but knowing this baby's mum will be my beautiful Ava...well, it's a dream come true. Now more than ever, I know I'm ready to marry this woman. I will love her until the day I die and forever after that. There is no I without her. She makes me want to be a better man, partner and now I know she will make me want to be a better father. She will be the best mum there is. I know she will love our boy or girl unconditionally and unapologetically. She won't expect too much from them, nor will she make them feel less of themselves. She will teach them how to be strong, independent and brave. She will teach them a love for books that she brought onto me a decade ago.

I know he or she will love her just as much as I do. There is no way you meet Ava and aren't taken with her. Her warmth, kindness, sassy and sarcastic attitude reel you in whether you want it or not. Her looks attract any man—*or woman*—with a brain and common sense. Our child will realize quickly how lucky we are to have Ava in our life.

I had begun to panic the first day she didn't wake. They explained that it was a significant trauma that she had experienced and would need time to have the strength to wake up. I wanted to correct the nurse and tell him that Ava will never lose her strength. Even in her weakest moments, she *is* strong and powerful.

In the ten hours of the unknown, I must have died a thousand deaths. Yet, I'm overcome with joy. The mixed feelings are exhausting, but I welcome it. It reminds me that it's real, I'm going to be a father.

She moans softly, and I stand quickly. I can hardly breathe as I wait for her eyes to open. She does this from time to time, almost to torture me. Even in her unconscious, she's stubborn.

"Ava," I whisper into her ear. "I'm here, angel. I'm not leaving, I'll be here when you're ready to wake up."

I want her—*scratch that*—I *need* her to hear my voice. I need her to know that I've been by her side and I will never leave. Every time I think she's going to wake up...she doesn't. As every minute passes, the ache in my heart intensifies. The hole in my chest continues to grow by not hearing her voice, her laugh, to see her beautiful brown eyes, her amazing smile. I would do anything possible to switch places.

"Gabriel," a soft voice says from the entrance of the private suite. I wasn't about to let Ava be in a shared room. I look to see my baby sister poking her head in. She's been coming once every two hours for two days now. My mum hasn't left my side—*until now*—since she arrived at the hospital. Today I put my foot down and sent her home to shower, eat and rest. I know she's healthy now, but in my eyes...I will always take care of her.

"Come in," I assure her and look back at my girl. She has bandages wrapped around her head and a small bruise on the left side of her face. Her body has no visible bruises except for her arms: no broken bones or internal bleeding.

It's a miracle that she isn't in worse condition, another blessing that our sunflower survived.

She walks to the seat on the other side of the bed. "Have you heard anything from Harris?" She asks worriedly.

When we arrived at the scene, Ava had just been taken away in an ambulance. We searched for any sign of the grey Ford and its accomplice but found nothing. Only one witness who had stuck around the scene had written the license plate down of the grey vehicle. I told Harris to find the fucker and rushed to the hospital. I know Tristan is behind this; he has to be. He went searching for Ava, meaning he's not ready to give her up. The fucker had a second chance and still managed to fuck it up. Now, it's my goal to make him feel the same pain he inflicted on Ava and my child.

I won't rest until I get revenge.

"Whoever it was rented the car. Obviously, they won't give out that information, so Harris is trying another way, "I mumble and scratch my now scruffy beard. I smile, knowing Ava would like the length of my beard. She doesn't like me clean-shaven. "We won't stop until we find who did this." I rest my hand on her stomach and wish I could feel something. I want to know if it's safe in there. Is the baby scared? Happy? Stressed? I just want to feel one kick, but the nurse informed me it was too early for that. At seven weeks, we would hear the heartbeat, and at eighteen weeks, we would know the sex.

Isabella gasps. "She never gave you the gift." She mumbles.

"What?" I ask, confused. Ava never mentioned getting me a gift. Why would she? I should be the one spoiling her.

She stands. "Where's her purse?"

I point at the table against the window where her belongings are. They just gave it to me this morning. She walks over to the purse and rummages through it. She pulls out a small box wrapped in yellow wrapping paper. There's a small little bow on the top.

My heart sinks.

She was going to tell me the day of the crash.

Isabella walks over to me and hands me the gift. "She wanted to give it to you after work that day."

I take the gift and swallow hard. This would confirm it. This is coming from Ava, not some doctor who I have to believe. Clearly, my baby sister knew about the baby before I did. I wonder who else knew.

"Should I open it?" I ask, unsure.

She gives me a soft smile. "I think she would want you too."

I look at Ava, who has a feeding tube attached to her. I hate seeing it, but the baby needs nutrients, and so does she.

I look back down at the gift and begin to tear open the wrapping paper. My heart is pumping with excitement and fear. I open the lid of the box and see a navy blue travel-mug that reads: *Best Dad.* I blink back the tears that threaten to escape. I clear the lump in my throat. I have no idea where this emotion is coming from. I've been crying more in the past month than my entire life. I take the mug out and see something white stuffed inside. I take the clear lid off the mug and pull out the fabric. It's an onesie that says: *Dad's number one fan.*

This time the tears can't be stopped. There's something about holding your future child's, future clothing in your hands. It all feels so much more real. I didn't think I had any more love to give after I found Ava again, yet here I sit with so much love for this unborn child.

My unborn child.

"That's adorable." Isabella mutters thoughtfully. I know she wants children of her own. Her arms wrap around me, and I look at her in surprise. "You're going to make an amazing father, Gabe; I know you will."

Her words hit deep within me. Will I be a great father? I had an amazing one for eighteen years, then out of nowhere, it stopped. What if the same thing happens between my potential son and me? The thought of hurting my child the way my father pulled me slices my heart in a way it never has been. It's almost hard to breathe at the thought. I could never hurt my child. It's my job to protect them from harm, to make sure they always feel safe.

I embrace her. "You're going to be an amazing aunt."

She pulls away with a grin. "Of course, I will. I'm going to spoil them rotten."

Them?

Would Ava want more than one baby? Will I? We weren't planning this one, and it turned out to be a blessing, but babies are hard. We both have careers, and I could never ask her to give it up to raise more babies. I will only want more if she wants more. Her needs come before mine in this matter.

"I know you will, Belle." She has baby fever at the moment. "Did she ask you to be her assistant?" I ask.

She pouts. "We're calling it business partners."

I smirk. *Of course,* Ava wouldn't want to call Isabella her assistant. That's not like Ava. She sees everyone as her equal, and I believe that's why my sister said yes. "I'm glad you said yes. You two can look out for one another."

Her face softens. "You *really* love her." She isn't asking, more like stating a fact.

I nod. "She's everything to me, Belle. I can't live without her...not again." I look over to her still body. It's uneasy to see her so still and pale. "I'm going to ask her to marry me."

She gasps. "*When?!*" She asks excitedly.

I chuckle under my breath. "I'm not sure. I need to pick out the perfect ring for her. Finding who did this is the first priority, then ring shopping."

Now, I'm going to have to go baby shopping. There's so much we need to get, so much we have to prep for. I've spent the past two days reading the baby book *What to Expect When You're Expecting* and many others. I want to make sure we're both educated and prepared. There's so much I didn't know about pregnancy, birth, and child care. We're also going to need a house if she says yes to my proposal. We can't have a baby in a penthouse, it's not safe. He or she needs a backyard to run and play with a dog.

First, finding Tristan and making him pay.

"Gabriel, why don't you go home, shower, eat something and come back?" She says. They have been trying to get me to go home since I got here, but I can't. What if she wakes up? She's going to need me.

I shake my head. "I can't leave them." I mumble, in distress. I left her once and look what happened.

She gives me a sympathetic smile. "I promise you I will call you the second she twitches. Any sudden sounds or movements. Do you want her to wake up and smell you?" Her nose scrunches up in distaste.

I sniff myself and flinch. I *do* smell. "Fine." I sigh and stand with my gift. I'm not leaving this behind. "The second she does anything, you call me."

She rolls her eyes. "I just said I would."

"I mean it, Belle." I warn.

She begins to push me toward the door. "*Go*. The longer you stand here talking to me, the longer you will be away. I will keep them safe."

It isn't easy leaving the hospital. I promised I wouldn't leave without her, but I know she loves to smell me. She hasn't said it out loud, but whenever I'm freshly showered, she inhales deeply when I'm close.

My phone rings in my pocket, and I take it out to see a message from Harris:

The car was rented in Elizabeth's name.

CHAPTER 19

AVA

Pain. That's all I can feel. My body is stiff as I try to move my fingers. The ringing in my head is still there as I try to pry my eyes open, but my body won't listen.

It's still tired.

My head throbbing from the crash.

I can hear a muffled voice coming in and out of focus. I only catch a few words here and there. I can hear Gabriel's voice. I'm fighting as hard as I can to open my eyes for him. A slicing pain rips through my chest and throat.

It feels like I'm choking. I gasp as the acid runs down. I want to cough, but I can't. My hands want to grab around my neck but can't. I want to try and stop whatever is choking me, but my body feels bruised from the inside out. My eyes open slightly, but the light is blinding. I squeeze them closed and moan loudly. My eyes feel like they haven't seen the sun or light in months. I try to pry my eyes open again and see white. I see silhouettes of people but can't make my eyes focus long enough to see who it is. I close them again and begin to cough, choking. My mouth feels dry, which doesn't help the choking. I need water.

"Ava." I hear someone mutter. I begin to swallow. Finally, the object causing me to choke is gone. "We are giving you something for the pain." Something pierces my skin, and the world is quiet again.

I open my eyes slowly, trying to adjust to the fluorescent lights. My head feels heavy and groggy. My ears adjust to the loud sounds coming from right next to me. I blink a few times before I can focus on the silhouette of the person sitting next to me.

It's Gabriel.

I smile softly as I watch his head resting in his hand, eyes closed as he sleeps. I look around the room and notice I'm in a giant hospital room...all by myself. Even my tired mind wants to fight him for spending this money, but I don't because if the roles were reversed, I would have paid any amount of money to make sure he's safe and secure. I look to the bedside table when something catches my eye. There are three books piled on top of one another. The books look outworn, but there's no way he didn't get them new. That's when it hits me.

He knows.

The three books are *What to Expect When You're Expecting, What to Expect in the First Year,* and the last book is *Dude, You're Gonna Be a Dad!*

If he's reading these books, that tells me our baby is okay. Our baby is safe. I died a million deaths, not knowing if he or she was going to make it. Even in my subconscious, I pray to God to watch over my little family. I fought so hard, and it paid off. We're going to be okay. He's going to be a father—*an amazing father*—and I'm going to be a mother. We're going to figure out how to be parents together. Tears fall down my cheeks as I pick up the first book and see circled paragraphs; highlighted sentences; corners of the pages folded down so he can remember the page.

I knew he would be this way. The doubt I felt toward him fills me with guilt. I should have told him sooner. If I didn't make it—along with the baby—Isabella would have been the one to tell him or my aunt. I wonder if he would have forgiven me...

"*Ava,*" I hear his voice say and for the first time—I don't even know how long I've been in the hospital—in what feels like a long time, I feel complete. I look from the book to him, and his eyes are red and tired. His beard is fuller than his regular five o'clock shadow—but still short. I love it at this length.

He stands and begins to kiss my face softly. I close my eyes and inhale his scent. I missed him. "I died a million deaths, angel."

I can hear the pain in his voice. "I'm sorry," I mumble.

He pours away and cups my face. "*Don't*. You have nothing to be sorry for."

Yes, I do.

"I didn't tell you about the baby," I say guiltily. I look away in shame, hanging my head.

I feel like shit.

He lifts my chin, his face soft. "No, you didn't, and I wish you had, but I understand. I had betrayed you once, and now you had someone else to protect, but I don't care about any of that, Ava. I care that both of you are healthy and alive."

I smile. "You bought parenting books," I mumble in adoration. Knowing he went to get these books because he wants to makes it so much more special.

His eyebrows narrow. "Of course, I did. I need to know everything, so I can protect the *both* of you. Now, rest your voice."

My eyes widen. "Gabriel, I'm capable of protecting myself and this baby."

He frowns. "Look what happened to you, Ava. I'm not letting anything or anyone else have the slightest chance to hurt you or my child. Starting with getting Harris to drive you to and from work. He's your new bodyguard."

My mouth drops for two reasons. "It's *our* child, Gabriel and absolutely fucking not. I do not need a babysitter." I'm almost twenty-eight; I'm a grown woman. Yes, Tristan is likely out there trying to hurt me, but that doesn't mean I change my whole life. I can't let him ruin my life again. He's done enough damage.

"Must you argue with me when you're on a hospital bed?" He asks annoyedly. He doesn't want to be annoyed with me at a time like this. He wants to be taking care of me, but I can't let it go.

"Gabriel, say it's *our* child," I demand.

He scowls. "I know it's *our* child, Ava, don't be ridiculous."

"Now, tell Harris I don't need a babysitter." I'm not backing down.

He clenches his jaw. "Ava," he says through his teeth. "Look at where you are. Do you have any idea what it was like to hear you scream and cry over the phone, knowing I couldn't do anything? I couldn't get to you in time; I couldn't save you. I had to sit there with Harris and pray to every God there is that you lived. I screamed your name, and you wouldn't answer me. I"— He swallows hard and looks away, out the window—"I thought you were dead."

My heart breaks for him. I felt my own pain as I came to terms—*while the car began spinning out of control*— with the fact that I would never have the amazing life I could have had with Gabriel. The pain crippled me, made it hard to breathe. I want to continue to argue with him on this but seeing the pain in his eyes tells me to give him a chance to breathe. He's been through enough already, and I know he won't rest until he finds out who did this to me.

I sigh. "Okay. You win...for now."

He exhales in relief and shakes his head. "You would think being out cold for almost three days would keep the stubbornness at bay."

I gasp. *"Three days?"* Somehow it felt so much longer.

He nods. "Yes, they took out your feeding tube today. That's why your voice is raspy."

That would explain the burning I felt earlier. Why it felt like I was choking. "And the baby?" I ask.

He grins, his eyes filling with pride and joy. "Healthy and beautiful. They did an ultrasound." He pulls out his wallet and opens it to see the picture slot has the ultrasound picture in it. My chest swells with love. This six-foot—*very muscular*—tattooed tough guy is reading parenting books and has a picture of our baby already. I already know he's going to be the type of dad in the front row cheering on our kids; he's the type to hang their drawings in his office because he genuinely believes their art is the most fantastic thing ever drawn. He would wear every Father's Day t-shirt or hat, the type to love every gift they give him.

I gasp. "I had a gift for you!"

He puts his wallet away and walks over to the table by the window, picking up the travel mug. "This is the only cup I'm going to drink coffee out of." He says with pride.

I've never been more in love with him.

"I love you," I say.

He grins and puts the mug down, making his way back to me. He leans down and presses his lips against mine softly. As if he doesn't want to hurt or break me. He pulls away and presses his forehead against mine softly.

I try not to wince in pain and succeed. I don't want this moment to end.

"I will always love you, Ava." He whispers.

"I don't know if you should be leaving the hospital," Gabriel says as he wheels me out into the parking lot—*which is totally absurd*—but he gave me two options: the wheelchair or he carries me out. The look of determination told me not to call his bluff. He looked utterly ready to scoop me up and take me out of the hospital. It's been a week since I woke up, and my body isn't as stiff, and my head has almost completely healed.

My doctor told both Gabriel and me that I was okay to go home but no work, stress, strain, exercise or sex.

The sex part is what made Gabriel and I frown at one another as he went on and on about the dangers. Everything would be allowed after one more week. Gabriel looked pained but also determined. He promised that he would follow those rules, and I believe him. If it comes to my safety and the baby's, I know he won't give in. For the past week, he has been getting on my nerves by shoving books under my nose. If it's not books, it's vitamins and nutrition. The nurse was the one who used to bring my prenatal vitamins, but now it's Gabriel. He goes on and on about folic acid, iron, and my calcium levels. When I stand, he stands; when I go to the bathroom, he hovers around me, making sure I don't slip and fall. It took me yelling at him and demanding to give me privacy when he wanted to be there while I showered. Most times, I would love him with me in the shower, but I hadn't been able to use the bathroom on my own in what felt like forever. I needed two-seconds where I could use the bathroom in peace.

The sexual tension between us isn't helping. He told me he wouldn't give in, and I understand why, but my baby hormones, along with my libido, don't understand why. My body burns for him. What's baffling is I'm getting turned on by everything he does, even when it's not sexual. There were times he was reading manuscripts at the hospital, he would be sitting in the chair next to my bed, one leg crossed over the other. The one end of his pen pressed against his bottom lip; his eyebrows furrowed as he reads the story. His strong and large hand turning the pages made it hard to breathe. He looked up at me, and his eyes darkened when he saw the look in my own eyes. I was basically panting, and all he was doing was reading. This man oozes sexy and confidence even when he's not trying to.

"Gabriel, the doctor said I was ready to leave," I mumble in annoyance. I know he's worried, but they wouldn't discharge me if I needed to stay...especially with Gabriel's money paying for luxury accommodations.

His mouth presses against my ear, sending chills down my spine. "Just because I can't fuck you doesn't mean I can't spank you, angel."

I let out a shaky breath. "Please do, Sir."

He groans frustratedly and pulls away. "Let's get you home."

He helps me into the car, buckling me in, then moves to the driver's side. He pulls away from the hospital with his hand laced in mine. I squeeze his hand as we're passing by cars. I'm nervous, I'm watching every person in every vehicle, reading every license plate. I wasn't expecting this type of anxiety or even *any*. After what happened with Scott, it only lasted for a few hours. I don't know why I was expecting to be okay after this. What I went through was traumatic, and it didn't help that I'm pregnant. My arm is wrapped protectively around my stomach as he drives.

"Did Harris find anything?" I ask, looking at him.

His jaw is tight; tense. "Not yet."

Harris is quick at his job because I know Gabriel demands it of him. I know there *has* to be something he isn't telling me to try and protect me. "Promise me." I demand. I'm watching his reaction.

His hands grip the steering wheel. "I promise." He says. He doesn't give anything away. His face is blank, his tone steady. Something in me tells me this isn't the case, but I know there isn't enough evidence for me to accuse him of anything.

I'm going to have to get answers myself.

He clears his throat. "We should probably discuss when to tell our families."

"About what?" I ask, blankly then I remember. "Oh... right, *the baby*."

He narrows his eyebrows. "You forgot about our sunflower." He growls.

My eyes widen. "Our *what*?" I ask, amused. I remember the sunflower tattoo. He chooses a sunflower because that is my favourite flower. Now, he's calling our baby sunflower.

He gives me a quick glance. "*My sunflower.*" He repeats, calling our baby just his again.

I roll my eyes. "*Our* sunflower, Gabriel." I hiss.

He exhaled loudly. "Yes, that's what I said."

I laugh out loud while shaking my head at my possessive man. I should've known he would be this way about our baby. "We both know you didn't say that." I say when I finish laughing. I place my hand against his cheek. "But, yes, *your* sunflower."

He nuzzles into my hand. "*My* Ava."

I smile. "*Always.*"

CHAPTER 20

AVA

"You never said when you wanted to tell our families." He repeats while he washes the back of my head. I'm sitting in the tub with Gabriel sitting outside the tub, on the floor. I begged him to join me in the bath, but he refused. He said he couldn't trust himself, and he knows I wouldn't stop him. *'Someone has to be thinking clearly'* is what he said to me when I tried to entice him. "I know Isabella and my mum know, but they promised not to tell my anyone."

I think about his dad and wonder if he would want to tell him also. His parents aren't on good terms, and he despises his dad more than anything at this moment.

Will Jack Warner want to be apart of our child's life? Will Gabriel or I want him in our child's life? Gabriel will have a more challenging time than I would.

"We can tell your family first. But..." I chew on my lip nervously. "Your father should be there."

His hands stop. "I didn't even begin to think about that." He mumbles. I turn, causing the water to splash out of the tub. He's frowning.

"Talk to me," I whisper. I can tell the cogs in his head are going lightning speed.

He looks at me. "What if I'm like him?" He asks nervously. "I don't know what it takes to be a father."

It destroys me to know he has so little faith in himself. They may look alike, but their hearts are different. Gabriel is hard and tough, *yes*, but you also see the gentleness in him. You see kindness, compassion, empathy and sympathy. There's nothing he wouldn't do for his mom, sister or even me. His dad couldn't even apologize to his own son if it meant saving his marriage. He's too proud to admit when he's wrong.

I press my dry hand against his cheek. "You are *nothing* like him. I don't think anyone knows how to be a good father or mother, Gabriel. You can prepare as much as possible, but you won't truly know how to raise a child until he or she is in your arms." He frowns, worry written all over his face. I think apart of him was hoping those books would be enough. "You have me. I'm going to be right beside you, trying to learn how to be a mother." I don't tell him how worried I am when it comes to my own experiences with moms. I despised my mom for as long as I can remember. I haven't spoken to her since I was in high school. Now, I have nine months to prepare and pray that I will be better than her.

He sighs. "I should tell you something." He mumbles nervously.

My heart begins to race. "What?"

"When your cousin called me, he never told me where you were. He said he couldn't betray you that way. I would have to figure it out on my own. I knew your father wouldn't tell me; I needed to find someone who might have a slight idea of where you could have been. I tracked down your mother, and she's the one who told me where to find you."

I inhale sharply. "You *called* her?"

He shakes his head.

"*Oh my god.* You saw her in person." I say after it dawns on me what he means. He knows how I feel about her. He's known since we were seventeen, and he hated her too. He couldn't stand how she treated me. That means she told him where I could be. She didn't turn him away at the sound of my name on his tongue. She didn't revolt or make a scene. She helped him find me, but why? She hates me more than one could hate a person.

He frowns. "I did...I swore to myself that if you forgave me, I would pass on her words..."

"*No,*" I hiss, standing up abruptly. I don't want to hear her words.

"Ava." He barks as he stands with me, his arms hovering around me to make sure they catch me if I slip. "Can you be more fucking careful?"

He's angry, but so am I.

"I don't want to hear a word from that woman." I step out of the tub and grab the towel off the counter, wrapping it around myself. I can't believe he's willing to pass on any sort of message for her. He follows me into the bedroom, and I know if I turn, his arms will be out, ready to catch me if I slip in my hasty steps. It's sweet but frustrating when I'm upset.

"Ava, I owe her." He mumbles.

I whip around to face him. "You don't owe her shit." I hiss.

He winces. "You shouldn't swear...the baby can hear you."

I clench my jaw, waiting for him to tell me he's joking, but it doesn't come. "Oh, fuck off," I mumble angrily and go into the closet, where my clothes have been moved and neatly organized. How could he possibly owe her anything?

"Ava." His tone is clipped. "I don't know what you expected me to do. No one would tell me where you were."

"They were doing that for a reason, Gabriel!" I spit angrily. I turn to face him and see the pain written all over his face.

"I deserve that," he mumbles. "I deserved the pain I felt when you left. I know you may not want to hear it, but I made a promise to myself that I would tell you. If it weren't for her, we wouldn't be standing here, back together."

"Gabriel," I warn.

"She misses you." His eyes finally meet mine. "She only wishes happiness for you."

I feel my heart constrict as it gets harder to breathe. I want to pretend that it doesn't phase me. I want to pretend that my younger self isn't affected by what she said. I needed these words from her as a child, not now. They mean nothing to me now.

"She didn't want me," I say sadly. "She can't decide now that I'm older and no longer need raising to be in my life." I look in the mirror to see my stomach beginning to shape itself. "Being pregnant with my own child makes her even worse in my eyes. I haven't even met this baby, and I adore it more than I can express in words. I will protect this child from the world. She has no excuse."

He comes up behind me and wraps his arms around me, placing his hands on my stomach. He kisses the top of my head. "I know," he mumbles. "I just had to...pass on her message...for my own conscious."

"I can't hear about her anymore," I whisper sadly.

"Of course." He says softly and rubs his thumb over my stomach. "Why don't we talk about when you want to tell your father about her?"

I frown. "About who?" I ask, confused. Is he still talking about my mom?

He frowns heavily. "My baby." He says, annoyed. As if I'm supposed to know.

I gape at him. "How do you know the gender of *our* baby?" I ask. Where the hell was I for this? "We don't find that out until I'm eighteen weeks." At least that's what my aunt told me.

He shrugs. "I just know."

I smirk. "You can't call *her* a *her* if you don't know yet. What if it's a boy?"

When I say the word *'boy,'* his face changes from annoyance to pain. He looks away from me, pulling away. Where his hands were placed is now cold. His body is tense; rigid.

"What's wrong?" I ask softly.

"I don't want a son." He says through his teeth.

The heartbreak I feel is unexpected. I wrap my arm around my stomach, needing to protect the baby from his words. What if it *is* a boy? How could he say that? As long as this baby is healthy, I don't care what it is or wants to be. He's *already* rejecting our child.

"How can you say that?" I ask, sadly. This is the same man that has been reading all the baby books without even having to beg.

"Ava, you see how my father is with me. My grandad died without seeing his son for twenty-something years. My father hit me. The last thing we need is to continue this curse."

He truly believes his words. I can hear it in his voice that he really thinks this is a curse. He believes if he has a son, no matter how great their relationship is, they will hate each other. I want to ease his thoughts, but how? I think the only way he will be eased is to actually have a son.

"Gabriel," I say sadly and wrap my arms around him, pressing my cheek against his back. "You will be an amazing father *because* of the relationship with your own. You know how it feels to be neglected, which means that is the last thing you'll want to do to our own child." He places his hand over mine. I can tell his mind is running wild. He doesn't believe in himself. "I'll be right by your side through it all. You and me."

He turns and cups my face, kissing me with no hesitation. My libido wakes from her long slumber and is now laser-focused. I wrap my arms around his neck, deepening into the kiss. I know what I'm doing. The doctor said no sex for one week, and only one day has passed, but how can I resist him? He pins me against the wall, his hands on my hips. Our kiss is going from gentle to hungry very quickly. I need him. I place my palm over his erection, and he pulls away.

"Ava, we can't." He mumbles breathlessly.

I frown. "I feel perfectly fine," I mumble.

He opens his eyes. "Ava," he says, pained. He doesn't want to reject me; I can see it in his eyes. "Please don't make me deny you."

His phone begins to ring, and he sighs. "I'll be back; it could be Harris, and I need to take this." He kisses my forehead. "Get dressed, and Ruth can whip you something to eat."

He leaves quickly, and I sigh heavily, leaning against the wall. I feel like we've gone from zero to one hundred in a matter of seconds but what honestly scares me is how comfortable I am with it. This all feels so natural with him. Now, we're about to be parents out of wedlock; we have to tell our parents; Tristan is after me; Elizabeth is in the hospital, and my baby daddy is having dad issues of his own. I wonder if other people have this much drama in their lives, or is it just us?

I get dressed and make my way downstairs to see Ruth cleaning. When she hears me, she looks up with a smile. "There she is," she says happily. "We've been worried sick about you."

I smile shyly. "Thank you, Ruth. How have you been?" I ask.

She makes her way to the kitchen and takes a water out of the fridge, placing it on the breakfast bar with pills next to it. "I'm well, sweetie, especially now that you're here. Come sit and take your vitamins." She isn't asking. Gabriel has wasted no time in telling his staff that I'm pregnant. I make my way to the barstool and sit, opening the bottle before taking the vitamins laid out before me.

"Why now that I'm here?" I ask curiously.

She frowns as she wipes down the countertops. I'm glad she hasn't offered me food. She sighs but doesn't meet my eyes. "I haven't seen him that distraught since...since Simon died."

I think back to the balcony. I swore I could hear him talking to someone, but I saw no one there with him when I stepped outside. I assumed he was mumbling to himself, especially when I saw the empty bottle in his hand. He was pissed drunk. Then he cried in my arms. My heart broke over and over for him.

"Were they close?"

She smiles slightly as she recalls a memory. "Yes. Gabriel replaced his father with Simon, and Simon replaced Jack with Gabriel. They needed one another without even knowing. I don't think it hit Gabriel how much he needed Simon until he was on his death bed." I frown as I imagine a young Gabriel in distress about losing someone else he loved truly. "When he passed, Gabriel destroyed everything in this apartment. I had come here to check on him to find him unconscious after drinking three bottles of scotch. I held him until he woke, and that's when he began to cry as he muttered over and over again that he lost the only person that's ever been proud of him. After that, he never grieved over Simon again."

I swallow past the lump in my throat, my baby emotions getting the best of me. If I didn't hate his father, I do now. Gabriel needed his father to help him get through this, and he failed him. "Gabriel says that his mom and Simon were close."

Ruth grins. "Very much so. Simon could be tough and stubborn but was charmed by Emilia. Everyone is when they meet her. He wrote her letters once a month when he found out she had cancer. Gabriel saved those letters because Emilia never wanted Jack to find them just in case he tossed them." She chuckles under her breath. "And Simon charmed Emilia. I suppose she saw a piece of her husband in him."

I wonder if Ruth dislikes Jack as well. "How do you feel about Jack?" I ask.

She sits down next to me. "I've spent enough time with him to know he's a broken man. He lost a giant piece of himself when Emilia got sick, and I think pushing Gabriel to step up and take care of them damaged him even more. He wasn't always like this— that's what Emilia tells me at least—he was kind to Gabriel and wanted a better relationship than he had with Simon. Sadly, they never got the chance."

Just because Jack loved Gabriel until he was eighteen doesn't mean he should be forgiven for how he treats Gabriel now. I can never understand how a parent can hate their child and hit them. All Gabriel wants is a pat on the back and hear that his father still cares for him.

"He's afraid he's going to repeat history," I say, trying to hide my doubt. Now, I'm afraid that it will be the same way, just like Gabriel predicted.

Ruth places her hand on mine. "If there's one thing I know about Gabriel is he loves passionately...when he *really* loves. It was a whole decade, and he hadn't even forgotten about you. Whether this child is a boy or a girl, I know he will love the child with all his heart. The same way he loves you."

"Talking my girl's ear off, Ruth?" Gabriel's voice fills the room, causing both of us to look his way. He's completely shirtless and wearing gym shorts. He is covered in sweat which tells me he must have worked out before finding me. I wondered if he still had time to work out with our...eventful lives.

Ruth kisses her teeth before standing. "Actually, I'm giving the girl a wonderful break from you."

I grin at her wit as Gabriel makes his way to me and kisses the top of my head. I try to keep my libido calm as she gawks at a sweaty Gabriel.

"Food, my boy?" She asks.

"Yes, please, for the both of us."

I clear my throat. "Uh, actually none for me, please."

Gabriel pulls away and is scowling. "You need to eat, Ava, that wasn't a question."

I frown. "I can't eat yet. The baby doesn't like to be forced to eat."

He looks at me like I'm crazy but nods. "Lunch just for me, Ruth, thank you." Gabriel sits down next to me. "Speaking of the baby... I found you an ob-gyn."

I gape at him. My god knows no bounds. "Gabriel," I say in disbelief. "Isn't that something I'm supposed to do?"

He smiles sheepishly. "Yes...but I figured you didn't tell me about Tristan visiting, so..."

I roll my eyes. I want to yell at him and tell him he's overstepping, but this is his way of taking care of me. In his weird overbearing way, this is what settles him; to know I'm safe. "I figured you made an appointment for me as well?" I ask before taking another drink. The ginger is helping settle my stomach.

He winks at me. "Would I be the man you loved if I didn't?"

I try hard to stifle a grin but fail.

CHAPTER 21

GABRIEL

If you told me a month ago that I would be driving the only girl I have ever truly loved to our baby's ultrasound appointment, I would have laughed in your face. Ava seems nervous. She argued with every piece of clothing she had and burst into tears after getting sick.

It's been a week since we arrived home from the hospital, and every second of it has been heaven, at least from what Ava has seen. I haven't been sleeping well. She's been falling asleep at eight or nine every night; working has tired her out. I fought with her about going back to work two days early, but she begged me that she wanted to feel normal. She wanted to embrace her career because she would have to be away for a whole year on maternity leave when the baby comes. I wanted to mention that I wouldn't want her to be working and want her home raising our child, but I didn't want another fight. Ava falling asleep early gave me a chance to spend most of the night trying to track Elizabeth down. She disappeared without a trace and won't answer any of my calls. I lied to Ava, and I know it's wrong, but I had to. I can't have her learning about Elizabeth yet. She will spiral, and I need her calm, especially after the accident. The last thing we need is for Ava to be bedridden. I wouldn't be able to function knowing she's at home by herself. I would have to make Ruth move in, which means Harris would be moving in too.

I'm already looking for our forever home and a ring, which I know will cause a scene. She's going to panic and say it's too soon even though we already live together and are welcoming a baby—that will connect us whether we like it or not. But she wouldn't be my Ava if she weren't dramatic.

I'm nervous.

When Ava was in the hospital, I told doctors that I didn't want to see our child without Ava awake next to me, holding my hand. I wanted that first time to be full of love, not dread that she wouldn't wake up. I wanted to see Ava cry in happiness, both of us staring at the pictures because we weren't ready to take our eyes off our bundle of joy. All I would take was an ultrasound picture but I could hardly even see the baby the nurse promised was there. Now, we are finally going together to see our baby. I wonder if they can tell if it's a boy and a girl early? The baby books all said eighteen weeks, but

I'm still hopeful. The anxiety that comes from waiting is crippling.

I meant it when I told her I didn't want it to be a boy. This curse needs to end here. My grandfather adored the women in his life, as does my father and as do I. We deserve to have a beautiful little Ava running in our home. The world does not need another Gabriel or, worse, another Jack.

I frown.

Does it make me more like my father for wishing for a daughter rather than a son?

"Gabriel?" Her voice breaks into my loud thoughts. I look over at her quickly, seeing a frown on her beautiful face. "You're tensing. What's wrong?"

The list is long, my love.

I shake my head, placing one hand on her hand. "Nothing...just nervous," I lie. It would be selfish to take this moment away from her with my sad thoughts. I knew how much it upset her to hear me say I don't want a son. I can't tell her again. I have to deal with this on my own.

She squeezes my hand. "I was nervous too at my first appointment."

It didn't even occur to me that she went to an appointment already. "When did you go?" I ask. The jealous side of myself wants to ask if she went alone. However, the logical side of me knows her cousin is the only one who knew about the baby. I would be okay if he went with her.

"In Texas. My aunt is an ob-gyn. I had taken a pregnancy test and knew the only person I could go to was my aunt." She's looking at me, and I wish I could see her eyes. I should have been there with her. She doesn't sound sad when retelling this story, but it makes me sad. I should have been there holding her hand, kissing her flat belly at the time.

"Stop." She says, causing my head to quickly whip her way then back to the road.

"What?"

"I can tell you're thinking something bad. Stop. This is supposed to be a happy time." She leans over the console and kisses my cheek.

"Sit properly, babe." I say worriedly, but she just scoffs.

"I'm kissing you."

I smile. "Yes, you are, but kiss me when it's safe to do so. We don't need more accidents." It already petrifies me, knowing her life is in my hands as I drive this car.

Once we're parked, I rush to her side, and I open the door for her and helping her out of the Jeep. She's wearing a beautiful light grey, long cotton dress that hugs every delicious curve. Her hair is long and shines in the sunlight. She's been using coconut oil for her curls —usually, something like that wouldn't catch my attention, but she smells fucking incredible.

It makes me want to lick her head to toe. I have
caught myself many times about to initiate sex, and then
I remember that she's still healing. The baby is still
recovering. I don't even know if we should be having
sex while she's pregnant. All the books say it's okay, but
apart of me doesn't trust it.

We make our way into the office, and I make my way
to the reception before she can. She's going to want to
try and pay for it or try and pay for a cheap option.
That's why I looked for the OBGYN; I wanted to pay for
the best my money could buy. That also means having
the best machines and best ultrasound pictures.

"Hi, an appointment for Ava Thompson." I hate that
I'm using her father's last name. It should be mine. "I'm
her partner Gabriel, and I'll be paying for anything and
everything." I slide over my Amex card before she can
say anything.

"Gabriel." Ava hisses and pinches my arm lightly.

I ignore her. The woman behind the desk looks at me
with desire in her eyes as if I'm not checking in my
pregnant girlfriend. She hands me a clipboard,
purposely passing with both hands on it so there's a
chance we will touch. I make sure I don't give her the
satisfaction and take the clipboard. I face Ava, who is
shaking her head disapprovingly.

"You know no bounds, Warner." She says and takes
the clipboard out of my hands and sits in a chair.

My heart is beating faster as every scenario possible races through my head. What if there's something wrong? I wonder if she worries this much.

"Thompson." A woman calls, and Ava stands without me, handing the clipboard to the receptionist and then makes her way back to me. She holds out her hand with a small smile. "C'mon, Warner. It's time to meet our baby under the right circumstances." I put my hand in hers, and we walk back with the nurse.

"Doctor, your patient Ava Thompson." The nurse says as we walk into the room. I scowl at her when she doesn't say my name.

It's my baby too.

Little does the nurse know I'm the one fucking paying for everything. I didn't tell Ava that either. I knew if I told her anything about Doctor Greene, she would have laughed in my face and told me to find somewhere else to go. Madison Greene is the best OBGYN in Seattle and happens to be a friend of my mum. Even though she is retired, my mom is still involved in community charities and programs for local schools. Madison is interested in the same thing because her mum was a teacher, and that's how they met. Even though they're friends, I'm still paying thousands of dollars for today. I'm hoping Ava won't argue.

Madison smiles at us and shakes both our hands. "I'm Doctor Greene; you must be Ava. Gabriel had told me all about you." I called Madison earlier and told her

everything about Ava. Everything we have been through
from our past, her first pregnancy to the accident she
went through just now. I make my way to the chair next
to where Ava will be sitting and take a seat.

Ava tells me not to call her a her, but I can't help it. I
feel it down deep in my soul that she is carrying my
daughter.

"You two know one another?" Ava asks

Madison gesture for Ava to take her seat. "I'm a
friend of Emilia's, but I met the Warners through charity
events—mostly for teachers and schools. Emilia and I
became fast friends." I can feel Ava's eyes on me,
looking for my explanation, but I'm too busy looking at
the screen, waiting for my child's face to appear.

"We got the 3D ultrasound machine like requested,"
Madison says, and I mentally curse. I was hoping she
would just do it, and it would be too late for Ava to
argue. Ava's head snaps in her direction.

Great.

"I specifically said I could only afford the 2D
machine. I don't have insurance." She mumbles.

I can't wait until we're married, and she won't have
to worry about that shit. I find it ridiculous that she
thought I would let her pay for this. Isn't it bad enough
that we are having a child out of wedlock, let alone will
I let her pay for everything? It's my job to provide for
and protect her and our future family.

"Ava, don't be ridiculous." I say and roll my eyes with annoyance. "First off, I would never let you pay, and secondly, it's my baby too, and I want 3D. I want to see her face."

She shakes her head in disbelief. "You have to stop calling the baby a '*her*', Gabriel,"

I wink at her. "Make me." I tease and look at Madison. "I'd like to see my baby now." I'm not asking. I've been patient enough.

I'm surprised my angel doesn't argue with me about paying for this. Maybe, she's learning, but that's wishful thinking. She will always be stubborn. I think she want's the 3D ultrasound just as badly as I do.

"Okay, Ava, just lift your shirt, and I'm going to squeeze this gel—*it'll be cold*—and then I'm going to use this wand"—she lifts the wand to show us, and it looks almost like a store scanner—"to rub the gel on your belly and the picture will start to appear on the screen. I'll freeze it and print out some good shots of the face." I'm listening to Madison's every word, making sure I don't miss anything. If something goes wrong, I need to be prepared.

Ava hisses when the gel touches her skin, and she winces when Madison presses the wand against her stomach. I'm about to tell her to stop hurting Ava, then Madison speaks, "I have to put some pressure for it to work." She warns Ava softly.

I take Ava's hand, not knowing what else I can do to take her pain away—*if* she is in pain. I want to ask her if she's okay, but I can't look away from the screen. I don't want to miss a single second of this. I can see Ava take out her phone in the corner of my eye and take a picture of me, but I still don't move or take my eyes off the screen.

Then out of nowhere, a thumping begins to fill the room. It's all I can hear as a lump forms in my throat. After a few minutes, a face appears on the screen. I can see her beautiful face and her small hand that looks like it's waving at us. I didn't think it was possible to love someone as much as I love Ava. I haven't even met this child, and I would die for her. All I can feel is love and happiness.

"*Holy shit,*" I whisper in complete awe.

Madison laughs softly. "Very healthy heart and healthily growing. You're about ten weeks, almost done your first trimester, eight more, and we can find out the sex. We're going to have an appointment every four weeks until you're around twenty-eight weeks." I already read that in the baby books, but I still make a mental note of everything she says.

I look at Ava, who has tears running down her cheeks. We have created something so beautiful. Not only has a love grown for this child, but my love for Ava has also increased. She is no longer just the woman I love; she is also the mother of my child. That's a love you can't describe.

I lean in a kiss Ava softly, needing to show her how grateful I am that she chose to forgive me. I will never take her or the life I have with her for granted. When I pull away, we are both grinning ear to ear.

"I'll give you two some privacy while I go get your photos." She hands Ava a towel. "You can use this to wipe the gel off."

Madison exits the room, and my lips are back on Ava's. My tongue brushes against hers out of habit, and that's all it takes for the both of us. She pulls me closer by the nape of my neck. My body tells me to take her right here in this office, but I know better than that.

"Easy, girl," I whisper as I rest my forehead against hers. "We're at a Doctor's office."

She scoffs. "When has being in public ever stopped you before? You almost fucked me in your parent's bathroom."

Why must she swear when her shirt is up, and our baby can possibly hear her. "One, don't swear when our baby can hear us. Two, we both know you can't have sex yet."

She frowns. "Gabriel, they said one week, it's been one week." I know we should be fine to have sex, but I can't risk hurting her. The thought of going too hard or losing control and making her injuries worse scares the living shit out of me. Or what if I hurt the baby? The sex

Ava and I have cannot be safe. We would have to be gentle and slow until the baby comes.

"Let's not talk about his now," I beg. "I don't want to ruin this moment."

She sighs, and I know I've got my way. "Okay," she whispers.

Madison enters the room with a handful of ultrasound photos. "Here we are," she mutters as she sits back down. "Now, you need to be taking prenatal vitamins. Folic acid is key while pregnant. Gabriel told me about the accident you were in, which means you're in a high-risk pregnancy. You have to take it easy for the next couple of weeks."

Ava bites her lip. "Can we still have...uh...rough sex?"

I nearly choke on my tongue in complete dismay. "Ava," I mutter but can't help my smirk.

I had no idea she would just come out and ask that.

Madison tries to fight her grin. "Yes, sex is completely okay...even, uh, rough sex but nothing too...eventful."

"Alright," I mumble and stand uncomfortably. "If that's all, I need to feed my girl."

Ava rolls her eyes. "I'm sorry he can be possessive."

"Have you spoken to your father yet?" Ava asks as we sit in the car eating burgers. She told me she was craving them, and I wasn't going to say no. As long as she eats, I don't give a fuck what it is.

I haven't spoken to him since we left after that terrible dinner. My mum had been begging me over and over again, especially after Ava's accident. She told me life was too short to be in this feud with my own flesh and blood. I think any other time, I would have listened to her like I always do but now that I've seen my baby and heard the heartbeat, I couldn't imagine ever treating my child the way my father treated me. My child could do everything wrong, and it wouldn't change my love. Like my grandad told me, they could run this company to the ground, and I would still be proud of them.

Why does my father get an exception? What makes his case so unique?

I shake my head. "It's not like he's calling me or knocking down my door, Ava. He knows how to find me."

She frowns while chewing. "How about your mom? Has she moved back home yet?"

I sigh. "No, she isn't speaking to my father either. She isn't backing down this time, and he can't get over himself for ten seconds to fix his fucking marriage."

She places her hand on my thigh to comfort me. "I wish I could do something. It's hard feeling helpless when it comes to you."

She has no fucking idea. I died a thousand deaths while she paid on that hospital bed. I thought of all the ways to punish myself if she didn't make it. Dark thoughts riddled my brain, and it wasn't until I was given the first ultrasound pictures where I felt a sliver of hope.

I take her hand and kiss her palm lightly. "You being by my side is all I need." I say honestly. Ava and this baby are now my family. I will fight heaven and hell to protect them, serve them, and make them happy, and I won't stop until I take my last breath.

Ava fell asleep pretty quickly, which gave me enough time to sneak out. I told Ruth to keep an eye on her, and the second she woke up, to text me. I needed to make sure Ava doesn't find out where I'm headed. I step into the jewelry store with John by my side.

"Mr. Warner, we're so happy to see you again. Follow me; your ring just got in." Brooke says as she comes around the counter to greet both of us.

"I can't believe you're doing this." John says as we follow her, and it makes me grin. I can't believe I waited this long, and I still have a bit more to wait.

All Ava has said is how desperately slow she wants us to take our relationship—*John knows this*—hence his disbelief, but this feels right. We belong to one another. We always have. I know the challenge will be convincing her that this has nothing to do with her pregnancy. I want to marry her because she is the love of my life.

She pulls out a small envelope and then pulls out a cream ring box. When she opens the box, my breath is taken away like the first time I saw the ring. I knew it belonged on my Ava's finger. It's a simple petite, vintage 18k rose gold band with an oval 2.0 carat oval diamond in the centre. Surrounding the main centre diamond is a halo of smaller diamonds that almost make the ring look floral or cathedral, as Brooke described it. It didn't look like the other rings I've seen around. It doesn't look like it belongs in this time but instead in the time of Ava's favourite books.

"Holy shit," John mutters as he sees the ring. "She's going to kill you when she sees the size of that diamond."

I laugh because I know for a fact that she *will* kill me. She will ask me how much I spent and tell me to return it. I probably did spend too much, to be entirely fair, but I can't think of anyone who deserves this work of art on their finger more than Ava does.

I put the box in my pocket as John squeezes my shoulder. "Gabriel Warner is getting married." He mumbles in disbelief.

I sigh. "Lets hope she says yes first." I say worriedly.

CHAPTER 22

JACK WARNER

"You wanted to see me?" Emilia's voice fills the yard where I'm cutting wood for a fire tonight. It's been weeks since I've seen my wife or even spoken to her. I look up to see her standing on the deck with her arms crossed over her chest.

She always does that when she's angry.

There are so many things I want to say to her, but I don't know where to start. "How is he?" I ask. Lia had called me when Ava went to the hospital. I was worried for my son that he would have the same fate that I thought was destined for me.

Wasn't it enough that he already changed his whole life because of me?

She sighs. "He's good. They're out of the hospital. They went to an appointment today for the baby."

I'm going to be a grandad...kind of. I can't really be a grandad if my son won't speak to me. "That's good," I mumble and scratch the back of my head. "I miss you, Lia."

She frowns. "You know how to get me to come home, Jack, no one is stopping you."

I clench my jaw. "You're stopping me. All you have to do is stop this shit and come home. I haven't slept in fucking days. Didn't we promise if you got better, we wouldn't let foolish fights get in our way?" I spent years fearing that I would lose her, and now we're spending nights apart for what?

She makes her way toward me with a scowl on her face. "*Foolish*?" She spits. "He's my son. He's *our* son. I'm not sure where this coldness is coming from, Jack. Maybe, Gabe is right, and you can't stand the sight of him because you see the man you have taught yourself to hate."

Her words cut me deep, so deep I physically flinch. I don't hate my son or...my father. How do I tell her that I'm lost, knowing I never got to say sorry to my father before he passed. It's my own fault; I know that; that's why I live the way I do. I don't deserve their pity or understanding. How can I look my son in the eye and tell him I love him when I have all this pain because of my own father?

I should have gone to the hospital that day. I should have told my father how sorry I was; how much I love him; how much I miss mom because I know he misses her too. I want to tell him how many times I died while watching Emilia lay in the hospital bed with no hair, needles piercing her skin, needing assistance to walk or eat. There are so many times I picked up the phone but could never push myself to dial his number. I'm reliving the same habit with my son now.

"What do you want me to do?" I ask, my voice wavering more than I would like it to. I had only cried a few times in front of my wife: when I saw her walking down the aisle; when Gabriel and Isabella were born. "I'm trying my fucking hardest to even keep breathing, Emilia."

She frowns. "I don't know, Jack, but I can't help you anymore. I can't be the one who continues to fix things between you and Gabriel." She walks over to me and cups my face in her delicate hands. Her wedding ring is still on, which is a good sign. "You have to find a way to let this anger go, Jack. You have to learn how to forgive Simon and forgive yourself. I know your heart, and I know it's eating you alive that you can't see Simon or Mary anymore." she leans in and kisses my cheek softly. "You know where to find me when you do."

Emilia doesn't wait for me to answer, and I don't beg her to stay. I know my wife is right, and no one knows me better than her.

I can't fix things with my father, so I hope it isn't too late to fix things with my son.

CHAPTER 23

SIMON WARNER

Gabriel's Birth

My first grand-baby, and it's a boy. I was hoping for a girl, but this will be okay. I have my Mary and Emilia; they will make sure my relationship with my grandson will be nothing like the one I have with my son. He has no idea that I'm coming; he only knows that his mum is coming to meet Gabriel.

What a beautiful name.

We walk into the hospital room hand in hand to see my son sleeping on the chair against the window. Emilia is lying on the hospital bed with my grandson in her arms. She looks at him the same way Mary looked at Jack when he was born. The same way I looked at Jack when he was born.

"There's our strong girl," Mary says softly, and Emilia whips her head in our direction with a grin. At least someone is happy to see me.

"You guys made it," Emilia whispers happily. She's breaking a lot of rules, too, by having me here.

"Of course," I mutter. "We wouldn't miss this for the world." I step closer to the bed, and she sits up, lifting the baby.

"Would you like to hold him?" She asks, and I nod.

I take Gabriel in my arms, and I don't bother wiping away the tears that fall down my cheeks when my grandson looks up at me. I brush back his tiny hairs with my finger. "I promise I will be here for you no matter what," I whisper to him even though I know he doesn't understand a thing.

Love fills me head to toe.

I look at Mary, who has tears in her eyes as well.

She wants nothing more than for me to fix things with Jack. She misses her son, and she misses how we used to be with one another. She thinks I hate my son, but I could never. I look over at my boy—*who is no longer a boy*—as he sleeps peacefully. He looks so much older, yet I still see the boy who needed my help to walk. See the boy who fell off his bike and cried when he thought he would never learn like his friends. How could I ever hate someone I love more than my own wife, someone I would die for time after time.

My pride and joy.

"Okay, my turn," Mary says and doesn't wait for me to agree. She takes Gabriel out of my hands and smiles lovingly at him. "Hi, my love." She whispers and kisses his forehead softly.

"How are you holding up, mama?" I ask as I sit at the foot of the bed. Emilia was the best choice for my son. He needed someone to calm down the fire I put in him. He needs someone who will call him on his shit, and I've seen her do it. She's strong, independent, and won't let anyone take advantage of her family.

She smiles sadly. "I was hoping he would change his mind—that's this baby would soften him, but"—she shakes her head with a sigh—"it seems to have made him even more stubborn."

She doesn't understand, not yet, but I do. He looks at Gabriel, and all he can feel is love. Suddenly, you would die and kill for this small child that has only been alive for a few minutes. Everything that you thought was important fades away. All you can see is your child, and that's why he's even angrier with me.

He wonders how I can treat my own child so harshly, but he can't ever see himself doing the same to his own son. I pray that he can't ever be mean, harsh or cold with his son. I pray that Gabriel only knows unconditional love.

I pat her leg. "Don't you worry about that. You worry about recovering and this child. I'll worry about my son and our relationship."

"Or I will," Mary says.

"What is his full name?" I ask as I watch my lovely wife coo at our grandson.

"Gabriel Simon Jack Warner."

I look at Emilia in pure shock. "He let you add my name?"

She nods with a smile. "I was surprised too."

"What are you doing here?" Jack's voice startles the women, but it's almost as if I was expecting it. I turn my head to see him sitting up, wide awake now.

"Jack, I invited them. I told you I would." Emilia says.

He scowls. "You told me my mum was coming, not *him*. Now, what the hell are you doing here? What makes you think you can see my son?"

"*Our* son," Emilia spits.

I stand with my hands up. "It's okay, Emilia; I don't want to cause any issues. I can go."

"No," Emilia argues and whips her head back at my son. "This baby has nothing to do with your issues with Simon. He deserves to know both of his grandparents, it's only fair."

Jack's body begins to shake with anger. "Emilia," he hisses with hurt and anger. He wanted his wife to be on his side, not side with the father he can't stand anymore.

"Sweetheart, why don't we step outside." Mary says as if she's asking, but she's demanding—*nicely*—for her son to follow her.

Jack nods and walks past me without a look or a word. Mary hands Gabriel back to Emilia, who looks distraught. Once they are out of the room, I look at my daughter-in-law with sadness.

"He will come around eventually." I mumble, ignoring the heavy ache in my chest.

"I'm afraid he won't come around until it's too late, Simon; the anger has such a tight grip on him. It's going to kill him." She mumbles.

I frown at the thought of this anger driving my son to the point of no return, and it's all my fault. I kiss Emilia's forehead. "You rest, and we will visit in about a month's time." It's hard to visit Portland with the business succeeding as well as it is, but I won't let work or my own son keep me from my grandchild. If Emilia allows me to see Gabriel, then I will. I refuse to have my grandson think I didn't want him.

I make my way out to the hall to see my wife and son in a heated discussion. "Honey, Emilia has a question. Why don't you let me and Jack speak for a second?"

She nods and kisses her son's cheek. He stands exactly where he is, leaning his side against the wall, staring straight ahead. I can't remember the last time we had a talk that lasted more than a few minutes and didn't end in a fight.

"What, dad?" he mumbles annoyedly.

For a grown man, he still has the same attitude he had when he was a teenager. Teenager Jack was a pain in our asses.

"You need to stop this. Emilia won't be able to handle the stress, and you know your mother won't either." I stand in front of him, and it's like I'm looking in a mirror. My boy looks just like me. "I want to fix things between us, but I can't do that unless you give me a chance."

His jaw clenches, and he stares at me like I'm shit at the bottom of his shoe. It hurts when your son looks at you like that because my heart expands with love and pride when I look at him. "I want nothing to do with you and the life you want for my son or me. You don't think I know what you're trying to do? You want to control him the same way you did with me, but I won't let it fucking happen, dad; he will get to make his own choices, his own decision, his own life. I won't make him do anything he doesn't want to do, and I won't be disappointed in him when he chooses a different path. All you ever did was look down at the life I chose."

I shake my head in disbelief. "That's not true, Jack. I have always been proud of you."

He scoffs. "Now, when I'm already grown and already fucked up from the pressure you put on me."

"I wanted you to be the best," I hiss. "I wanted you by my side running a father and son empire. Was I upset when you chose a different path? Of course, I was, and I didn't handle it well, but that doesn't change the fact that you're my son, Jack, and I love you unconditionally; I would die for you."

He looks away, and I know it's because my son is just like me—or at least how I *used* to be. He can't handle intense emotion or the solemn words I'm saying, so he has to break eye contact.

"You shouldn't die for someone who wouldn't die for you, dad." He mutters and walks away with no regret.

"What did he say to you?" Mary asks as we drive back to Seattle. Her hand is laced in mine like it always is when we drive anywhere. I went to the car after my conversation with Jack and cried like a fucking baby. I mourned the young boy who loved me more than anyone in this world. I mourn the relationship I had with my only child.

Emilia is right.

He won't forgive me until it's too late. I won't stop trying, though. I will never stop fighting because that's what parents do, right? I will fight for my son until I can no longer go on. I will let him know that my love for him and my grandson is irreplaceable and cannot even begin to be described. I need to do something that will prove my love for him even after I'm gone and can no longer beg for his forgiveness and love. I will leave something behind that he can cherish forever even when he claims he hates it and wants nothing to do with it.

I shake my head. "Nothing I didn't already know." I say. I can't tell her what he said because, as a mother, it would crush her. She has to choose between her son and her husband, and it's pulling her apart.

"He loves you, Simon; I *know* he does." She states and brings my knuckles to her lips. "I never stopped loving my own father."

My wife's story is a heartbreaking one with many trials and tribulations. Her relationship with her parents was worse than my relationship with Jack, but there will be days where she talks about them fondly. Some fond memories of her childhood get brought up due to a particular place, song or smell.

"I know, love," I mutter and kiss her knuckles in return. "I love him too."

CHAPTER 24

AVA

"Do we have to invite all these people?" I ask as I stare down at the blueprint Isabella has laid out on the breakfast bar. It's been three days since our doctor appointment, and Isabella has kept me on my toes planning our grand pregnancy reveal for The Warner's friends and family.

Gabriel didn't want to wait any longer, even though I suggested it just in case of miscarriage, but he wouldn't hear it. The second I began talking about miscarriage, he would angrily start walking away, muttering under his breath that I shouldn't speak of such negative things. I told him that ignorance is not bliss in this case, but he refused to listen to that, also.

"Belle, I told you to keep it small," Gabriel states annoyedly as he wraps his arms around me from behind.

She pouts. "This *is* me keeping it small."

"Seventy people is keeping it small?" I question with a smirk.

She nods. "Yes."

"You had like twenty-five people at John's birthday!" I accuse.

She gasps. "But we live in an apartment. Mom and dad's house is a lot bigger."

John is watching us argue with an amused grin.

Bastard should be helping us.

"Belle," Gabriel replies sternly.

She sighs. "I can cut it down to fifty." She's sulking.

"Thirty," I argue and give her a grin.

"Ugh, fine." She mutters and begins to cross people's name's off one by one.

Gabriel kisses my neck below my ear. "That's my girl."

I shiver and swat him. We haven't had sex in weeks, and these baby hormones aren't helping. I'm about to purchase a toy if Gabriel doesn't get over this fear of hurting me.

"Are you inviting dad?" Isabella asks, and I look up at Gabriel to see what he's going to say. He hasn't spoken to his dad yet and refuses to talk about it with his mom. He just wants his mom to move back in, but I understand why she's doing this. I place my hands protectively over my stomach as I wonder what I would do if I were in the same scenario.

I love Gabriel with every fibre of my being, but I would choose my child over and over again. It would be no comparison.

Emilia is doing what she thinks is best for herself and her children. She's doing the one thing that may get Jack and Gabriel to end this feud.

"It's at his house, Belle; I don't think I can really leave him out, sadly." He complains and takes a swig of his drink.

She frowns. "Gabe, you don't mean that. He's still our dad."

Gabriel glares at his sister. "It may be the same man, but we have two different fathers. The last time I checked, dad worships the ground you walk on and has never punched you in the face."

She sighs. "I know. I'm sorry."

"Gabriel," Ruth announces as she steps into the kitchen. "Uh, your father is here."

We all whip our heads to Gabriel, who looks at Ruth as if she has two heads.

"My mum is at Isabella's house," Gabriel responds as if that answers this confusing situation.

Ruth shakes her head. "He's here to see you."

I stand, and I'm not sure why but I take Gabriel's hand. I don't know how to protect him or help him; this is all I can think of. He looks down at my hand and squeezes it softly. "Tell him to give me a second to change." He mutters and takes my hand, pulling me upstairs quickly.

GABRIEL

Why the fuck is he here to see me? Has he not done enough? I haven't called or even visited. I thought that was a clear indication that I want nothing to do with him. We were all taken back that my father travelled all this way to speak to me. The man hardly calls me.

Yet, here I am, changing out of my shorts and t-shirt into jeans and a sweater to go speak with him.

"What are you going to say?" Ava asks as she watches me undress.

I have no fucking clue.

"No fucking clue, angel," I mutter as I pull my head through my hoodie. I put on a pair of old boots and lean down to kiss her forehead. "I promise I won't be long."

I'm anxious, and it won't fade until I see him and start talking. She follows me and tugs on my hand to try and stop me.

"Wait," she mutters, and I turn to see her eyebrows furrowed with worry, and she's chewing on her bottom lip. "Promise me you will keep an open mind."

I'm taken back.

I thought Ava would understand better than most. She hates her mother. "Not what I thought you would say. You know better than anyone that we don't have to love our parents."

She frowns. "I know, trust me, I understand that," she says and takes my hand, placing it on her stomach. Even though I don't notice the bump. "But my mom didn't want me, Gabriel, from pregnancy to birth to adulthood. She despised that I had ruined her life before I was even in the world. Your dad loves you and wanted you the second they found out about you. That's the difference. I just think he lost his way."

Knowing that my hand is protecting our child fills me with emotion. I hear what she's saying but looking down at her stomach, I can't imagine ever treating my child the way he treats me. I would kill anyone who laid a finger on my child, let alone would I ever be the one to hit them.

"Gabriel," she whispers to bring my attention back to her. She cups my face and kisses me softly. My body instantly melts, and there is no room for anxiety. I bring her body flush against mine.

Fuck, I miss her body.

She pulls away, and we're both breathing heavily. "Just imagine yourself in his shoes."

I nod. "I promise that I will do my best," I whisper and kiss her one last time before rushing downstairs to see my father.

He looks older. It's been only a few weeks, but it has aged him being apart from my mum. All he did was nod at me and proceeded to walk to the elevator. We have been walking down the street in complete silence, but I refuse to begin. We make our way to a baseball field, and he sits down at one of the benches. I don't sit down next to him, needing space from him.

He's my father, yet I look at him and hardly recognize the man. My grandad used to tell me stories about a kid who was full of light; when I look at my dad now...it's hard to ever imagine him that way.

"Remember when you tried out for baseball?" He asks out of nowhere. "We practiced for hours at the baseball field at your high school."

"Our hands had blisters," I mumble as the memory comes flooding back. My father loved baseball, so of course, I tried out for the team. I loved it for a short time, then girls became a priority.

He laughs, and it catches me by surprise. "Your mom was so angry with me that I had kept you out all night, but it wasn't me who wanted to stay. It was you. Every time I said we should wrap it up, you told me *one more swing, one more pitch.* You wanted to get it just right. At that moment, I saw your grandad in you. The hours he would be up working while my mom would say it's time to eat, time to sleep, and shower. It was the same drive I saw in you." He looks at me, and his eyes are full of sorrow. Sorrow I have never seen before. "It scared the living shit out of me, Gabriel, to see the man I hated the most in *you*. You are my boy, my son, the greatest love I have ever come to know, and you were turning into Simon. He would have killed for me to be that way. I had drive and determination but nothing like you and him. I fucking envied it, I wanted to be as successful and as driven as him—I had some of it, but I was more, my mom, than anything. I had his ugly temper, though, which you also have. I knew my father would love to hear that his grandson was exactly like him."

I sit down next to him. "Why are you telling me this?" I ask.

He sighs. "Because I have to. Now, hush and listen." He mutters. "When your mum got sick, I had panicked. I wasn't speaking to my father, and now I was losing the one person who made my life worth living at a time where it felt like it wasn't. I wasn't an idiot. I knew your mom was letting your grandad see you, kids, once a month since you were born, so I knew he would help us if I called him. The day you were born, Gabriel, I made a promise to him that I would never control you; I would let you make your own decisions the way he never let me. Then eighteen years later, I took it all back, and I forced you to move and begin to work to take care of a family that I was supposed to take care of.

Your mother is *your* mother, but to me, she is my best friend, my partner in crime, my shoulder to lean on, my lover, my supporter, my college sweetheart, my everything, son. Before you kids, I never loved anyone more than her and all of a sudden, she had cancer. She was dying right in front of my eyes, and I couldn't do anything. I had to sit there and watch her waste away, and I thought I would have to watch it until she took her last breath at such a young age. We had planned to spend forever together, and now the clock was ticking. I had no idea how to be a father, a husband, and keep it all together at the same time. I was failing you kids and her. I went to my dad and cried like a baby; I was going to take my own life that night, son."

I look at him in shock and instantly feel sick to my stomach. I stand, needing to feel my legs under me. How could he say he was going to take his own life? We're us kids not enough? "You were just going to leave us?" I ask angrily.

"How did you feel when Ava was in the hospital?" He asks.

My anger slowly slips away and is replaced by heartbreak. "I died a million deaths," I whisper. I also wanted to kill whoever did this to her in various ways.

He nods. "I felt the same only for four years, Gabriel. Not only was your mum dying, but I had destroyed my son. I was watching you grow up when you didn't have to; I was watching you be put in the box that your grandad tried so hard to put me in. I became the same man I swore I wouldn't. I let you down in more ways than I can count, my boy, and I'm sorry. I needed to be the one to help our family but I was so consumed on your mom, I forced you. I will never be able to forgive myself for how I've been treating you but you deserve to know it has nothing to do with you. It's because I couldn't face you and my broken promises." His voice is raw with emotion as tears begin to fall down his cheeks. "I can never take it back, all the things I've done, but I refuse to let history repeat itself. I will never be able to tell my own father how sorry I am. I will never be able to say good-bye to him, and let me tell you that eat's me alive every fucking day. I love my father, Gabriel, but I let this hatred, anger, jealousy, and envy get in the way. I will never get him back, and I refuse to wait until one of us is on our death bed to fix things."

"I don't understand. Why now? What's changed?" I ask. Did my mum's plan actually work?

He wipes the tears off his face and reaches into his shoulder bag, pulling out a giant brown book. "I found this the other day when I was cleaning out the basement. Simon must have given it to your mum to give to me, but she never did. Probably assumed I would have thrown it out. Smart woman." He hands it to me, and I sit down again before opening it up.

The front page says. '*To my son, Jack.*' I flip the page to see photos of my grandad and dad when he was a baby. Photos upon photos, drawings, paintings, every card my dad has ever made for my grandad. There are newspaper clippings from when my dad won contests or tournaments; various items taped with a short description written beside it exposing what each one represents. My father's first loose tooth, first haircut. There are DVDs that must be old home videos tucked in between pages.

On the last page, it has written,

You are my greatest joy. Not one day has gone by where I don't think about my son. I know you will do amazing things with your own. You're right, you will love Gabriel and never pressure him the way I did with you, and that makes me forever grateful. My grandson will only know love and never know what it's like to not have his father by his side. I can die happily, knowing that. I love you, my son. Forever and always.

I look at him to see that he's still crying. I had never seen my father cry. "You may not forgive me, and I understand, but I'll be here every day waiting for the day that you do." He stands and places his bag over his shoulder. He leans down and kisses the top of my head. I'm completely frozen. "I love you, son." He walks away without another word. I watch his back until he disappears into the crowd.

I keep watching until it gets too dark to see anything anymore.

AVA

We're all sitting in the living room in Gabriel's penthouse, waiting for any sign, any tip that he's still fucking alive. Isabella even called Jack, but he told her that he left Gabriel hours ago, and the conversation they had may have pushed him to need a drink or two.

I've called Gabriel more times than I can count. I've sent text after text, begging for him to tell me he's safe. "Here's some tea, sweetheart; it helps with the sickness," Emilia says as she sits next to me with a mug. My morning sickness has gone from morning to night, and this situation is not helping. They don't know, but I know Gabriel and I are in danger. There is someone after us, and they could have gotten him. What if it was Tristan? He's capable of anything.

What if he killed...

I stand and go over to the piano, needing to calm my breathing.

"Ava, I'm sure he's completely fine," John says, but it doesn't help. If he's fine, why won't he answer us?

Where the fuck is he?

I hear the elevator ding from the front door, and I don't waste time running past everyone and down the hall. I don't care if it turns out to be someone else. If it is him, I need him now. I swing open the door, and there he is. He's still in the same hoodie, jeans and boots he left in. The only difference is his hair is a mess, and he reeks like liquor.

Like whisky.

"Where the fuck have you been?" I hiss and punch his arm.

"Ow, Ava," he hisses and rubs his arm.

I throw my arms around his waist and squeeze him tightly. I inhale his scent even though it's mixed with alcohol. I just need to smell him. I need to know I'm not dreaming, and he's actually here. "I was worried sick, Gabriel. We all were." I mumble with my cheek against his chest.

His arms wrap around me, and he kisses the top of my head. "I'm sorry I worried you. Wait, did you say 'we'?" He asks. He has a slight slur to his voice.

How drunk is he?

I nod and look up at him. His eyes are glossy and red. "Your mom, Isabella and John are here. Your dad has been calling every ten minutes to see if you've come

home. You nearly killed us all." I let out a breath of
relief. "Never do that again, Gabriel."

He frowns deeply. "I'm sorry, angel, please forgive
me. I wasn't thinking." He cups my face and kisses my
forehead. "I'll never do it again. Now, let's go inside so I
can calm my mum's worries." He takes my hand and
pulls me into the penthouse, closing the front door
behind us. Emilia stands and runs over to us, throwing
her arms around Gabriel. Her hands can barely touch
due to how muscular he is. She begins to hit him, lightly
and he blocks her hits.

"Where the hell have you been, boy? Just like high
school all over again. What was the point of buying you
that God damn phone if you weren't going to use it? It's
the same thing with you kids. Worrying me half to
death..." She goes on and on, and I can't help but laugh
under my breath. I make my way to sit next to John,
who is grinning—clearly enjoying the show as well.
Gabriel rolls his eyes as she continues to scold him and
Isabella does the same.

It's amusing to see them get in trouble like they
aren't grown adults. I can see high school Gabriel
getting in trouble every day after school. Probably
because he was out with me all the time and not
answering his cell phone.

"I'm sorry, mum, but I spoke to dad, and I just
needed a drink after. My phone had died on the way to
the bar, and I didn't even think about anyone worrying.

I'm sorry." He kisses his mother's cheek and pulls her to the couch. I just noticed the brown book he's carrying that looks like a photo album or a scrapbook.

"What is that?" I ask as I point at it.

He places it on the coffee table and sits down beside me. He puts my feet in his lap and begins to massage circles into my heels. I'm hardly pregnant, but my feet have been so sore lately. I don't even want to know how sore they will be when I'm eight months pregnant.

"Grandad made dad a scrapbook of all their memories together from birth to when they started fighting. Even after that. Photos that mum sent to grandad when we were kids. Dad just found it." Gabriel says, and Emilia reaches for the book with tears in her eyes.

She must have had such a strong bond with Simon.

"Dad gave it to me after our talk."

"How was your talk?" I ask nervously. I wasn't sure if I had the right to tell him to give his dad a chance. I would never give my mother another chance. She made her choice a long time ago. She doesn't get to decide to come back when I'm grown and no longer need raising. My dad had to do it all on his own.

"It was...eye-opening." He mutters as he looks off in the distance. He then looks to his mom and gives her a reassuring smile. "I think it's time for you to go home, mum."

She looks at Gabriel in awe. "He apologized?" She asks in disbelief.

He nods. "He did a lot more than that. I'm sure he would love to tell you everything." He lifts my feet off his lap and stands. "You're all welcome to stay the night. The guest bedrooms are open to you. Now, I have to take my girl to bed. It's late." He reaches for my hand and helps me stand. He kisses his mom and sister goodnight, and John gives him a brief hug. After saying goodnight, we make our way upstairs and to the bedroom. After closing the bedroom door, he reaches for the remotes and starts to close the curtains.

"Not so fast," I mutter. "You need a bath. I'm going to get drunk just by sniffing you."

He gives me a wicked grin. "Very funny, Thompson." He mutters.

I lead him to the bathroom and begin to draw the bath. "Why don't you put that song on you played on the night of our first date?" It's hard to think about our first date and not picture Elizabeth sucking...but I've been trying to remember what was amazing. I chose this man, which means I'm going to have to let go and forgive the past. He can't change it, but he's making up for it now.

"It's by Frank Ocean." He says as he walks over to the sound system mounted into the wall. After a few seconds, the familiar melody begins to play through the speakers softly. I leave the water running and walk over to my God and begin to undress him. I start with his hoodie, then his jeans. Before I can continue, he takes off my t-shirt, my sweatpants, and my panties. He kisses my thighs and then kisses my belly before standing up.

"I truly am sorry I worried you, angel." He says softly as he takes off his boxers.

"I thought that Tristan had…" I swallow hard.

"Hey," he says sadly and cups my face. He brushes his nose against mine. "I'm safe. I'm right here. C'mon, let's take a bath." He walks over to the tub and stops the water. He helps me in and climbs in behind me. We both hiss as the hot water touches our skin but then begins to soothe my achy body.

I rest my head against his chest. "How did the conversation with your father *really* go?" I ask. He didn't tell his family anything other than the fact that he apologized. Gabriel went to go drink for a reason.

"He told me he wanted to take his own life." He mutters.

My heart sinks. I turn to face him to gauge his reaction, and he's frowning. "Did he tell you why?"

He nods. "He couldn't handle losing his dad, wife, and he felt like he was failing us, children. He said he failed me." When his eyes meet mine in met with the unexpected.

He's beginning to tear.

"Baby," I whisper sadly and straddle him, causing water to spill out the wides of the tub.

"He started to cry and told me how sorry he was and how much he loves me. How much he loves and misses my grandad. When I looked at him, I saw so much pain. I didn't know what to say to him or even know how to feel, so I went to the nearest bar and started to drink. I listened to what you said and pictured myself in his shoes and pictured our baby"—he places his hands on my stomach—"and it broke me. It broke me thinking about him or her never wanting to see me again. I will never make the mistakes my own father made, but I'm still human. I'm going to make mistakes, there are times I may let them down, and I want them to forgive me. I even thought about everything I did wrong by you, and that took me down another whirlwind of emotions."

He rests his head against my chest, and I rest my cheek on the top of his head. "Our kids will always forgive you, but you don't even have to worry about that. You're right; you will never hurt our kids the way you've been hurt. The same way I will never treat this child the way my mom treated me."

"How can you be so sure?" He mumbles worriedly.

"Because even though we both like to pretend we aren't hurt by our parent's actions, I know that we are. I remember how I felt as a child when my mom wouldn't give me the time of day, and I wouldn't wish that feeling of loneliness on my worst enemy." I stroke and play with his hair. He doesn't say anything more; we just sit in the tub listening to the soft and beautiful melody. I listen to the words, and it makes complete sense why he chose this song our first night together. Each word slices me deeply, knowing what Gabriel was trying to tell me through this song.

He can only express how he feels through songs and quotes from books that he loves.

So far, I've made the mental note that he is only this emotional and vulnerable when he's drinking. It's the only time he really feels something, and it's usually pain.

What I would do to take his pain away...

"So, what now? Are you going to try and fix your relationship with your dad?" I ask softly.

He takes a deep breath. "I suppose." He mutters.

"And how does that make you feel?" I ask.

I need to make sure he's okay and won't spiral out of control.

He shrugs slightly. "Good, I suppose." He mumbles.

I look down at him to see his eyes closed as his cheek rests on my breasts. He has a slight smile touching his lips.

I decide to leave it there. He's done enough sharing and has been vulnerable enough for tonight. I know deep down, the younger part of him is happy about this, but the grown part of him won't admit it. Gabriel has told himself for ten years that he doesn't need his dad's approval or love; it's going to take some time for him to forget that mindset.

We stay like this long after our song is done playing. It isn't until the water starts getting cold when he decides to move. He dried me off slowly and carefully like I'm a piece of glass. I happily watched and memorized every tattoo that covers his skin.

This is the most we have gone without speaking, yet our eyes and actions are saying everything.

We curl up in bed together, my head on his chest with his arm wrapped around me—his hand resting on the small of my back.

And just like that, we both fall asleep in blissful love.

CHAPTER 25

AVA

Today is the big day.

Isabella has been calling me all morning to fill me in on every new detail about the party tonight. Gabriel laughed as I begged him for help. He doesn't want to deal with his sister either.

He's been hiding something all day. He and Harris have been locked in Gabriel's office. He comes out to make sure I'm okay, fed, and to kiss me but then goes straight back into the office.

I asked him if there was anything wrong, and of course, he brushed me off with a kiss and his charming smile that makes me melt. This means I'm going to have to find out for myself.

The party isn't until seven which gives me enough time to do what I have planned. We haven't had sex in way too long, and my pregnancy hormones are about to cause me to explode. I have to show Gabriel that I'm perfectly okay and healthy now.

Enough time has passed.

While taking a shower, I sent Gabriel a quick text to bring me the towel from the dryer. I know he'll have a hard time denying me while I'm naked and wet.

I hear him walk into the bathroom, and my stomach begins to twist and flip as if we haven't slept together a bunch of times. This time he may reject me...

I open the door, and he stops in his tracks, his eyes scanning my body from head to toe. His eyes darken with lust.

"Why don't you take a break and join me in the shower? The party starts in three hours." I'm hoping he doesn't catch on too quickly.

He sighs. "You're right. I'm sorry." He mumbles and places the towel on the rack, and then strips out of his t-shirt and shorts.

"You're just walking around with no boxers?" I ask while raising my eyebrow, but my eyes are glued to his manhood.

He scoffs. "It's my house, Ava."

I roll my eyes.

He steps into the shower, and I almost jump with glee. I've got him now; there's no way he can reject me. He turns on the other shower heads, so neither of us are out of the hot water.

"Are you nervous for tonight?" He asks as he grabs his shampoo.

I shake my head. "Only because you're the one who is going to announce it." I give him a cheeky smile.

He rolls his eyes. "Of course."

I watch his arms flex as he washes his hair. His stomach tightens, and it all goes straight between my legs. It really is unfair for someone this handsome to exist. I have no idea why he chose me, and would he have chosen me if we didn't meet as teenagers?

No longer being able to wait—as he rinses the shampoo out of his hair—I step closer to him until our bodies are pressed together. I kiss his chest as my hand cups his semi-erection.

He hisses and grabs my hand. "Angel," he whispers harshly. "Not yet."

I frown but continue to kiss his chest. "Please," I beg. "You know we have the all-clear." I drop to my knees and look up at him through my lashes. He cups my face and shakes his head slightly as he mutters a curse under his breath.

Mental note: *he likes it when I look up at him while on my knees.*

I stick my tongue out and lick the tip causing all his muscles to clench and flex. I tease the end of his cock until his hand fists into my hair. When he looks down at me, his eyes are dark and hooded.

"Stop teasing me," he says through clenched teeth. He tugs my hair back until my mouth falls open, and he slowly sinks into my mouth. I don't wait and begin to bob my head, swirling my tongue around his thick length. He's thicker and bigger than usual—*probably due to the lack of sex*—which makes this a lot harder, but I'm not about to stop.

I look up at him as I gag over his length and his hips buckle. "*Fuck*, you dirty girl." Those words—*that he's never said or I have never had said to me before*—go straight to my clit. I slip my hands between my thighs, and he bites his lip while exhaling heavily through his nose. "She loves my dirty words, doesn't she?"

Unable to answer, I moan around his length, and he throws his head back on a groan. "Keep your head still," he demands, and both of his hands cup my head. I do as he says, and he begins to move his hips back and forward, thrusting in and out of my mouth. I watch him the whole time as I rub delicious circles over my clit. His head is hanging back, his mouth parted slightly while he groans and curses. He looks mouthwatering as he gets off on fucking my mouth. I want this image burned into my brain forever.

It's the definition of erotic.

"Don't swallow," he says hoarsely.

I narrow my eyebrows and pull my mouth away, but my hand continues to work over his length. "I want to,"

I argue. I enjoy it as well. I don't wait and begin to suck his cock again.

"Ava, you're pregnant." He gasps, and his hips buckle again. His tip thickens against my tongue, and I know he's close. "Don't fucking swallow it."

I know he's probably right, but I don't listen. Knowing he's so close is all I can think about.

"*Fuck!*" He yells and pulls out of my mouth and comes all over my face. When I open my eyes, I see him breathing heavily, but his eyes focus on the marking he left on my face. "I could take a fucking picture of this and stare at it forever."

He picks me off the floor and stands me under the water, so he is washed off my face. Once my face is clean, his lips smash against mine, and he presses me against the shower wall. Water is spraying all over his back, but he doesn't stop worshipping my mouth with his. My hands touch him everywhere, my nails digging into his back, then my hands tugging his hair.

"You want hard fucking or soft?" He asks, and his lips go down to my neck. He doesn't usually ask, but I guess it's due to my pregnancy.

"Hard. Make me scream," I pant.

"Not much of a challenge," he mumbles, and I can feel his smirk against my skin. Before I can argue with him, his lips wrap around my nipple, and he bites down.

"*Yes!*" I cry out, and he chuckles. He sucks, licks, and bites until I'm thrashing my head with pleasure— pleasure so intense it's almost painful.

"Gabriel, I can't," I pant as his tongue circles my pebbled nipple. "I can't take it."

He hums. "Let's see if we can get you to come this way, shall we?" He challenges.

"Fuck," I whisper and run my fingers through my hair. He is trying to kill me. "I won't be able to take it."

He doesn't pull away, just continues to worship each nipple as his hand slides down my waist to my hip then to my sex. When his fingers brush over my clit I jump and moan loudly.

"Please," I beg as my toes curl. I won't be able to stand for too much longer, especially if he makes me orgasm.

"Please, what, angel?" He asks. He brings his lips to my ear, and I shiver. His fingers are still drawing small circles over my clit. "Do you want me to make this pretty pussy come? Do you miss how good I make you feel?"

"Yes," I whisper. "*Yes, yes, yes!*"

"So, fucking sexy," he snarls, and his mouth is sucking on my nipples again. It takes only a few seconds for me to throw my head back and scream as my orgasm rips through me. It's so powerful I don't even notice that Gabriel is now carrying me with my legs wrapped around his waist.

"Hold onto the bar," he instructs as he presses me tightly against the wall. "This is going to be hard—exactly what you asked for."

My libido is awake and so ready for another orgasm. I've missed this. I've missed my powerful alpha man who takes what he wants. I don't want him to treat me like I'm glass. Things don't have to change just because I'm pregnant.

I hold onto the bar like he says, and he slowly sinks into me. "Holy shit," we both say on a pant. He's so deep it's hard to take a breath.

"You feel so fucking..." he swallows hard and gasps. "You feel different, and it's fucking amazing," Veins begin to pop out of his neck. He pulls back and drives forward so hard I go up the wall on a scream, and he yells as well.

"I told you it wasn't much of a challenge." He says through clenched teeth, and I grab his hair, tugging and he groans.

"Shut up and move already," I threaten.

He grins wickedly. "Your wish is my command." He grabs my hips and drives wildly with an animal-like fierceness. We're both swearing and crying out with every thrust. All I can focus on is him, how good he makes me feel, how badly I've missed this, how I ever thought I could live without this...without him.

"I'm—

"I know, angel, I can feel you fucking squeezing me." he hisses. "Squeeze your nipples." He demands. I do as he says, and I throw my head back.

"Gabriel!" I scream as my body shakes intensely. This orgasm rips through me intensely; tears come to my eyes and fall down my cheeks—getting lost in the water from the shower.

When I open my eyes, we are in the bedroom, and I'm on the bed. His lips kiss me softly, but when he pulls away, he gives me a smirk. "I'm not done with you yet, angel. You asked for hard, and I told you your wish is my command." He flips me onto my stomach on a yelp and covers me with his body. He smacks his length against my ass on a groan.

"When we have more time," he mutters mostly to himself and then slowly sinks into me once again.

His lips touch my ear, which causes him to sink even deeper. "Be a good girl and come again for me."

I don't think I could stop it even if I wanted to.

Deep breaths.

Gabriel's hand is intertwined with mine as we walk into his parent's home with Harris behind us. I thought Harris would have waited in the car, but Gabriel

informed me he's an actual guest tonight, and so is
Ruth.

Gabriel said to dress causally even though tonight is
catered. He promised that no one would be dressed
fancy. He's wearing jeans, a dark grey crew neck
sweater, a beanie and dark brown boots. He has about
two pairs of sneakers, tons of dress shoes and tons of
boots. He is the first guy I've ever been with that wears
boots outside of winter.

He looks so much younger and a lot less serious but
still as sexy as when he's wearing a suit,

Finally, no gowns, skirts or tight blouses, or high
heels. I decided on a light wash jean jacket on top of a
thin white knit sweater, black leggings, a cream beanie
to match Gabriel, and white sneakers.

Looking at us right now, it feels like we're back in
high school.

We walk into the house that is packed with people. I
only recognize about ten people. The people that are
standing by the door notice us and walk over to Gabriel.
The woman hugs and kisses Gabriel's cheek.

"Ava, this is my mum's sister, Lauren. Aunty, this is
my girlfriend, Ava." Gabriel introduces us. I had no idea
he had an aunt.

I smile and stick out my hand, but she ignores it
entirely and hugs me tightly instead. "So, nice to meet
you, Ava. Isabella and Emilia have told me all about

you." She pulls back to get the full view of me. "She's stunning, Gabriel."

I blush and look over at him, and he's smiling with pride. "I know, she is."

"Your mom is upstairs. She's been waiting for you." Lauren says.

Gabriel takes my hand and brings my knuckles to his lips. "I'm sorry, but I'm going to leave you with Harris, or you can go find Isabella. I won't be long."

He takes off toward the stairs, and I look at Harris, who pats my arm. "Go mingle. I'm sure Mrs. Owens is waiting for you."

I politely excuse myself and make my way to the kitchen. I wish I could have a glass of wine more than anything. I need something to calm my nerves. Everyone watches me as I pass them, giving them polite smiles and nods to not come off rude. I grab a water bottle off the counter and sneak to the backyard for fresh air. I've only been here for a minute, and it's already too much.

"Ava," a deep Australian voice says, and I look out by the fire to see Jack sitting around it. I make my way over to him and sit on the chair opposite the side of him.

"I thought you would be inside," I say as I sit.

I wonder if he made up with Emilia yet.

"I was waiting for you and Gabriel to get here before I came inside. I'm not a fan of all these people in my house, but my wife and daughter don't know subtlety if it hit them in the face." He mumbles with a sulk.

I know Gabriel and him had a talk, but I don't know how much of him I can trust. I have to protect Gabriel and his heart. I refuse to let him be hurt anymore than he already has been. "How are you doing?" I ask.

He sighs. "I should be asking you that. I hear you're going to have my grand-baby."

I bite my lip nervously. I'm not sure how to word this without coming off rude. "Jack, there are three people in this world that I love more than anything and anyone. This baby, Gabriel and my dad. That means I will do whatever it takes to protect those people. I know you and Gabriel had a discussion—*I don't know all the details*—but I still need to let you know that I will choose Gabriel and this baby every time. If that means I have to take them away from you, I will." I don't want to offend him, but he needs to know I won't tolerate him hitting Gabriel anymore.

He looks at me with a serious expression then his lips begin to turn into a smile. He chuckles and shakes his head. "My father would have loved you," he mumbles. "He would have seen a lot of Emilia in you. I can sleep peacefully at night knowing my son and my grand-baby will be well taken care of. I can't take back all that I've done, but I promise you from here on out, I'm going to try and make a difference."

I smile genuinely. "Then do you prefer grandad or grandpa?" I ask.

He grins. "What about pop?"

I grin. "I love it."

"Ava?!" Gabriel's voice calls out to the darkness. I look over at the back door and see his silhouette.

"At the fire!" I call out.

He makes his way toward us, and I look over at Jack, who has a worried expression on his face, but he's watching the fire.

"It'll be okay," I whisper to him.

When Gabriel reaches us, he looks at Jack in surprise. "What're you two doing out here?" He asks, confused. Clearly, he wasn't expecting me to be out here talking to his dad.

I smile as I take Gabriel's hand. "We were just discussing that your dad would like to be called pop."

Gabriel is taken back as his head whips over to his dad, who stands.

"Of course, if that's okay with you," Jack says.

Gabriel looks at me with uncertainty. I nod and give him a reassuring smile. His dad is trying, and Gabriel should too.

He looks back at Jack with a sincere smile. "I like pop."

Jack grins and wraps his arms around his son, patting his back. "I'm so happy for you, son." Jack mumbles. Gabriel may not be able to see his dad's face, but I can. His eyes are closed tightly as he savours every second of hugging his son.

Gabriel's arms hesitate, but they slowly wrap around Jack. "Thanks, dad." He mumbles with a sense of discomfort. It's going to take getting used to for him.

When they pull apart, I swear I see tears in Jack's eyes, but his face gets lost in the darkness. "Alright, let's go inside and make this announcement so Isabella can relax," Gabriel says and reaches for my hand. He helps me stand, and the three of us make our way back inside the house. I stop in my tracks, but Jack doesn't notice. Gabriel, on the other hand, does and stops beside me.

Standing in front of me is Elizabeth. My body is shaking with anger. All the sympathy I felt for her when she was admitted to the hospital is gone; these baby hormones are why. All I feel toward her is the anger I tried so hard to bury.

When she spots us, she gives me a slight wave with a sly, smug smile. I turn on my heel to face Gabriel, who doesn't look the slightest surprised by her presence.

That tells me he knew she was going to be here. "You invited her?" I hiss.

He frowns and looks down at me. "Ava, you have to trust me. I would never do anything to hurt you or ruin this announcement."

I want to laugh in his face.

If that was true, he wouldn't have fucking invited her!

"How dare you invite her on our special fucking night!" I say through my teeth. "She's the last person I want here."

He grabs my shoulders. "Angel, you need to trust me, please. I know you don't want her here, but I need her here for a reason. Just please believe me when I say I know what I'm doing."

I was right. He was hiding something from me, and it has to do with Elizabeth. How could he think doing this on the night we announce our pregnancy would be a great idea?

"Gabriel, doing this right now is completely inappropriate," I say through my teeth.

He frowns. "I know, I will make it up to you, but it had to be this way." he leans down and kisses my cheek. "Trust me, angel." He whispers, pleading with me again.

I sigh. I have no idea what he's planning, but if Elizabeth has anything to do with what's been happening to us, then I have no choice. I have to let him do this.

I nod. "Okay."

He takes my hand, and we walk right past her without a glance. I'm glad he isn't going to be friendly with her. I can't stand her smug face. We make our way to the living room, and Isabella is standing by the piano in the living room with John.

"Are we ready?" Gabriel asks quietly to his sister.

She grins with excitement. "Of course. Are you guys ready?"

I exhale loudly. "I suppose."

Gabriel clears his throat and takes my hand while Isabella hits her glass to get everyone's attention. The quiet chattering silences and everyone's eyes are on us. I feel a sense of relief when I see Skylar and Denise in the crowd next to Emilia and Jack. Jack's arm is wrapped around Emilia's waist, which also fills me with a sense of peace. I know how stressed Gabriel was about his parents being apart.

"My lovely girlfriend, Ava, and I have an announcement to make," Gabriel says, and he looks down at me with a small smile. His eyes are bright and filled with love for me and our unborn child. "We're pregnant."

Gasps, cheers, screams, clapping erupt in the room. People don't wait and begin to make their way to Gabriel, hugging or kissing him tightly. He introduces me to each person, and then they hug and kiss me as well.

Emilia embraces me and sniffles. "I've waited for him to find someone for so long," she whispers. "I was worried about him."

My heart swells. "I've waited for him for so long."

Ten years to be exact.

She pulls away and cups my face. "I'm happy he found you."

Jack walks over to us. "Alright, stop hogging my daughter-in-law." His words cause me to stiffen. Am I his daughter-in-law? Just because I'm having Gabriel's baby doesn't mean he's my husband, nor do I expect him to propose. It isn't the olden days, we can have a baby out of wedlock. If he proposes, I want it to be when he's ready and only to do with the love we have for one another.

I fake a smile as he wraps his arm around my shoulders. "Jack said he's going to be *pop*. Do you have a name in mind?" I ask Emilia.

Her eyes light up at the mention of what her future grandchild will call her. "*Nan*, oh, please, can they call me *Nan*."

I grin. "Nan, it is."

I look over Emilia's shoulder to see Gabriel walking out the front door with Elizabeth.

What is happening?

Skylar and Denise make their way to us, trapping me here for a bit longer.

Skylar wraps her arms around me as Denise says hi to Emilia. "I'm so happy for you guys! Isabella told me how lonely Gabriel was and seeing him with you...he's just a different man." She says happily.

I smile as much as I possibly can. I want to enjoy this moment of congratulation, but my mind is focused on what Elizabeth and Gabriel are talking about outside.

"We're blissfully happy," I say and give Denise a hug when Skylar lets me go. "Will you guys excuse me?" I make my way through the crowd, saying *hi* and *thank you's* on my way to the front door. When I step outside, I see that Gabriel and Elizabeth are further down the lawn. The light from the porch barely shines off them. I can hear Gabriel's harsh voice. I step closer, hoping my feet don't give me away. Their backs are to me, which means I can get close enough to hear before they see me.

"Tell me then Elizabeth why the car that nearly killed her was rented out in your name." He whispers harshly.

"I don't know, Gabriel. I almost overdosed. Do you really think I had the strength to do any of that?" She argues back.

He pulls something out of his pocket. "Your fucking signature is on the document that rented the vehicle. Harris tracked it down and found it. You've been caught red fucking handed, and I'm trying to allow you to come clean."

"You're crazy!" She yells. "I was framed; it was probably, Ava, trying to make me look bad. You don't know who she truly is, Gabriel."

"Enough!" He yells. "I'll look into your story about being framed but believe me when I say I have eyes on you everywhere. If you try to even make a plan about fleeing anywhere, I'll know about it. Now, go."

She doesn't argue and doesn't wait. She races to her car that's parked on the side of the street and drives off. Gabriel runs his hand through his hair as he turns around. He jumps when he sees me.

He sighs heavily. "I should have known you were going to follow me." He mumbles frustratedly.

It's hard to calm my emotions. I know I should think before I speak, but it's hard when I feel anger, sadness, fear, hatred in one giant ball in my chest. "You had the evidence that she was the one that nearly killed me, and you let her go?" I ask with confusion and anger. "I asked you over and over again, Gabriel, if you knew anything about the accident, and you told me no!"

When will the lying stop?

"Ava, will you lower your voice?" He scolds.

"I don't think you want to tell me to lower my voice, Gabriel!" I yell even louder.

He grabs my arm and pulls me to the side of the house, where it's pitch black. "I am trying my best here to protect you, Ava, to find out who the fuck is after you without causing too much attention to this fucking company," he barks as he pins me against the wall. "Keeping you in the dark is my way of protecting you. I need you to worry about taking care of yourself and our baby. That's it."

He can't get off that quickly.

"No," I hiss, and he narrows his eyebrows. "This isn't protecting me. You're lying to me! I need to know what's

going on, especially if it concerns my own safety and my
baby's."

He scowls. "*Our* baby." He hisses.

I swat him. "Gabriel! Focus!"

He groans. "Ava, I know you're right, but you have to
believe me when I say I'm doing this because it's what I
believe is right."

I hit him again, and his jaw clenches. "You believe
her when she said she was framed!" I say in disbelief.
"You have got to be kidding me! You can't be this naive!"

"I know her, Ava!" He yells, causing me to flinch.
"She can be fucking cruel and heartless, yes, but she
isn't capable of killing someone!"

"She didn't kill me; she almost did!" I scream.

"Lower. Your. Fucking. Voice." He warns.

He's basically telling me to calm down, and that
infuriates me even more. "Fucking make me!" I yell even
louder.

He groans and covers his body with mine, smashing
his lips against mine. I pull at his sweater and wrap my
legs around his waist. Our tongues are thrashing, our
lips moving quickly, his hands squeezing my ass as he
holds me up.

"You need to stop lying to me," I mumble against this
lips as my hands tug hard on his hair, knocking his
beanie off his head.

He curses under his breath. "I'm trying to fucking protect you." He says through his teeth, and his lips make their way to my neck. He sucks softly and bites.

"Well, stop, you ass." I moan.

"Frustrating woman," he mumbles frustratedly and sets me down. "Take your fucking pants off." He commands as he pulls down the fly of his pants.

"You're going to fuck me out here?" I ask in shock.

He scowls. "Do you have a problem with that?" He pulls his length out through his jeans, and suddenly I don't care where we are.

I shake my head. "No," I pant and take off my sneakers, then my pants.

"Leave your panties on." He demands.

He pins me against the wall again and lifts me. "You drive me fucking insane." He groans and moves my panties to the side, pushing himself inside me.

I throw my head back on a moan. "*Jesus*," I whisper.

"No, angel, you call out my name and only my name." He grips my hips and begins to thrust with force.

"Fuck, *Gabriel!*" I scream, and his hand covers my mouth.

"There we go," he groans and continues to drive into me. We're both panting, moaning and gasping. "Rub your clit. This needs to be quick."

I do as he says, and it isn't long until my toes begin to curl, and my breathing accelerates. "Gabriel," I gasp.

"I know, angel," he says through his teeth. "Me too." He covers my mouth with his hand again and buries his face in my neck as we both cry out in pleasure.

"If I had known that sex is the way to get rid of your attitude, I would have been doing this a long time ago," Gabriel says as he puts his beanie back on, and I adjust my pants.

I roll my eyes. "Don't think you're off the hook for lying just because I'm—

"*Thoroughly fucked*." He says with a grin, repeating what I said after our first night at White Collar, and I swat his shoulder.

"I was going to say *relaxed*." I huff.

He chuckles and wraps his arm around my shoulder. he kisses the side of my head. "I promise I won't keep things from you anymore, but you have to trust me with Elizabeth. Harris and I know what we're doing."

I narrow my eyebrows. "Harris is involved too?"

It eases my anxiety knowing Harris is involved. He wouldn't let Elizabeth off the hook just because Gabriel has been married to him. I can trust Harris to make the right calls.

He scoffs. "Of course he is. Bastard wouldn't let me do it on my own even if I wanted to."

"Do you really have eyes on Elizabeth?" I ask as we make our way back inside.

He nods. "Since you were in the hospital. As I said, I'm handling it, love."

We walk inside and spend the rest of the night mingling.

It's about one a.m. by the time we get home. I met all of the Warner's family and friends, and I'm almost certain all of them wanted to touch my belly.

Gabriel wasn't a fan of that.

I thought I would have to argue with people about boundaries, but everyone that asked had to deal with possessive Gabriel.

"Are you nervous for tomorrow?" He asks as we lay in bed together. His arm wrapped around me.

"You mean am I nervous to drive to Portland tomorrow to tell my dad I'm pregnant once again by the same man out of wedlock?" I ask and look up at him to see a concerned look on his face.

"You really think he would be upset?" He asks.

"The last time he saw you was in Texas when you came to ask for forgiveness, and now I'm ten weeks pregnant." Does he not see how badly this could go?

"Ava," he says with a slight smirk. "You know you're not seventeen. You're twenty-seven-years-old, meaning that you're an adult. We both have jobs, and I have so much money we won't ever have to worry about staying afloat."

"So, you're saying I'm overreacting?" I ask.

He shakes his head. "I would never say that. I'm a smart man." He kisses the side of my head, and I begin to play with his fingers; that's when I notice it. Under the tattoo of Simon's initials is a fresh tattoo that I have never seen before.

S.G.T

There's no way it is what I think it is. "Gabriel, when did you get this tattoo?" I ask.

"A few weeks ago," he mumbles. "when we were apart."

I trace each letter with my finger as emotion builds up in my chest. I blink back tears and bring the tattoo to my lips, kissing it softly. I don't think a woman truly moves on when losing a baby. Yes, I may not talk about it as much, and it doesn't hurt nearly as bad, but that sense of loss is always there. Whenever his due date is coming up, there's a heavy ache in my chest. I've been going through that loss and pain on my own for years. I never truly knew how Gabriel felt about losing our first child that he didn't get the chance to know or bond with. I wouldn't have held it against him if it didn't affect him the way it did me. Seeing this tattoo tells me that it hurt him in one way or another.

His other hand covers my stomach. "I don't think there's a minute that passes where I'm not terrified history will repeat itself." He whispers sadly.

I can't tell him that there's no chance it won't happen. Life is mysterious and can be cruel. I can't give him false hope, but it would be different this time if history *did* repeat itself. I cup his cheek. "If the world is cruel to us again, at least we have each other." That is what I can promise him.

"Forever?" He asks.

I hope we get the chance. "Forever."

CHAPTER 26

AVA

I wanted to surprise my dad, but I had to make sure he didn't go fishing like he usually does on Saturdays, so I called Valerie as soon as we woke up, and she promised to keep him home. I didn't want to just tell my dad about the baby; I wanted it to be more special than that.

Before driving to Portland, Gabriel and I stopped at a baby store to get a frame for his copy of the ultrasound; a t-shirt that reads *'Best Grandpa'* and a onesie that says *'I love my grandparents'*. I told Gabriel we would have to make custom shirts or onesies for the baby that says *'nan'* and *'pop'* for Gabriel's parents. All he did was shake his head with a grin while paying, so I took that as an *okay*.

Gabriel offered me to drive his beautiful Mustang, but I told him I needed to wrap these gifts. I couldn't trust him with the task.

I begged him to let Harris have time off, but the most they could do was have Harris follow us in the Escalade.

I took what I could get.

What I wasn't expecting was nausea when we pulled into my dad's driveway. Harris went to the nearest hotel —that took a lot of pleading.

"Ready?" Gabriel asks.

This home isn't my childhood home that Gabriel was familiar with, but it's still strange to have him in any house that belongs to my dad now that we're so much older.

I look at him and shake my head.

He chuckles and takes my hand in his kissing it softly. "I'll be beside you the whole time. I think he'll be thrilled."

I scoff. "I think you mean, I *hope* he'll be thrilled."

He shakes his head while rolling his eyes and steps out of the car, making his way to the passenger side— opening the door for me. I step out holding the gift and feel bile coming up my throat.

"I can't do this," I whisper.

He closes the door and cups my face. "Hey, if you can't do this, then we can wait, but I promise you no matter what his reaction is, all that matters is *we're* excited for this baby. I have never been happier, Ava, and I refuse to let anyone else make you feel as if this isn't a special time for us."

He's right.

This baby came from a place of love. Gabriel may have made mistakes, but that doesn't take away from what he's done and doing right. All this baby will ever need is our love.

I take a deep breath. "No, let's do this."

He smirks. "That's my girl." He takes my hand and leads me to the front door. We don't have to bother knocking when the door swings open and Valerie comes rushing out. Her arms wrap around me tightly.

"I missed you, bug." She mumbles and lets me go to admire my handsome God. "And I have really missed you, Gabriel."

I groan with embarrassment. "Val," I whine.

Gabriel grins and kisses her cheek. He isn't helping; if anything, he loves how much my step-mom praises his appearance. "Nice to see you again, Val; you look amazing."

She blushes, and I want to throw up. I make my way inside and leave them to flirt. "Dad!" I call out, and I hear the tv in the kitchen mute. He must be cooking; he always cooks with a game on.

He steps out from the kitchen and gasps when he sees me. "Bug! What are you doing here?!" He yells as he makes his way to me and hugs me with a small chuckle.

"I miss my old man," I mumble as I wrap one arm around him, the other still holding his present.

"I missed you. I was planning on calling you while I was on the lake, but Val told me we had some important date." He mumbles, and Val laughs.

"I made the man sweat. I knew if I lied to him about a date, he would pretend he remembered," she says as her arm is linked with Gabriel's.

"Ray, it's good to see you," Gabriel says and sticks out his hand for my dad to shake.

"You brought my girl home after not seeing her for weeks. You get a hug." My dad says and embraces Gabriel, who is caught by surprise.

"Are you scared?" Val whispers in my ear.

I look at her worriedly and nod.

She frowns. "Don't be. He'll be worried like any parent, but I know he will be happy."

How is everyone so sure?

"Gabriel, you want a beer?" My dad asks.

"I would love one." Gabriel answers and they make their way to the kitchen.

What is happening?

"Look at boys. So simple-minded that all it takes is a beer to bond." Val says and pulls me to the couch. "How are things with you two, now?"

I feel guilty for not telling my family what's been happening. My dad has no idea about the accident or that I'm in any danger. "Things are...really good between us." That isn't a lie. I'm on cloud nine whenever I'm with him. "He's excited to be a dad."

Val grins. "Of course he is. That man is *devoted* to you. I can tell by the way he looks at you."

God, I hope she's right.

"Okay, now something has brought you two here. What's going on?" My dad asks as Gabriel and him walk back into the living room with their beers. He sits on his recliner, and Val joins him, sitting on the armrest. Gabriel sits down next to me as I put the gift in my father's lap.

"We got something for you. Consider it an early wedding gift." I take Gabriel's hand as he opens it.

"Our wedding is still weeks away." My dad mumbles in disbelief. His face drops when he opens the gift and sees what's inside. He looks up at me and then to Gabriel and then to Val, then back to the box.

"You're pregnant?" he asks in shock.

I nod, not being able to speak.

He lifts the frame, and when he looks back at me, he has tears in his eyes. "Is it a boy or a girl?" He asks.

"We don't know yet. We find out in eight weeks." Gabriel says for me.

I'm so thankful for him.

My dad looks at Val, and a sob escapes him. "This is the best news..." his voice breaks.

"Daddy," I mumble as tears roll down my cheeks, and I walk over to him, wrapping my arms around him. Val claps with excitement.

"I'm getting my camera. We need a picture with you in the shirt." She says and runs upstairs. Gabriel's phone begins to ring.

"I'll give you two some privacy." He says and excuses himself.

I pull away and sniffle. "Are you really happy about this?" I ask.

He scoffs and rubs his red eyes. "Me crying isn't enough? When's the last time you've seen me cry?" he asks, his voice husky from emotion.

I grin. "You have a point."

He cups my face and wipes my tears. "Are you happy?" He asks like a concerned father.

I sniffle and nod. "So happy." I choke out. "It's almost scary."

"You don't have to be afraid anymore, bug; he loves you. We can all see it, and even if something were to go wrong, I will always be here. Just like last time." He kisses my forehead. "I can't believe how grown you are."

"Believe me, dad, neither can I." I mutter.

"Okay, I got the camera!" Val yells as she makes her way down the stairs. "Where's Gabriel?"

Right on cue, Gabriel walks back inside. "Right here." He looks over at me and gives me a small smile.

I nod to reassure him that everything is okay.

"Ray, go change. We will be here waiting." Val demands.

After my dad changes into his shirt, he grabs the onesie and the picture frame. "I need this in the photo." He explains.

My heart swells with love as Gabriel wraps his arm around my waist. "I told you so," he whispers in my ear.

I roll my eyes, but I can't fight my smile. *"Yeah, yeah."*

Val sets the camera on a timer then runs toward us. We all smile, and I can't help but look up at Gabriel with so much love as he looks down at me with a grin as the flash goes off.

My dad insisted we stay the night in my second childhood bedroom. I insisted we could stay at a hotel, but Gabriel happily agreed that he would love to stay here. He already planned on it. He called Harris to book himself a room for the night while I was cooking dinner with Val. Turns out Gabriel had packed us an overnight bag before we left.

This man is always one step ahead of everyone.

We make our way upstairs after saying goodnight, and I lead him to my old bedroom that still looks like it did when I lived here. Gabriel's grin is immediate when he steps inside. My walls are a lavender colour with posters, pictures, and book pages taped to my walls. He walks over to the cork board that's over my old desk and grabs a picture before I can see what it is.

"What is it?" I ask as I sit on the bed, dropping our bag onto the floor.

"It's us," he whispers. He turns the picture so I can see. My heart aches at the sight of the picture. We both look so young and so much scrawnier. He has no muscles, and I'm nearly not as curvy as I am now. He's wearing a Lincoln High School hoodie, and I'm wearing one too. It looks like we're at a football game.

The memory comes flooding back. This was the night we...

I look up at him, and he's giving me a knowing look. "I took your virginity that night."

I bite my lip and nod. "*You did.*" I mumble.

He sits on the bed and takes the picture. "Our school team had won the game, and we all went to the cabin for an after-party."

"My *first* party," I interject.

He chuckles. "It was. I remember how nervous you were. You thought I was going to be rough and careless."

"In my defence, the talk of the school was how rough you were in bed."

He laughs loudly, throwing his head back. "Those girls have no idea, and clearly neither did I."

I giggle. "You are a *lot* better now." I tease.

He pokes my side causing me to scream and laugh. "Very funny." He says dryly. "So, you hated me, yet you kept this photo." We both lay across the bed—me on my back and Gabriel on his side.

I nod. "I got rid of everything else but this photo. I couldn't let you completely go, but I couldn't hold onto more than just one thing. That night was so special to me."

I hate now that I got rid of all the memories we had together, but I had no idea that I would have found him again. I had lost all hope.

"Well, it's my photo now." He mumbles and tucks into the overnight bag.

I narrow my eyebrows. "I don't think so. It's mine."

He shrugs. "Well, what's yours *is* mine." He stands and continues to peruse through my teenage things. He walks over to my old stereo. "There's a tape inside." He presses play.

"There's no way it still works." I mumble and sit up.

He turns the volume knob, and the music begins to fill the air. The sound of the piano starts to fill the room, and he smiles.

"Of course, young Ava was listening to Tony Bennett," he says while shaking his head in disbelief. He walks over to me and sticks out his hand for me to take. "May I have this dance?"

I blush. "How can one deny a God?" I ask as I place my hand in his. My dad loved this song and used to sing it when we would cook together. It was his tape which is why I thought it wouldn't work anymore. He places one hand on my waist, and the other holds my hand, and we begin to sway.

"How did you learn how to dance?" I ask.

"My grandmother taught me. She loved to waltz… any kind of dance, really." He spins me and pulls me back to his chest. "My grandad said a way to a woman's heart are words that help them blossom; novels about love and dancing. Is he right?"

"I think my opinion is quite biased," I say as he dips me down. His lips lightly kiss mine, and he lifts me back up. "I love novels; your kind words and dancing with you make it a lot more fun."

He grins. "So, he *was* right." He confirms.

At Last, begins to play, and Gabriel groans in appreciation. "Who's tape?" He asks.

"My dads." I giggle.

He spins me again and begins to sing. I'm lost in his beautiful voice accompanying Etta's. He pulls me back to his chest and continues to sing.

"Your voice is *too* beautiful."

A slight blush—*which I've never seen before*—touches his cheeks. "Thank you," he whispers.

"Has no woman complimented your singing before?" I ask in awe. Indeed, I can't be the first one.

"I've never sung in front of anyone before…until that night with you. It was something I kept to myself. It felt too personal."

I can't contain my glee. "I'm the only woman you've sung to?" I need to hear it again.

He rolls his eye as he dips me down again. "You're the only woman I've sung to, the only woman I've loved and the only woman I want to carry my child."

Words cannot begin to describe the happiness I feel right now. "I love you."

He kisses me lightly again. "I love you, my Ava."

Some Years Ago...

Gabriel and Ava have been dating for six months now, and Gabriel can't even begin to remember the last time he was this happy. All his friends call him stupid for devoting himself to a girl who won't even *"put out"—as his lovely friends put it—*and at such a young age.

Gabriel, however, ignores them because when he looks at Ava, all he can see is love. How could he not devote himself to the one person who makes it feel like he could fly? That's why he hasn't bothered pressuring her about sex. Of course, he wants it but being in Ava's presence is enough.

Cold showers also help.

He was expecting her to say no when he told her about the cabin trip after the game. Win or lose, everyone will be heading to Corbin's cabin on the lake for a huge party. He knows partying isn't her thing. She would rather stay indoors watching movies and reading, but he would still ask her. If she said no, that would be the end of it, and he would explain to his friends that this girl comes first.

They wouldn't understand, but he couldn't care less.

What he wasn't expecting was Ava to say *yes* with excitement. She went on and on about what to pack and how long we would be there. When Gabriel told her it would be overnight, Ava was filled with anxiety.

Ava has never been away with a boy. Gabriel has slept over a few times, but she would never do anything under her dad's roof, even if he *is* out of town. Before Gabriel picked her up for the football game, she decided that she would make love with Gabriel tonight.

Gabriel has been so patient and so kind, stopping whenever she feels too overwhelmed or afraid. Lately, the ache between her legs has gotten worse whenever she cut's their make-out session short. She knows she's ready, and there is no one she trusts more than Gabriel.

On the other hand, Gabriel has no idea what his girlfriend has planned after the party, but he has something planned himself.

"Are you sure?" He asks softly as they stand outside the bedroom door that Gabriel had reserved for them for the night.

He's nervous, and his heart is racing a thousand miles a minute. He hasn't been this scared since it was his first time. So many thoughts are running through his head.

Ava nods. "I want you.."

"*Fuck*," Gabriel whispers and presses his lips against her's again. He opens the door and walks her into the bedroom, not breaking the kiss even for a second. He pulls away, and when she opens her eyes, she gasps when she takes in the room. She turns around and sees the candles he has set up everywhere with real rose petals scattered all over the floor and bed. His arms rub her arms lightly, and he brings his lips to her ear.

"To be loved to madness—such was her great desire." He whispers in her ear. She shivers and turns around to look at him in awe. She recognizes Thomas Hardy's work any day. What shocks her is that Gabriel is the one quoting him.

"Thomas Hardy?" She whispers in awe.

He nods. "I've been trying to educate myself on romance novels and authors. For you."

She has never loved anyone this much, and she doesn't think she ever could. Gabriel has stolen her heart with his words and actions.

She presses her lips against his, and he kicks the door shut with his foot. He backs her up to the bed and lays her down gently, his body covering hers.

He brushes his nose against hers. "If at any point you change your mind, all you have to say is stop, okay?" He says in between kissing her neck.

"Okay," she whispers as she arches her neck to give him better access.

So responsive, he thinks.

"I love you, Ava." He whispers as they lay in bed together, wrapped up in the blanket, hiding their naked bodies.

"I love you, Gabriel," she whispers before they kiss softly.

CHAPTER 27

GABRIEL

Ava fell asleep quickly like she has typically been doing since she became pregnant. Her body becomes tired a lot more rapidly than before. I played with her hair for a few more minutes after she fell asleep before I snuck away. Coming here to announce the pregnancy to her father isn't the only reason I'm here. The love she has for her father is strong, and I know she would never do anything significant without talking to her father, minus this surprise pregnancy that none of us saw coming.

I knew before I proposed I would have to ask her father for his blessing.

He's sitting in his recliner with a beer in his hand, the tv illuminating off him. "Still up, I see," I say as I sit on the sofa across from him.

He looks at me in surprise. "You too. Bug, hogging the bed? She tends to do that." I want to laugh and tell him he doesn't have to tell me that. I share a bed—not just now but also long ago—with her and know exactly what she's like when she sleeps.

"No, nothing like that. I was just hoping we could talk."

He leans back in his chair. "Shoot."

I reach into my pocket and take the ring box out. "I want to propose to your daughter. I love her and our baby more than anyone in this world, and I will do whatever it takes to protect both of them or any other future child we have. I want to give her the life she's always wanted..." I open the ring box, and I'm taken back by the ring all over again. "I wanted to ask for your blessing before I did anything because she loves and respects you, I think more than she does me."

I look at him to see him watching me with his mouth agape.

Shit.

That doesn't seem like a good sign.

Maybe, I've messed up too many times.

"Can I see the ring?" He asks with a hoarse voice.

I stand, and hand him the ring. His eyes widen at the side of the diamond—I'm almost certain. The halo diamonds aren't too big, but the muddle diamond is what made the ring costly.

"Holy shit," he mumbles and takes his baseball cap off. "I'm getting a grandchild, and now my only daughter is getting married."

I breathe a sigh of relief. "I take that as your blessing?" I really didn't want this to go the hard way. It would have crushed Ava.

"Of course, you have my blessing. Shit, not that, bug would have cared if I said no. That girl does what she wants when she wants. Stubborn like her mother."

I laugh out loud now. "You're telling me." I mumble.

The girl is going to give me grey hairs before I'm even thirty.

He stands and hands me thing ring, then shakes my hand. "Welcome to the family."

"She hasn't said yes yet." I remind him.

She could think this is going way too fast. That seems to be her popular opinion.

He scoffs. "You got nothing to worry about. She's going to say yes."

"What makes you so sure?" I ask.

He shrugs. "Because I know my daughter, and I know there's not one day that went by where she didn't think about you. I could see it in her eyes, and when she lost the baby, that pain got even worse."

"I'll never forgive myself for not being there when she lost him." I mumble.

"There's nothing you could have done. She was too young; you both were. You two never would have provided for the child the way you can provide for this one now. This one will have an amazing life and not the life Ava had to have for her first few years of life."

He has a point, but that doesn't take away the guilt I feel. "Do you have any advice? Dad to dad?" I ask.

I'm going to be a father...Holy shit.

He nods. "Just show up even when they don't want you. All Ava wanted was her mom to be there when she needed her. That's all a child wants."

If that's all it takes, I will be there and walk miles for my child. I'll have my arms out, ready to catch them when they need it and help them stand back on their feet. If she screams at me to leave her alone, I'll wait outside her door just in case she changes her mind.

I will do whatever it takes to be the best dad.

Val and Ray stop in their tracks as they pass by his daughter's old bedroom. Every night Ray walks his future wife to bed and kisses her goodnight before heading back down to finish whatever game he's watching. Ava and Gabriel don't notice the two older adults spying on their moment.

Ray's heart swells in his chest as he sees Gabriel twirl his daughter. Ava has a grin on her face as her eyes sparkle with delight. Gabriel pulls her back to his chest, and Ray sees it right there and then. He knows this young man will marry his daughter and spend the rest of his life with her.

The love they feel for one another isn't some childish love or fantasy they are trying to relive. They are devoted to one another.

Ray didn't get things right until his second marriage. His first marriage was a disaster. He was worried that would be his baby girl's life too. His fears are gone when he sees them dancing.

Val takes his hand and squeezes it. "They're going to make it." She says quietly.

He nods. "If it's not him, it's not anyone." He knows his daughter well enough to know that she has loved Gabriel all her life. She was just too stubborn to admit it. She couldn't swallow her pride and try to find Gabriel or listen to him when he wanted to give her the letter.

He wraps his arms around Val and walks her to their bedroom. "I can't believe I'm going to be a grandpa." He mumbles in disbelief as he tucks her in bed.

"Believe it, old man." She teases.

When he looks at Valerie, he wants to scold himself for trying to stay with his first wife. He could have had this happiness so much earlier.

"She really is happy, huh?" He asks as he sits on the edge of the bed.

Val nods, "Yeah, Ray, she is."

"Then why do I feel so sad?" He asks as tears come to his eyes. His only baby girl is grown, and he doesn't know how to handle it.

"Aw, Ray," Val whispers and wraps her arms around her further husband. Val knows Ava was his only family for so long. Yes, he had his brother in Texas but only saw him once or twice a year. For the longest time, it's been Ava and Stephen Ray Thompson side by side. Now, she is starting her own family. Gabriel is her partner and her confidant now, and Val knows Ray is beginning to feel unneeded.

Ray wishes he could reverse time just for a second to hug his baby girl a little longer.

AVA

"So, you're going to call us when you find out the gender, right?" My dad asks again as we eat breakfast before heading back to Seattle.

"Wouldn't you rather I tell you in person when we come for the wedding? It's literally the weekend after our appointment." I mumble while shoving bacon in my mouth. Gabriel has been watching me with amusement since they put the food on my plate. My morning sickness is beginning to fade, and I'm taking advantage of it.

"Are you crazy?" He asks. "That's three days after the appointment. Everyone you know in Seattle will know, but I won't. You call me right after the appointment."

Gabriel scoffs. "Yeah, Ava, Jesus. Of course, we will call you, Ray." He's teasing me.

I roll my eyes. All of a sudden, Gabriel gets to call my dad Ray now too. Only family call my dad by his middle name, which was my grandpa's name. Everyone else has to refer him by his first name Stephen.

"Okay, daddy, we will call you," I promise.

"Have you guys thought of baby names?" Val asks.

I shake my head. "Not really."

Gabriel clears his throat. "I have a few in mind."

"What?' I ask in shock. "tell me."

He shakes his head. "Not yet." He mumbles.

How can he keep me in the dark?

Now I feel guilty for not thinking about names. I figured we would wait for the day and see what he or she looks like.

Apparently, I have to start looking for ideas asap.

"What are you hoping for?" My dad asks.

"A girl." Gabriel says.

My dad raises an eyebrow. "*Really?*"

"What's wrong with having a girl, ray?" Val asks, and I scowl.

"Yeah, dad."

Gabriel snorts a laugh and takes a swig of his coffee to hide his amusement.

"Oh, God." My dad groans, and Val and I roll our eyes.

"So, we will see you at the wedding then." My dad says as he hugs me tightly.

"Of course, dad, we wouldn't miss it." I mumble and kiss his cheek. "I'll text you when we're in Seattle."

"You better." He warns, and he hugs Gabriel good-bye, and I hug Val.

"Call me if you need me for anything." She says, and I nod.

"I will."

Gabriel opens the car door for me, and when he's in, we speed off with my dad and Val waving bye in our review mirror.

He rests his hand on my thigh. "So, everyone knows," he says with a smile and puts his sunglasses on. It's unusually sunny for Portland.

I nod and bite my lip. "Everyone knows." I confirm. It feels a lot more real now but apart of it still feels like a dream. It was like this last time too. I don't think it will truly sink in until I'm holding him or her. "Are you really not going to tell me the names you're thinking about?" I ask.

He nods. "Not until we know if it's a boy or a girl."

I pout, and he looks over at me. He chuckles. "Nice try, but I'm still waiting." He says and squeezes my thigh.

"I can't wait to come back," I mumble while looking out the window. I miss my dad a lot more than I thought I would. When I'm around my dad, it feels like Texas.

"All you have to do is say the word, and we can come whenever you want, angel." He reassures me.

I smirk. "How will you get any work done?" I tease.

"It's going to be very hard, baby, trust me," he says with a grin. "But every second will be worth it."

CHAPTER 28

AVA

"Do we have to go?" I mutter sleepily into the pillow. Gabriel opened the curtains when I didn't wake up to the alarm. I showered last night before bed, specifically so I could sleep in. He left me to sleep and went to shower but opened the curtains.

Bastard couldn't have let me sleep a little longer?

He straddles me and spanks my bare butt. "Yes, we have to get dressed, and you still need breakfast."

"Or we can skip breakfast and make love," I suggest, hoping he'll give in but knowing he won't.

His damp body covers mine, and I inhale his scent. He smells like fresh mint. I can't wait until he puts on cologne. It's something that's been turning me on lately due to the pregnancy. He bites my earlobe softly, causing me to moan.

"Tempting, but I have a company to run, Miss Thompson. You said so yourself." He kisses under my ear then smacks my butt again. "Up you get."

I groan and roll out of bed.

I watch a completely naked Gabriel saunter to the walk-in closet. I bite my lip, watching his muscular legs and tight butt. I follow him and lean against the doorframe, watching him rummage through the drawers.

He smirks at me. "Enjoying the view, baby?"

I nod. "I could take a bite out of your bum."

He laughs hard, his beautiful green eyes shining with amusement. "Could you now?" He walks over to me and kisses me chastely. "These pregnancy hormones are making you insatiable. I could also say the same about your bum, love."

He begins to get dressed, and so do I. It's bizarre how quickly we have found our rhythm. As if we have lived together for years. We don't get in one another's way, and the other knows precisely what the other needs.

I roll up my stocking while resting my foot on the bench. I see Gabriel buttoning up his light grey dress shirt, but his eyes are fixed on my hands sliding up my leg. I switch to the other leg and do the same thing but slower. I turn my back to him, knowing his eyes will go straight to my ass—that is hardly covered in a white lace cheeky panty with a matching bra. I take my hair out of its ponytail and tussle it.

I feel his body against me, his hands caressing my hips. He brings his lips to my neck, and his erection presses against my behind. I watch him through the mirror; his hands slide to my front and down my panties to my sex.

"Already so wet," he whispers in appreciation. "Open your eyes and watch yourself." I peel my eyes open as his finger begins to draw circles over my clit. I thought it would be uncomfortable to see myself be pleasured, but it makes it more erotic. I look between myself to him, and his eyes are full of desire. He loves this, and that's all I need to know. My mouth drops open.

"Fuck, we're going to be late now," he hisses and bend's me over. "Hold onto the edge of the bench." He spanks me, and we both moan in pleasure.

Being late will be worth it.

"I'm so sorry I'm late." I run into my office to see Isabella waiting inside, writing notes down. She looks up at me with a sly smile.

"You get a pass cause you're carrying my niece or nephew in there." She says and hand's me my half cup of coffee.

Yes, not one cup but half a cup.

It's all Gabriel will let me drink while pregnant. The books say I can at least have one cup, but he doesn't trust it. Those were his exact words.

"What's on the agenda for today?" I ask as I take my seat and fire up my laptop.

"We have ten manuscripts that we need to look through today, conference call at three with a poet Neil and their agent. They were supposed to fly in but couldn't last minute. Violet Reed has also booked a meeting with you to discuss working together with an author."

I look at her in awe. "Violet Reed wants to work with me?" I ask in disbelief. We only met once during the meeting I filled in for Scott.

Isabella grins. "Looks like it."

I shake my head. "Do you ever get used to the extravagant life you guys live?"

She shakes her head. "Not, really no. I mean, you tend to stop fighting it at a certain point, but it still feels surreal. That's why Gabriel donates a lot of his."

Gabriel donates his money?

I give her a puzzled expression. "I didn't know he donated his money." I assumed he held onto it and spent it like most rich people. That's how you stay rich, right?

Isabella looks at me like I have two heads. "You're joking, right? Of course, he does. I don't know all the charities and foundations, but I do know he's involved in a few foundations that have to do with teachers, breakfast clubs, food banks, and any cancer foundation."

I had no idea, but Gabriel doesn't discuss his money. He doesn't hide it by taking people on magnificent trips and driving fancy cars, but he never discusses how much anything costs or where he's really spending it.

I make a mental note to ask him about it later.

My email pings and I open it to read that we have a late conference call with an author in New York.

Perfect.

"We may need to order dinner in," I mumble.

She sighs and writes in the day planner. "Great," She mutters.

"Well, let's get started. We have a long day ahead of us." I say as I remove the elastic's from the manuscript and grab my red pen.

At about four fifteen, I emailed Gabriel explaining that Isabella and I would be staying late, and she would give me a ride home. I didn't want him stuck here if he didn't have to be. At five-fifteen, he came to kiss me and say goodnight to Isabella before heading home with Harris.

The conference call finishes at seven which was a lot earlier than we were expecting. Since we already ordered dinner, we decide to head back to my office and read the rest of the manuscripts while waiting for the delivery driver to arrive at the building.

Isabella's phone begins to ring while we're both on the couch, with the radio playing softly in the background while we edit. "I'm heading down! I'll be back," she says to me as she walks out of the office, answering the phone.

I continue to read, circling the few mistakes I find here and there or writing notes when something should be changed or rewritten. I hear the office door open behind me. "That was quick," I mutter and look over my shoulder to see Elizabeth standing there.

If you have ever been in danger, you know how it feels for the hairs to stand up at the back of your neck, and adrenaline begins to flow through your veins. It's almost the same feeling I got when Scott had attacked me; however, I know I can protect myself better this time.

"What are you doing here?" I hiss.

So much for Gabriel having her followed.

If looks could kill. "I can't wait any longer for this to proceed," she slurs. Her eyes are glossy, which tells me she isn't sober. I can use that as an advantage; that means she's weaker.

"What do you mean?" I ask, hoping to get more information out of her. She knows something. I'm certain she wasn't framed. Gabriel can believe her sad puppy act all he wants, but I'm not that stupid to fall for her fake tears.

Evil is Evil.

"You came along and took everything from me. *Everything!*" She screams and pulls out a knife.

It doesn't scare me like it should. I won't let her get close enough, and she doesn't have the balance to charge at me. I would see her coming before she got too close.

"Elizabeth, think about what you're doing. You could go to prison for this. *I'm* not worth this." I try to negotiate as I take a few steps back. Isabella will be walking through that door any minute, which means I need Elizabeth to step away from it. If Isabella is quiet enough, Elizabeth may not notice her—giving us the element of surprise.

Elizabeth steps forward with each step I take back— exactly what I was hoping for. "You're right, you're not worth it, but *he* is." Isabella walks in with a smile and stops when she sees what's unfolding. Elizabeth is too focused on her hatred for me to even notice.

I give Isabella a knowing look, hoping she will do something to take Elizabeth down while I distract her. That way, we can detain her.

"Gabriel said he has people following you. Don't you think they will be here any second?"

She lets out a trembling breath. "Don't worry about that. They're distracted long enough for me to take care of what should have been done long ago."

She's going to attack, be ready.

Isabella grabs the vase off my bookshelf and, with all her force, smashes it over Elizabeth's head. She falls to the ground, dropping the knife. I run over as quickly as I can—*not knowing if she's conscious or not*—and grab the knife before she has another chance to. I toss it to the other side of the room.

I look over at Elizabeth, who is lifeless on the ground. "Call Gabriel," I tell her. I refuse to take my eyes off this woman.

"She is bat shit crazy. I don't know why my brother ever married her crazy ass." Isabella says while dialling his number.

She isn't working alone. I need to tell Gabriel that. Gabriel was sort of right in the sense that she isn't capable of creating this mastermind plan on her own. Her being drunk means she didn't have the courage to do it sober. She doesn't have the stomach to hurt anyone. She's being fed information and directions. I'm confident Tristan is helping her. I have no evidence but the gut feeling that's nagging at me. Why else would she have mentioned that she can no longer wait? Whoever this is clearly has a strict plan to get to me.

I grab the scarf I wore today and tie up her hands for our own safety. "Gabriel is coming with Harris. They were already on their way. One of Harris's men got in an accident. He was following Elizabeth who set up some sort of decoy."

This woman is clearly willing to go to any length.

"What the hell is going on, Ava?" She asks as she sits down next to me at Elizabeth's feet.

I'm exhausted as the adrenaline begins to fade. "Someone is after me, but I don't know who. Neither does Gabriel. We have been trying to figure it out, but now I'm certain that it's my ex who I think got to Elizabeth. I have no proof, but it's the only thing that asks sense."

She frowns. "Why would your ex be after you?" She asks.

"He abused me, and I charged him. We went to court, and he got three years but then was released early. He found me when I left Gabriel. When he was released, all this started and Elizabeth is sent on a crazy rampage." She takes my hand and squeezes it softly.

"Why didn't you tell me? I would have helped any way I could." She says sadly.

"This isn't your burden. The last thing I want is you or John in danger. I would never be able to forgive myself." I didn't even consider my family and friends getting hurt. Would Tristan go that far?

The door swings open, and I see Harris but no Gabriel. I waste no time and stand, throwing my arms around Harris, who is taken by surprise. "It's clear," he mumbles lowly and then his arms wrap around me. "You're safe, Miss Thompson. I'm sorry this continues to happen. Mrs. Owens, are you okay?"

"Yes, Harris, she didn't get the chance to hurt us."

"What happened?" He asks as I pull away.

"She tried to attack me with a knife, and then Isabella broke the vase over her head." I finish by pointing at the broken glass that surrounds us.

He gives Isabella an impressed smile. "Well done, Isabella." he praises her and takes cable ties out of his pocket and ties her arms and legs up.

"Where's Gabriel?" I ask.

"In the lobby talking to the police. They will be up any second, so why don't you two clear out of here." He says and helps Isabella stand. "Go on. I will stay here."

Isabella links her arm with mine, and we exit the office, making our way to the elevator. When we're in the safety and security of the elevator, emotion hits me out of nowhere. Tears well up, and a sob rips through me from deep within my chest.

"Please don't cry," Isabella begs as her arms wrap around me.

"I'm sorry," I sob. "It's just the baby hormones. I cry a lot more than I used to." The elevator dings, and I open my eyes to see Gabriel standing there.

"Ava, are you hurt?" He asks worriedly and hits the button that stops the elevator before hugging the both of us. "Are either of you hurt?"

"No," Isabella says. "We knocked the bitch out before she could do anything."

He pulls back with surprise. "You guys knocked her out on your own?" He asks.

"Isabella did," I mumble as I wipe away my tears.

"Belle, can you give us a second? Why don't you tell the police your story?" Gabriel says, and she squeezes my hand before walking out of the elevator.

He cups my face, and his thumbs wipe away my tears. His face looks tired and hurt. "I am..." he shakes his head. "How many times am I going to apologize? How many time's am I going to fail you?"

My heart breaks for him. "Gabriel, none of this is your fault or mine. There is no reason for you to apologize. I didn't even get hurt; it's just the baby hormones making my emotions crazy."

His hands go to my belly. "Are you sure you two are safe?" he asks worriedly.

"Yes, I promise." I place my hands on his. "What's going to happen to Elizabeth now?" I ask.

He sighs. "I charged her."

My eyes widen in shock as I look at all the police. "I thought you didn't involve the police?"

"Harris used to work for the FBI. I think part of him still has a foot in the door, but he won't tell me. I've always had the law enforcement's help. I just didn't want anything in the papers. I told you I had to handle this my way." He runs his fingers through his now long hair. He hasn't gotten a haircut in quite a bit. "I called them as soon as Marcus called me to say she slipped away."

His words spark the memory of Elizabeth's words in my office. "She said something to me when we were up there. She told me that she couldn't wait any longer for this to proceed. I think somehow—*I know I have no proof, but*—Tristan has been hiding behind Elizabeth."

His eyebrows furrow. "How could Tristan have found her?" He asks, unsure.

"He followed me all the time when we were together, and I didn't even notice. It wasn't until he showed me pictures of me walking around that I found out he had been following me basically every day. If he did it then, he could do it again." Chills run up and down my spine as I imagine him following me around Seattle.

Does he know that I'm pregnant? If he's been following us, that means he must have followed us to Doctor's appointments and then Elizabeth was at our announcement. If she really is working with Tristan, he knows for sure now.

Gabriel runs his hands over his face as he sighs heavily. "We can't fucking find him. After he left Texas, he disappeared so he *could* have been using Elizabeth's name to hide."

Guilt is all I feel when I see how stressed he is. This is all my fault. Gabriel didn't ask for this, and how much longer will he be able to take?

"Angel, why are you crying?" He asks sadly.

I didn't even notice that I was. I wipe away my tears. "This is all my fault," I croak. "Tristan is *my* ex-boyfriend —

"Stop," he says, interrupting me and cups my face. "This is not your fault. I'll find this fucker, and this will all be over, I promise."

He kisses me softly, and my body melts against him. "We got a long night ahead of us." He takes off his boots and his socks. "Put these on and take off your heels. I'll carry them." I'm hardly pregnant, but my feet have been killing me more and more.

I beam at him, and he winks at me. "I know how to treat my girl."

Elizabeth was sent to the hospital after taking everyone's statements. The officers reviewed the tapes from the building and my office. Elizabeth was charged and would be arrested. It isn't until two a.m. when we finally lay in bed for the night.

"Five hours until we have to wake up for work," I say with distaste.

He chuckles softly. "At least you aren't the face of the company." He says tiredly.

I look up at him in the dark. "I've had something on my mind," I whisper.

I can't see him, but I know he's rolling his eyes. "And that is?"

"Your birthday is coming up," I whisper. We never celebrated his birthday because he left, but we did get to celebrate mine when we first began dating. He had told me, though, that his birthday was September fourteenth.

It's a week away.

He shifts, and he's looking at me now. "You remembered my birthday?" He asks, surprised.

I scoff. "I was in love with you and still am, Gabriel, of course, I remember. Do you remember mine?" I bite my lip nervously.

He scoffs this time. "March twenty-first." He mutters like it was the easiest question I could ask him.

I smile. "I'm impressed."

"As am I."

"So, what would you like to do?" I ask.

He shrugs. "What we do every year." He says as if I should know.

I swat him. "Stop teasing me and tell me!"

He laughs. "We go to Australia every year for my birthday."

My eyes widen. "Australia?" I ask in disbelief. "You said you weren't rich when you were younger."

"My grandad would pay for it and send everything to my mum. My dad couldn't say no, and he tried."

I frown. I guess I can plan something for him when he gets back. I'll decorate the penthouse and bake him his own cake. "When will you be back? I would love to do something for you."

He's quiet, and I can't see his expression in the pitch black. "Gabriel?" I ask.

"Ava, it's my birthday." He says as if it's common sense. "You're coming."

I'm taken back. "Coming where?"

He sighs but I can sense a smirk on his face even in the darkness. "To Australia, Ava."

"Pardon?"

He groans and pushes me onto my back, straddling me, then begins to tickle me. "You, Ava Thompson, are coming to Australia with me—*Gabriel*—and my whole family for my birthday," he says while I squirm, hit and laugh obnoxiously. He finally lets me take a breath, and I can tell he's grinning down at me. "Do you understand now?" He asks.

I take deep breath's with a goofy grin on my face. "Yes, I understand, please, no more tickling." I beg. "Can I at least pay you for the trip?"

"You asked for it," he mutters.

"Gabriel, no!" I bark out a laugh and try to escape his grasp. "*Okay, okay!* You can pay! You can pay!"

He stops and kisses each breast. "Good girl." He mumbles and gets off of me, falling to his side of the bed.

After I've caught my breath, I rest my arms on his chest and my chin on my hands. "Can I at least buy you a gift?" I ask.

"Ava, you and this baby are gift enough." He argues.

I won't accept it. "Please," I beg. "Otherwise you won't be able to get anything for me when my birthday is here."

He sighs. "Fine, but I promise you I have everything I have ever wanted."

I'm sure he's right, but I don't care. I get to spoil him too.

"When do we leave?" I ask excitedly.

"Saturday, and we will be gone for a week. You're going to love it. I'm going to try and take you everywhere in the short time we're there." He even sounds excited.

"Tell me all about it." I can't wait.

He chuckles. "I have to leave some surprises for the trip. Besides, we need our rest." He wraps his arm around me and kisses the top of my head. "I love you."

I smile. "And I, you."

CHAPTER 29

GABRIEL

Ava was shocked when we checked into the Four
Seasons hotel, but our view took her breath away. I
walked her to the window, and her gasp made this all
worth it. From our room, you can see the Sydney
Harbour Bridge and the Sydney opera house. She shook
her head in disbelief as I wrapped my arms around her,
needing to touch her belly. This is the first time we have
stayed in a hotel this nice. Usually, we stayed at a local,
small hotel, or we stayed at my grandad's house he
purchased here.

This birthday is different, however, and it called for
luxury. On this birthday, I have Ava beside me, who is
carrying my little sunflower. Standing with her,
watching the view of the harbour makes the dream I
had even more vivid.

One day we will take our children here, and they will
learn where their father comes from. Then take them to

Texas, so they see where their beautiful mum comes from.

Our night came to a close quickly when we arrived due to the long flight—that's typical when you're flying to the other side of the world. I made sure to order Ava breakfast for when she wakes up while I go on a morning run. It was and still is my favourite morning ritual when we're here. Running along the harbour while the sun rises is a sight to be seen.

"I'm surprised you actually woke up, mate," I say with a grin when I see John in his workout gear waiting for me in the lobby.

He rolls his eyes. "Fuck off, it's ten in Seattle." He argues. "Now, are we going to run or not? Your sister will be up soon, and I gotta *attend* to her."

I will never get used to my best friend being married to my sister. It was even worse when they had first started dating. They couldn't keep their hands off one another, and I would catch them in unforgivable scenarios.

"Please don't, mate." I shiver with disgust. We exit the hotel and begin to jog lightly.

"Are you still going to propose this week?" John asks.

I was planning on it until Elizabeth had fucked everything up. After she tried—*and failed*—to attack Ava, she was arrested but posted bail. The question is, who the fuck had fifteen-thousand to release her? When I close my eyes, I can still see Ava's reaction when I broke the news to her. We're both trying hard to live life as normally as we can, but it's fucking impossible when shit like this keeps coming up. We have now decided that Harris will be Ava's bodyguard and driver. I don't seem to be in as much danger as her—if it all. She broke into tears when we told her and blamed it on the baby hormones, but I know her well enough to know it was more than that. Not only is she losing her freedom, but she's trying to protect herself, my...*our* sunflower, and myself. Now, she feels like she's burdening Harris—that he didn't sign up to babysit.

I'm not sure what she thinks he was doing with me that makes it any different. Technically, he was babysitting me as well, especially as a teenager.

I had it all pictured in my head that I would propose on this amazing trip. Australia is my home away from home; it's where my family has been at its happiest. However, it doesn't feel right now with the weight of Elizabeth and Tristan over our heads. I would have to come up with a plan that is just as meaningful and just as special.

"No, not anymore. Not with this shit still fresh. She can't even drive a car yet, mate, without freaking out at the wheel." My heart breaks at the memory. I gave her permission to drive the Ferrari, and when she got behind the wheel, she was no longer with me. It was like the night Scott had attacked her when she forgot where she was. Her breathing began to accelerate, and her nails dug into the steering wheel as if her life depended on holding on. We didn't even make it out of the parking garage.

When she went to bed that night, I snuck into my office and researched PTSD. From what I read, it seems like Ava shares the symptoms, but I'm no doctor. I would have to convince her to speak to someone about what she's been through. I need to make sure she's well taken care of.

"Fuck," he breathes. "I'm sorry, man, I know how badly you wanted this."

I narrow my eyebrows. "Hey, I'm still doing it; we just got to be creative about it. Now, enough talking and let's see if you can beat me in a race yet."

"You're on."

We both start running as fast as we can, but he can't pass me as usual.

AVA

I can't get over the view. No city should be this beautiful; it isn't fair, and it definitely doesn't feel real. I woke with breakfast waiting for me with my vitamins on a small plate, and a note that reads:

On a run with John.
Please eat.
Xoxoxo Gabriel

I can't believe how far we have come. Choosing to forgive him was the best thing I could have done for either of us. This child is going to be overwhelmed with love just from him alone. The past week he's been talking about cribs, strollers, photoshoots, and nursery sets but then talks himself into waiting until we find out the sex. I know he's doing it to distract me from my episode in his car and Elizabeth getting out on bail. It's been hard to sleep, knowing deep in my gut that Tristan and Elizabeth are working together.

"I can hear the cogs in your mind running in overdrive," Gabriel says, "from all the way over here."

I turn to see Gabriel wearing a grey muscle shirt that is sticking to his sweaty body. His hair is slicked back, his cheeks flushed, and the shorts he's wearing shows off his muscular-toned legs.

"Just enjoying the view." I'm standing where the tub is that looks out at the Opera House. He walks over to me and kisses me chastely. "How was your run?"

"A breeze compared to John, who can hardly breathe right now." He smirks to himself in amusement. I roll my eyes.

Men.

"How was your breakfast?" He takes off his shirt, and suddenly my answer to his question vanishes from my mind. The sweat on his body is causing his tattoos to glisten. He strips out of his shorts and boxers, leaving him in all his naked glory.

I'm instantly wet and no longer care about our conversation or what he may have planned for the day. I place my coffee cup on the bathroom counter before walking to him and putting my left hand on his chest and my right hand on his manhood—that begins to harden instantly. His eyes darken, and his hands pull at the belt of my robe, exposing the front of my body.

"Seems like my girl is still hungry," he whispers with desire.

"How can I not be when you look this good?" I ask while panting. He pushes the robe off my shoulders and groans at the sight of my body.

"I'm the one who has a hard time resisting your body," his hands run over my hips. "We're supposed to be getting ready, but I've been meaning to do this since we got back together. Turn around." His voice is husky with desire, and it causes my thighs to clench in anticipation. I do as he says and turn so my back is to him.

"Hang on to the edge of the tub," he whispers in my ear, and I follow instructions. I'm bent over and exposed for him. I feel his hands caress my ass, and it makes me nervous. I've never had a man this close to my ass before or want to do anything with it. Gabriel's obsession knows no bounds, and I don't want to stop him. Even though it makes me nervous, it also excites me. "I dream about this ass, angel, and all its curves."

His lips are trailing kisses on my skin, and then his palm collides with my ass, causing me to gasp and lunge forward. Then again, on the other cheek, and I'm instantly wet for him and ready for sex. Gabriel's fingers slide through my folds, and he groans in appreciation.

"Already so fucking wet. Do you like it when I spank you, angel?" His fingers slide into me, and I moan loudly.

"Yes," I pant.

"I'm going to eat this sweet pussy now, Ava." His mouth is on my sex as his hands still caress and squeeze my ass. I throw my head back as I cry out, and my legs begin to shake with intense pleasure. His moaning and groaning sounds aren't helping, he's acting like I'm a five-star meal.

I gasp when he sucks over my clit. "Gabriel, I'm going to come already." My body isn't climbing slowly like usual. It's moving at the speed of light, and he doesn't even have time to answer when I close my eyes and scream out his name while pleasure rocks through my body in waves.

"You will never know how much I fucking love how responsive you are." His voice is rough as he positions himself behind me. I stand and turn around, pushing him back to the couch. He falls with a thud and a smirk on his face. His hands cup my breasts, and his thumbs brush over my nipples until they're hard. "Your tits are going to get so much bigger, and I'm really fucking excited about that, baby."

I roll my eyes at my possessive caveman as I straddle his lap. His mouth is now busy sucking and biting on my nipples. I throw my head back on a cry as I sink down on his hard length.

"Fuck," he hisses. His nails digging into my hips. "I want you to grind on it."

Way ahead of you, my love.

I rest my hands on his knees and begin to grind against him like he asked. I let my head fall back, my mouth dropped open as my next breath is knocked out of me. He's so deep I can feel him in my stomach. My body is flushed and overheating; his thumb rubs over my clit, and I begin to feel faint from the intense pleasure.

"Oh my god," I moan and look at him to see his hooded green eyes watching his thumb pleasure me. When his eyes meet mine, something in him shifts. He lifts me up, throwing me down onto the couch, his body covering mine. He hooks one leg over his shoulder and begins to drive wildly.

"You feel so fucking good, I can't fucking control myself," he barks out, the veins on his neck popping. He kisses and nips at my ankle while his free hand goes back to its favourite spot: my clit.

"Jesus!" I scream and throw my head back. With every thrust, he grinds his hips, dipping them low to rub a new and very pleasurable angle.

I hear a deep chuckle. "Wrong name, angel."

He thrusts forward with such force my orgasm comes crashing through me in a giant wave. "Gabriel!" I scream as my body trembles.

"That's more like it." He grunts and drives forward three more times before calling out my name.

"Snorkelling? In the sea? With sharks?" I ask on a gulp as we stand on a dock before a giant white boat.

Gabriel chuckles from behind me. "It's the Australian experience, love. You have to."

I look up at him with a scowl. "What happened to the man that wanted to protect *his* baby?"

He looks down at me with his eyebrows furrowed. "I will always keep *my* baby safe, don't question that. This is safe; we used to do it as kids."

I want to knock the fucking fedora off his head. I want to be mad at him, but I'm distracted by how good he looks in his tan shorts, light blue button-down—that hugs his shoulders so tightly I'm sure if he flexed, he would rip the shirt. His aviators hide his beautiful green eyes that I know would look breathtaking against the sea's blue.

"Do I have to?" I ask.

He kisses the top of my head. "You'll love it, trust me." He takes my hand and walks me onto the boat where the rest of the Warner family is waiting for us.

When the boat begins to set sail, I forget all about my fear of swimming with sea creatures. The water is so blue and so clear you can see everything as we speed past it. This is when it hits me that I never would have seen water like this in person without Gabriel. I never would have seen Bora Bora or Australia, nor did I realize it was something I *wanted* to experience.

He will never know how grateful I am.

"There you are; I thought you sneaked away." Gabriel says from behind me. I look over my shoulder to see him walking up beside me. "You okay?"

I nod. "Just...savouring this moment." I look back at the water and rest my head on his arm.

He kisses the side of my head. "We can always come back. Especially when she's born."

I roll my eyes.

He sighs. "I know, *she* could be a *he*." He mocks me, and I swat him causing him to laugh.

"I love that sound." I mutter.

He's taken back at my compliment, and a slight blush touches his cheeks. "My laugh?" He asks.

I nod. "I love everything about you, but that sound makes my insides melt."

He blinks in surprise and tries to stifle his smile.

"Are you not used to compliments?" I ask teasingly.

"No, I am, it's just different when it comes from you...it makes me feel...unconditionally loved." He finishes his sentence in a soft, sincere tone.

I place my hand on his cheek. "That's my goal."

"Guys! It's time!" Isabella says as she pops her head onto the deck.

Gabriel grins. "Here we go." He says excitedly.

My stomach squeezes with fear and excitement. "Promise me you'll keep me safe?" I know he would never put me in danger, but I need reassurance. It's different now that I'm pregnant. There are two lives to think about now.

He kisses me swiftly. "Always, c'mon."

The instructor goes through all the steps as we change into wet suits. Isabella and John are the first ones to jump in with two instructors, then Jack and Emilia.

"You two ready?" The woman asks us with a giant grin on her face. I know for a fact that my face does not match hers. Gabriel takes his hand in mine.

"Hey, you will be with me the whole time. I won't leave your side." Gabriel says to reassure me.

I swallow hard and squeeze his hand. I can't find my words right now.

"We're ready," Gabriel says, and we put on our goggles and the mouthpiece of the snorkel. We walk up to the edge of the dock, and when Gabriel jumps, I close my eyes and follow his lead.

Water washes over me, and I wait to touch the ground, but it doesn't come. The need to panic is strong, but when I open my eyes, I see the Warner's swimming around us, but they aren't the only ones. There are various kinds of fish swimming around us as if we aren't invading their natural habitat. I can see every creature through the clear, crisp water.

I am in complete awe. This can't be real; life *can't* be this beautiful. This is what you see in the movies or read in books. I never thought in my entire life that I would be swimming in the sea with the most beautiful creatures around us. I look at Gabriel, who sticks his fist out for me to bump with my own.

He was right, and he knows it; he wants his credit.

My fist meets his, and we begin to swim as if we belong down here. The coral is as vibrant as you see in pictures.

It's *too* magical.

Gabriel stops and takes my hand, pulling me to him —my back against his front. Everyone gathers around us, and I see what has caught everyone's attention. Sharks are swimming peacefully along with the fish, and one is coming our way. Everything tells me to panic, but when I see the instructor's hands glide along the top of the shark I relax and watch in awe. Gabriel lifts my hands, and the shark passes by, hitting my hip and tears well up in my eyes when my hands glide along with the shark the same way the instructor did.

I turn to look at Gabriel in awe, and we swim up to the surface. I remove the snorkel from my mouth and begin to laugh in pure awe and gratitude.

He does the same and flashes me a cocky grin. "What did I say?" He teases.

"You've given me more than I could have ever dreamed of." The joy I feel is overwhelming.

His eyes fill with love. "That's all I have ever wanted to do."

CHAPTER 30

GABRIEL

I never realized how privileged my life had become until now. Seeing the look in Ava's eyes when we were on the boat and then when we were snorkelling almost made me weep. She looked at me as if I made the sun and moon just for her; she looked at me like I had given her the world, but in my world, this had been normal. I never even began to realize that my home away from home would be a trip of luxury for others.

It filled me with a sense of pride that I never felt before, knowing I could give her the experiences she had only dreamed of.

I have the power to give her what she desires, and it makes the caveman in me want to beat on his chest.

After snorkelling, we had dinner on the boat over the sunset, then Ava and I had a romantic dance on the deck of the ship while the song we sang at John's birthday played in the background.

It was a moment I had dreamed of many times in our decade apart. I wanted to fall to my knees and sob in gratitude because Lord knows I don't deserve this Goddess of a woman. She should hate me and my bad habits, lies, and betrayal; instead, she decides to love me and all my flaws.

Tonight is our last night in Australia, and I saved the best for last. After visiting the bush, surfing at bondi beach, dinner and a show at the theatre, it is now time to climb the Sydney Harbour Bridge. I'm not sure how Ava feels about heights; however, this should be a breeze compared to petting a shark.

My birthday this year was more than I could have asked for. Ava had promised me that her gift for me was coming, but I would have to wait for perfection. Her words, not mine. However, my sexy Goddess made sure I wasn't left empty-handed. She gave me a blowjob that men only dream about. When I came on her face, I was expecting sex, but her mouth had wrapped around my cock again, and I felt my heart in my fucking throat. My balls had drawn up so tight I thought I was going to pass out. My second orgasm winded me, and I collapsed on the bed.

"What if I throw up?" She asks as she bites her lip. We are all harnessed and ready to go with me upfront and Ava behind me. My family had wanted to tag along, but I needed fucking alone time. The only alone time we have gotten is at night when we make our way back to our hotel room. Even then, Belle finds a reason to make five short visits to our hotel room, but Ava finally has a friend, so I bite my tongue.

All for my girl.

I laugh. "You won't throw up. Where's the girl that touched the shark?" I ask.

She frowns. "She can survive a shark attack but can't survive that fall."

I roll my eyes, but I can't help my smirk of amusement. Her worries are irrational. It is entirely safe. I would never put her in danger, yet she still doubts me. "I promise you will love it. Have I been wrong yet?"

She narrows her eyebrows, but there's a sense of playfulness in her eyes. "Not *yet*."

I kiss her hard, leaving her breathless. "Trust me." I whisper.

Just like that, we begin to climb, the wind is welcomed, knowing this will probably make the both of us sweat. By the time we get to the top, the sky should be a beautiful pink-orange, and we will watch the sun begin to set in the sky.

If I wasn't so concerned about her mental well-being, I would have stuck to the plan and proposed right now.

"Gabriel!" She shrieks. "We're so high!"

I laugh. "That's the point!" I yell over my shoulder.

When we get to the top, I turn to look at her; she's looking out at the sky as if it holds all the answers she's looking for. She looks at me, and there are tears in her eyes.

"*Wow*," she whispers and sniffles.

I wrap my arm around her shoulder, tucking her into the crook of my armpit. "We can have this forever." I kiss the side of her head. She needs to know that I want this forever and only with her. There will never be anyone else.

We were meant to be the second I saw her in that library.

"I want this forever," she says as she looks up at me the same way she looked at the sky.

Like *I'm* all her answers.

AVA

"So, do we want to find out the sex?" Doctor Greene asks as she squirts the gel onto my stomach. Gabriel's eyes are glued to the screen even though nothing is happening yet.

Australia was a dream come true, but our life in Seattle was waiting for us.

"I don't think Gabriel will let us wait," I say and snap my fingers in front of his face to catch his attention.

He scowls. "Let's not fuck about here, ladies, please. I need to know, and I can't wait any longer."

I swat at him. "I'm sorry for his language. He tends to get like this when he is impatient."

Doctor Greene grins. "I think it's sweet he wants to know so badly." She grabs the wand and presses it against my stomach, spreading the gel with the same pressure I've come to be used to.

The same familiar sound of our baby's heartbeat fills the room, and I get the same feeling I did when I had first heard it. Tears roll down my cheeks before I can even see the figure on the screen. I look at Gabriel, but he isn't crying; instead, his eyebrows are furrowed as he focuses intently on the screen.

"There *she* is." Doctor Greene says, and I gasp at the screen. The baby's face is so much more defined from the last time we were here.

"Oh my god," I say in shock and laugh in awe as I take out my phone to record.

"*Wait*, what did you just say?" Gabriel asks, blurting it out.

"I said there *she* is. You're having a girl."

"Holy shit," Gabriel gasps and when I look at him, he running his hand through his hair; his eyes are red as tears fall down his cheeks. A soft sob rips through his chest as he rests his forehead against mine.

"We're having a girl?" I whisper, needing to hear it again.

He was right this whole time.

She nods, and I can't help but laugh with pure joy. I kiss Gabriel, who wraps his arms around me and sobs with no shame.

"I'm happier than you can ever imagine," He whispers just for me to hear.

Gabriel asked for way more photos than we needed, but he wanted various angles of *his sunflower.* His words to Doctor Greene. Usually, I would argue with him and tell him he is overbearing, but I understood. I wanted every angle of our beautiful little girl as well.

When Doctor Greene left to give us some privacy to compose ourselves, he didn't fail to rub it in my face how right he was.

When I asked him how he knew, he shrugged and said he just knew.

He could feel it.

I was expecting to feel disappointed when finding out we were having a girl because I didn't want to repeat my mom's mistakes. I shared the same fear Gabriel does but the second I saw our daughter on that screen, none of that mattered. I don't care if it's a girl or a boy; my fear no longer existed because I know for a fact that I will never hurt my daughter the way my mom hurt me. There is no way I could fail her because the love I feel for her right now is all-consuming. I would already die for her before she is even in the world.

All she will ever feel is love.

"Where are we going?" I ask as I notice we aren't going the usual way home. I was busy admiring the photos of my daughter. "Why are we in Arroyo Heights? I ask.

"I want to show you something." He says as we pull onto Marine View Drive, and he pulls into a driveway.

Are we visiting friends?

There is no For Sale sign on the lawn, which tells me we aren't here to buy this house. We must be visiting.

He gets out of the car and walks over to my side, opening the car door for me and taking my hand, helping me out of the vehicle.

"Who lives here?" I ask.

"A friend of mine." He says vaguely, and we walk through a black gate. The exterior of the house is black with wood accents. We walk up a few steps and walk down a small path hidden with shrubbery and trees. The white glass door is open, and I already can see the luxury of this home. The floor is a beautiful light tile, and the first thing you see is a small bench and a giant floor-to-ceiling window. You can see a tree through that window and see the clear water with boats sailing on by.

We walk deeper into the home, and there is a beautiful brick wall that I can imagine a family portrait hanging on...*our family portrait*. We now enter the carpeted living area, and I gasp at the sight. The roof is a cherry wood; there's a small section of a beige wall, but to the left of us, only windows and beside the wall are all windows and wall again. In the corner facing the view of the windows is a black piano. I can see Gabriel playing and teaching our daughter and any other future children we have together.

There's a fireplace next to the beautiful cream sofa that's close to the piano. I can see myself reading by the fire while Gabriel is at the piano. We pass by the long eight-person dining room table that seems like it's in its own section of the house. Instead of boring, blank walls, however, the room is all glass. There's a door to the left that leads to the wide porch that looks out to the water.

Meals will always be breathtaking.

The kitchen is all mahogany wood with stainless steel handles and black marble countertops. The stove is built into a separate island that is in the middle of the kitchen. Even when you're cooking, you can see the beautiful view. Then off to the side is another living room with a flat-screen mounted to the wall, a fireplace underneath it, surrounded by a giant black sectional couch that almost looks like a bed. It could fit nearly a dozen people on that couch. I see us laying in our pyjamas, cuddling under the blanket while watching a movie.

He continues to pull me along, and I wait for him to say anything about what we're doing here, but he doesn't. He leads me up a carpeted staircase that also has a view when you get to the top of the stairs. He takes us into what looks to be the master bedroom. And again, I can see Gabriel and myself lying in the king-sized bed that sits across from the brick fireplace. The walls are a soft grey, and there is a small window that faces the beautiful forest, garden.

"I think you'll like the bathroom," he finally says as he opens the bathroom door. He was right. It's smaller than the one at his apartment, but it's way more beautiful. The wall to the left is where the double sinks are located. It's all made with walnut. The stand-in shower—with teal tiles—has a rain shower head just like he has back at home, and beside the shower is a gorgeous deep soak oval tub. I can see Gabriel and I bathing together like we usually do. I see Gabriel bathing our infant in this bathroom.

"There are three other bedrooms and a basement, but there is one bedroom, in particular, I want you to see." He laces his hand with mine once again and pulls me out of the master bedroom, down the hall to a closed-door, then opens it, revealing a light brown crib and a white bassinet sitting in the middle of the room with a small window facing the backyard on the wall behind. "You told me that you didn't like my office because of it's boring white walls. So, when I was looking for a house that is suitable enough for my future wife and my future family, I needed to make sure that you weren't just staring at white walls."

I cover my mouth and look at him in shock as tears pool in my eyes. This time I can't blame it on the hormones. My first theory was correct, he's showing this house because he wants to buy it for me...*for us*. I knew my heart was going to break when we left this house. I didn't understand why we were here, but I fell in love with this house the second I could picture our family portrait on the brick wall by the entrance.

But Gabriel is standing here telling me that I never have to say goodbye to this house. He really can sit at the piano teaching and playing with our daughter while I sit by the fire, reading but really watching them with pride. We can bake while watching the sunset or sunrise. While I do dishes or make dinner, I can watch Gabriel sit around the fire with our children or watch them setting the dinner table. I can see myself sitting in this room singing our daughter to sleep or passing by to see a shirtless Gabriel holding a tiny infant in his arms, rocking it to sleep while he looks out at our backyard. Our backyard is big enough for a swing set; where our friends and family members will get together for birthdays and barbecues.

"This house could be ours?" I ask in awe.

He gives me a sweet smile as he pulls keys out of his pocket, holding them in the air. "It already is, angel."

I leap into his arms on a shriek, and he catches me, his hands going straight to their favourite place: my ass. He laughs as I kiss all over his face in pure love, happiness, and appreciation. "You bought me a house!" I say in shock. My face already hurts from grinning, but I can't stop this is the happiness I have always wanted with him.

He grins. "I bought *us* a house, angel. A house we can grow old in if you want. I will live here; I will live in Texas. I don't care."

My heart swells in my chest, knowing he would leave this life behind and move to Texas if that's what makes me happy.

"You would move to Texas for me?" I ask as I swallow past the lump in my throat.

"Ava, wherever you are is where I want to be too. All I've ever wanted in life is you. Texas, Seattle or Portland, I don't care as long as you're always beside me."

I cup his face, and when I look into his eyes, it's on the tip of my tongue. I want to marry him; I know it now more than ever. There is no doubt in my mind that this man is the man I will grow old with

"I love you." I whisper and press my lips against his.

"Is that a yes to the house?" He mumbles against my lips.

"Yes."

CHAPTER 31

AVA

My father's fall wedding is finally here. I have been dying to call my dad and tell him he's going to get a granddaughter, but Gabriel suggested waiting until we saw him in person since it was only a few days away... even though my dad gave us specific instructions to call him. We decided to say that our appointment was rescheduled and we would have to wait. He was not happy with that phone call but Gabriel was right. I wanted to see his face when I told him. Tonight is the night we finally announce it, and I know I'm going to cry all over again.

Elizabeth and Tristan have been burning in my mind since we came back from Australia. Gabriel and Harris, however, won't tell me anything that is happening with the police. Apparently, everyone decided it was best that I stay in the dark due to my pregnancy. Harris has been driving me everywhere, and I thought by now I would have drawn something out of him; sadly, I was heavily mistaken. His loyalty lies with Gabriel, and he wouldn't dare betray him.

The fact that it's been too quiet is what makes me so anxious. Gabriel has suggested therapy, which caused me to laugh out loud, but I knew he was serious when he didn't join in laughter.

He gave me pamphlet after pamphlet on the benefits of speaking to someone about traumatic events. It never occurred that I might need help until he reminded me about the driving incident before we left for Australia.

Before I could even say I was going to think about it, he informed me that he signed us up for couple counselling so I could get a sense of therapy.

"Bug!" Drew yells as he runs to me, leaving his luggage—picking me up and spinning me.

"I missed you." I mumble as I squeeze him tightly. When he sets me down, his hands go to my belly, which has now finally begun to pop out.

"I can't believe my eyes," he mumbles in shock. "You're actually pregnant."

I understand his shock. It *is* starting to feel a lot more real now that I'm beginning to show. "I know; wait till my dad sees."

Drew looks over my shoulder at Gabriel and nods. "*City Man*, good to see you again under the right circumstances."

Gabriel nods. "Good to see you too, Drew."

"Boy, you could have waited for us!" My uncle scolds as he comes up behind Drew with Margi by his side.

Margi runs past her husband and kisses my cheek before her hands are on my belly. "Look at my baby girl, not so baby anymore." She is already welling up, and I'm hardly pregnant.

I give her a sweet smile. "You know I'll always be your baby girl." I mumble. Then she spots Gabriel, and her eyes light up like a Christmas tree. She has no shame whatsoever. I roll my eyes as she makes her way to my baby daddy.

"Gabriel you are looking handsome as ever," she says and wraps her arms around him. I narrow my eyebrows at him, but he just winks at me as his arms wrap around my aunt.

Neither of them have shame.

"Margi, you look stunning."

My uncle throws his arm over my shoulders. "Be ready for this for the rest of your life, kiddo. My wife has no shame."

For the rest of my life?

That makes me wonder when he'll propose if he *ever* will. Will we continue to have kids out of wedlock? Does he ever want to get married?

"Alright, Margi, let the man breathe and let's get on the road. My brother is getting married tomorrow, and at this rate, we're going to be late." My uncle rants.

My aunt rolls her eyes, and we begin to make our way to the car.

We're all sitting around the fire while my uncle and dad argue about the proper way to barbecue. Gabriel is sipping on his fourth beer while he and Drew talk about a movie that I don't recognize. Val and Margi are singing along to the radio—*very badly*—due to already being drunk off two glasses of wine.

This is all I have ever wanted in life. This is what I wanted a decade ago with this same man. The amount of happiness I feel is powerful.

I clear my throat. "Everyone, we would like to make an announcement." I call out, catching everyone's attention.

Gabriel looks over at me with a soft smile and squeezes my hand. My eyes are on my dad because I know he's the one who will be the most emotional. "We had our check-up, and we figured out we're having a girl." I finish with a grin.

Everyone gasps and cheers. Drew begins to applaud while my dad stands, coming my way. I stand and wrap my arms around him while he cups my face. Tears are streaming down his cheeks unapologetically.

"I'm gonna have a granddaughter." He says in awe and kisses my forehead. I expected him to be upset that we hid this from him but he isn't. He's too over come with joy.

I let myself cry as I rest my cheek against his chest. "Are you happy?" I ask, needing to hear him say it.

He kisses the top of my head. "Beyond," he croaks.

"You're gonna have your hands full, son," my dad says to Gabriel, who chuckles and shakes his out stretched hand.

"I already do, Ray."

I laugh on a sob. "Please, I'm going to be nothing compared to *your* daughter."

His green eyes light up. "*My daughter.*"

My dad laughs. "You never get used to it."

CHAPTER 32

AVA

I have been a mess all day. I knew I wasn't going to stand a chance, especially with the new set of hormones it seems like I get every day. The second I saw Val come downstairs for breakfast and kiss my dad's cheeks, I began to cry.

Drew rolled his eyes, and Gabriel comforted me with a teasing smile. What can they expect when my dad is getting married to the woman of his dreams? I live and breathe romance novels and have made a career based on them. That alone should have tipped everyone off that I would be emotional today.

"Val," I gasp when she walks out of my dad's master bathroom in her wedding dress. Tears well up in my eyes as my hand covers my mouth. This dress was made for her. The dress is a white silk, satin material that pools at her feet and leads to a small, simple train at the back—with thin straps.

"Do you love it?" she asks as she smoothed out the dress with her hands.

I blink back the tears. I have my makeup done which means I can't cry. "You look so beautiful."

She smiles and helps me stand from the bed, looking at me in my bridesmaid dress. "Look at you, pregnant and still hot."

When Val told me to find a bridesmaid dress, I wanted a form-flattering dress since I won't be able to wear dresses like that for a few months. I chose a burnt orange silk dress that matches Drew's suspenders—who is my dad's best man.

"Wait until my stomach is so big that I can't see my toes. I won't be hot then." I'm not looking forward to that part.

She kisses her teeth. "Oh please, that hot man of yours would still take you to bed."

My cheeks flush. "Val!" I scold, and there is a small knock at the door.

Drew's head pops in, and he is almost unrecognizable. His messy hair that usually is hidden under a cowboy hat is now gelled and groomed to the side. He isn't clean-shaven like normally; instead, there's a five o'clock shadow that makes him look so much older.

"Ya'll almost ready? Ray and *city man* are getting impatient waiting for their women."

Val takes a deep breath and grins. "Let's go," she whispers and takes my hand, leading me out of the room. Drew hooks his arm with Val's, and I stop when I see Gabriel standing in my bedroom. I lean against the doorframe and watch him flip through the old books I have on my bookshelf. He read every single book on that shelf at first to impress me but secretly fell in love with them just as much as I had.

When he turns, it feels like the wind is knocked out of my body. His hair his gelled back, his beard perfectly groomed and trimmed on his strong jaw. He's wearing a white dress shirt, a black tie, a tweed light brown vest and a burgundy wool jacket with bottoms to match and light tan dress shoes. This is a suit I have never seen him in before, and this suit doesn't compare to his work suits. Even through the layers, this vintage suit hugs his body in a very yummy way.

He looks like he belongs in the English Countryside. He would be the town's most eligible bachelor that all the mother's want for their daughters. He looks like my very own personal William Darcy, and my heart—*and libido*—are swooning.

"Ava, you look..." he walks over to me, taking my hand and twirling me in my spot. "Fuck. I'm going to like what pregnancy does to your body."

My body flushes. Lately, all his compliments do one thing to me, and it's getting me horny. He's been complimenting that my hips are flaring out, which I don't see, but he insists it is happening. Whenever I bend over, he's usually pressing his pelvis right against my ass, and then he ends up taking me in that same position. He's been trying to be gentle—*worried that he would hurt the baby*—but whenever my ass is in the air for him, he loses control. He becomes more animal, wilder but my libido lives for it. Before I was pregnant, I wanted soft sex, but now my hormones need it hard and rough. Even then, my hormones are hardly satisfied.

"I figured you would like the way this dress hugs my hips." I pant. His hands go from my hips to my ass, and he squeezes on a groan.

"I already know I'm going to love the way you look from behind." He whispers in my ear.

I'm going to pass out.

"Gabriel," I breathe. "We have a wedding to attend."

He kisses my neck. "Until later," he whispers against my skin, causing me to shiver.

"I love you in this suit." He needs to know. I want all his suits to look like this. "You look like Mr. Darcy."

He smirks. "That was the plan, angel." He kisses me swiftly and takes my hand. "Let's go. You can't be late." He escorts me downstairs through the kitchen and through the glass sliding door that leads to the backyard. This isn't their first marriage, so they wanted to keep it small. Val and my dad both agreed on a backyard wedding with only thirty guests. However, backyard doesn't mean simple when it comes to Val. The

backyard is covered with twinkle lights and beautiful
fall-coloured flowers. There is even a rented wooden
dance floor that is in a tent built just from twinkle lights.
The dining room tables are rustic mahogany with
burgundy roses running down the centre of the table.

"Okay, this is where I leave you." Gabriel says to me
and kisses me deeply, dipping my body down. When he
lifts me and lets me go, I'm winded and flushed. "I'll see
you out there." He walks over to his seat, and Val enters
the kitchen.

"You ready?" I ask.

She nods as she holds her bouquet of dark burgundy
roses, burnt-orange roses, and light orange. She's now
wearing a cream boho straight brim, felt fedora that
goes beautifully with her dress. "Baby girl, I've been
ready to marry this man since the day I met him."

My heart squeezes, knowing how loved my dad is.
"Lets go," I whisper, and I face the aisle. The guitar
begins to play, and I take my bouquet—made of dark
burgundy and burnt orange roses.

I begin to walk, and tears come to my eyes when I
see my dad standing there, waiting for his future wife.
He smiles lovingly at me and wipes away a stray tear.
My dad is wearing a dark brown suit with a white dress
shirt, a skinny black tie, and an orange rose tucked into
his jacket pocket. His unruly hair that is usually hidden
under his baseball cap is now perfectly trimmed and
groomed. When I reach the alter, my dad kisses my

cheek, and I stand in place. I look down the aisle as everyone stands, and Val begins to walk down the aisle. The look on my dad's face says it all.

He has been waiting for this all his life. He thought he had this when he met my mom, and his heart was broken, but now we all know that Val and my dad were destined for one another.

When she reaches the end of the alter, my dad leans in and kisses her cheek, whispering something in her ear. My uncle clears his throat and opens his bible.

"Thank you for gathering here today to celebrate the most important day in this couple's life. The scripture reads..." I look over at Gabriel who's eyes are on me, but I expected that. This is all I want; *he* is all I want. I want to be his wife; I want to take his name and shout from the mountain tops how much I love this man. How much he has consumed me, devoured me, and how much he has loved me. My heart has belonged to him the second I looked up at him in that library, and those green eyes sparkled. No distance, pain, or person can keep us apart.

I look back at my dad, who is now beginning his vows. "Everyone knows this isn't my first marriage. When that one ended, I had given up and devoted my life to my only beautiful daughter. She was my only love and only concern, and I was okay with that. Then I met this woman who came into my life as just a friendly neighbour and slowly became my best friend without me even knowing. It wasn't until my lovely daughter had set us up on a blind date."

Val laughs. "More like ambushed us." She sniffles.

I had told her that I needed help with an essay, knowing for a fact that my dad would be home and I wouldn't be. It was the date that started it all.

My dad laughs and winks at me. "You saved me without even knowing that I needed saving. I had lost who I was, and you brought me back to him. You showed me that there really is such a thing as having a soulmate. It took us a few years to find one another, but now we have forever."

I wipe away my tears with my tissue and look at Gabriel, who has so much intensity in his gaze.

"My dearest, Ray. Not only have you shown me what true love is, but you have also given me the greatest gift, the gift I have always longed for"—she turns and takes my hand with tears streaming down her face—"you have given me the beautiful daughter I have always wanted. You're the only man who can handle me at my worst and who enjoys the challenges I throw at him. You are strong, loving, caring, and most importantly, you will be my husband until my dying day. My heart has always belonged to you."

My dad doesn't bother to wait and cups her face, pressing his lips against hers—everyone cheers and hollers. I look at Drew, who has tears in his eyes himself.

"Alright, alright, now, let's get the rings on." My uncle says with a grin. I hand Val my dad's wedding band, and Drew hand's my dad Val's.

"Do you Ray take this woman to be your wife, to love, and hold through sickness and health until death do you part?" My uncle asks as Val slips the ring on my dad's finger.

"I do." My dad says.

"And do you Val—

"You know I do, Dev." She says, interrupting my uncle, causing everyone to laugh as my dad places her ring on her finger above her engagement ring.

"I now pronounce you husband and wife. You may kiss."

My dad cups her face, and she cups his, kissing one another as everyone stands, cheering and celebrating their love.

"It was a beautiful ceremony," Gabriel says as we sway on the dance floor—our hands intertwined as I rest my cheek against his chest.

It was more than beautiful.

"It was perfect," I mumble.

"Do you see us getting married?" He asks, and I look up at him in shock. He's not grinning or showing any indication that he's joking.

Is he just saying this because he knocked me up?

"Of course, one day...if that's what you want." I bite my bottom lip nervously.

"*One day*," he whispers as if tasting it on his tongue. My dad walks over to us and kisses my cheek, but his eyes are focused on Gabriel.

"It's time." He says and nods. Gabriel nods and stops swaying his body. "Let's take a small drive."

I frown. "No, I'm not leaving my dad's wedding."

"Bug, it's okay, you'll be back in an hour—max." My dad explains. "I have a surprise for both of you, and he's going to take you to it."

I narrow my eyebrows. "Really?" I ask with doubt.

"Yes now go." He instructs and pushes us along.

I look at Gabriel in confusion, who is too busy walking to our car to even look my way. "Where are we going?" I ask.

He shrugs.

I scowl. "If you don't know, then how will we get there?"

He holds a piece of paper. "Your dad gave me directions."

My curiosity is running wild, wondering what my dad could be surprising us with.

After driving fifteen minutes, he pulls into a familiar parking lot. I gasp and whip my head in his direction. "What are we doing here?" I ask.

"I guess we'll find out." He mumbles as he stops the car in front of the back entrance of our old high school. He opens the door for me, and we climb the familiar steps and enter the school. The lights are still on, but the halls are bare. I have never seen it this empty.

We walk down the hallway past the cafeteria and into the hall of lockers. "Let's find our old lockers!" I say excitedly and jog down the hallway, remembering exactly where my locker was. I stop in front of it, and when I look down the hall to see Gabriel strolling to me with his hands in his pocket, I'm suddenly back in time. Kids are walking around us, their voices buzzing in my ears as I see their figures zoom on by, but Gabriel is perfectly clear in my vision. He's no longer the twenty-eight-year-old, but he's now seventeen with a backpack hanging off his one shoulder. His hair is short and spiked up at the front. He's clean shaven but his jaw is still chiseled and defined. People nod and say hi to him as he walks toward me. My locker is open, and there are pictures of him and me, my dad and me, and quotes from my favourite novels cut up and taped on my locker door. All the girls are watching him, but his sunflower eyes are locked on me. He flashes me a crooked grin that makes my heart skip a beat.

I blink, and we're back in the present. I look at my locker and stroke it as if that door holds every memory he and I have ever had together in these halls.

I gasp and look his way again. "The library." He sticks out his hand for me to take.

"Let's go check it out." He says, and I take his hand as we make a right then go up a flight of stairs where the library is. He opens the familiar door, and I step in, looking around in pure confusion. Hanging from the ceiling are book pages, hundreds of them. There are rose petals, vases of sunflowers scattered around the library and LED candles. I walk further into the room, reading each book page that is hanging. Each book page has a quote I love from my favourite novels. I turn to face Gabriel to see him on one knee, holding a ring box in his hands, but it's closed. My hands cover my mouth as they tremble.

"I have for the first time found what I can truly love —I have found you. You are my sympathy—my better self—my good angel—I am bound to you with a strong attachment. I think you're good, gifted, lovely; a fervent, a solemn passion is conceived in my heart; it leans to you, draws you to my centre and spring of life, wrap my existence about you—and kindling in pure, powerful flame, fuses you and me in one." He quotes *Jane Eyre* by Charlotte Bronte. He opens the ring box, and I gasp again at the sight of the ring as tears roll down my cheeks from his words. In the velvet cream box is a beautiful diamond ring surrounded by a halo of smaller diamonds. It looks vintage and rustic. Something that would have been worthy of any woman in the novels we have read. "Ava Thompson, will you marry me?"

My heart is beating so loud, I'm sure he can hear it.

There is so much we have to fear, so much against us, but when I look down at him and look into those green eyes, none of that matters. We are strong enough to face anything, whether it be life in general or what Tristan is trying to do to us. We have survived abandonment, neglect, loss, trauma, sickness and will continue to survive anything that comes our way. As long as I have him by my side, I can do anything.

I walk over to him and cup his face. "Yes, Gabriel, I will." Tears fall down his cheeks, and he kisses my belly before taking the ring out of the box and taking my hand, slipping the ring on my finger.

He stands and wraps his arms around me, kissing me with so much passion and love.

"Mrs. Ava Warner," he mumbles against my lips. "I love the sound of that." He grins as he rests his forehead against mine.

I do too.

SNEAK PEAK TO FOREVER WITH YOU—BOOK #3 IN THE FALL SERIES

PROLOGUE

I did everything in my power to make them think Ava was in danger. It wasn't fucking easy. Finding Elizabeth was the easy part but getting her to betray Gabriel was the challenge. Then she found me and was pissed drunk, spewing on and on about how much she hated Ava. I hated hearing her bad mouth the love of my life but I knew the mission. I had to hold my tongue and not beat the shit out of her so she would do what I tell her.

That's when I told her that I wanted to take down Ava. Her eyes lit up with delight at my plan and she agreed easily... as long as we didn't hurt Gabriel. That was her one condition.

I wanted to hit the bitch for even giving me conditions but again I clenched my twitching palms. I agreed and that's when we came up with our plan.

What I was not expecting was the bitch to go crazy and fucking try to attack *my* Ava. Having to pay fifteen-thousand dollar to get her out of prison was the last straw. She could sense the anger vibrating from my body. I proceed to beat the shit out of the stupid bitch until she was begging me to stop. She told me she would make things right.

Little did I know that Elizabeth going off the rails led us to our end goal earlier than planned. Gabriel was no longer protected. His main bodyguard was now protecting my Ava the way it should be. She needs to be protected even though she's a whore who is sleeping with someone else. She promised she would wait for me and yet I see her belly growing bigger and bigger with someone else's child.

That's okay though, that just means I'm a father a lot sooner than planned.

Now, it's time to do exactly what I wanted to do since I saw them together.

Kill, Gabriel Warner.

GABRIEL AND AVA'S STORY FINISHES IN BOOK 3...
...*FOREVER WITH YOU* COMING SOON...

ACKNOWLEDGMENTS

My husband, where would I be without you? These books wouldn't exist without you, or they would just be for my eyes like they always have been.

To my cousin who sent me Snapchat's of her going on and on about my book and how much she loved the characters. For gifting my book on any occasion you possibly could—to people who didn't ask nor wanted my book. You truly understood everything I wanted to get across. You validated my talent, my writing and my imagination. You love these characters just as much as I do, and it means the world to me. I love you.

When I published my first book 'Fall For You' on Amazon, all my friends and family members shared, purchased, reviewed, gifted, and spread the word about my book. It went from #2,000 to #27 overnight. I owe everything to you guys. To everyone who purchased a copy, thank you so much from the bottom of my heart.

Thank you to the beautiful creators and artists I featured in this book; they get all the credit for their work! Frank Ocean's rendition of At Your Best is the song Gabriel plays, and it summed up his feelings for Ava perfectly. This book would be nothing without that beautiful song and artist.

Thomas Hardy, Jane Austen, Charlotte Bronte are the legends of writing romance and the reason why I fell in love with romance novels, to begin with. Every book quote mentioned has been created by those authors and have all the credit. Without their work, romance novels, including my own, wouldn't exist.